Pieces of
Happily Ever After

Pieces of
Happily Ever After

Irene Zutell

St. Martin's Griffin
New York

PIECES OF HAPPILY EVER AFTER. Copyright © 2009 by Irene Zutell. All rights reserved. Printed in the United States of America. For information, address St. Martin's Press, 175 Fifth Avenue, New York, N.Y. 10010.

www.stmartins.com

Library of Congress Cataloging-in-Publication Data

Zutell, Irene.
    Pieces of happily ever after / Irene Zutell. — 1st ed.
       p. cm.
    ISBN 978-0-312-54009-8
    1. Divorced women—Fiction. 2. Hollywood (Los Angeles, Calif.)—Fiction. I. Title.
    PS3626.U84P54 2009
    813'.6—dc22
                                              2009016671

10 9 8 7 6 5 4 3

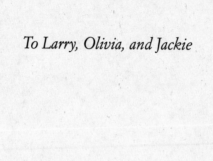

To Larry, Olivia, and Jackie

Acknowledgments

Thanks to Andrea Barvzi, Jennifer Weis, Jane Liddle, Hilary Teeman, Anne Bensson, Joe Goldschein, Joan Higgins, Felicity Blunt, Emma Lewis, Katie McGowan, Stefanie Wilder-Taylor, and Larry Bleidner, who all helped get the book to where it is today. And also thanks to the people who—unbeknownst to them—provided me with great material, including Larry Bleidner (of course); Catherine and Raymond Zutell; Jeannine and Dave Schwing; Joan Zutell; Renee Lipp; the Sagebrush regulars; the residents of Candy Cane Lane; the former neighbors on Calderon; the St. Mel moms; and all the denizens of the San Fernando Valley. And a special mention—or perhaps apology— to Olivia, whose expressions and insights I stole.

Part One

The Really Bad Stuff

I

Once Upon a Dream

I spy on them. They're clustered in the driveway, sipping lattes and chais from Starbucks and Coffee Bean while smoking or talking into cells or thumbing at BlackBerrys or chatting with each other—most likely about me. I straighten up a bit to get a better look and open the blind an inch wider. A straggly looking guy on his cell phone locks eyes with me. I blink, and suddenly they're furiously snapping away at my eyeball peering through a tiny slit in the blind. This appears to be the most exciting event they've ever witnessed. I slide my finger off the Venetians and dive to the floor as if I'm dodging bullets instead of cameras. My heart pounds.

"Alice! Alice," I hear them yelling. "Alice! Give us something. Come out, come out. You can't stay in there forever."

Maybe I'll prove them wrong.

It's Day Three and the paparazzi are still staked outside the brand-new rambling ranch home my husband Alex and I had built.

"I'm starving to death," Gabby, my five-year-old daughter, yells from the living room.

I have never been much of a bulk shopper, even though it's a religion out here. Be fully stocked so you're prepared when the Big One hits, they say. Everyone swears by Costco or Sam's. You can buy a whole cow for half the price of one supermarket steak, they giddily tell me. So because I'm not a believer, Gabby and I are stuck inside with hardly any food, except for some pasta, cereal, American cheese, strawberries growing fuzzy beards, and three liver-spotted bananas.

"How about some cereal?"

She answers without turning her head away from *Rugrats*.

"I hate cereal."

"You can even have some Froot Loops. I know you love them." My voice sounds like a crazy falsetto. Until just now I didn't even know my voice could sound so fake. It frightens me. Hollywood living, I suppose.

Gabby turns toward me and rolls her eyes like some bored teenager. "That's before you made me eat it like one hundred and twenty-six times, du-u-uh."

She's speaking like Angelica Pickles, the snotty oldest Rugrat. During the last three days, Gabby has been sitting glassy-eyed in front of the oversized flat-screen with surround sound that Alex couldn't live without.

Before the day that changed our lives, I had forbidden Froot Loops and had limited Gabby to two hours of television a week. By Day One-and-a-Half I had surrendered the clicker.

So while Gabby learned how to perfect her Valley Girl lilt, I curled on my bed and cried.

I click off the TV. "Draw. Play with your dolls. Do something."

"I wanna go outside and catch butterflies."

"You can't go outside today."

"I wanna play outside. I haven't been outside in one hundred and thirty thousand years. I wanna go outside. NOW. Why can't I go outside?"

How do you explain any of this to a five-year-old? She's too old to fool yet too young to know the truth. A year to go before the age of reason, the experts say. She still believes in Santa but doesn't quite buy the chimney part. And she already has strong doubts about the Easter Bunny.

Instead of waiting for some inadequate response, Gabby plows ahead.

"Play with me, Mommy."

I open my mouth but no sound comes out.

"I know what you're going to say. You never want to play with me. I want to play princess. Then we can talk my Barbies and make Easy Bake cookies. I'll find my Polly Pockets beadmaker and we can make neck-a-laces and brace-a-lets. Then we can make teacups and saucers with my pottery wheel."

That's all, I think. Time management is not my five-year-old's forte. "Well, maybe in a little while."

Gabby puts her hands on her hips and scowls at me. "Maybe. Maybe. Maybe. You know what maybe means? No! You are no fun. Daddy's fun. When's Daddy coming home? I want Daddy. Get me my daddy. Now!"

I bite my tongue.

"Daddy is just taking a little vacation, but he'll be back very soon." The crazy falsetto invades my vocal chords again. "He loves you very, very much."

Gabby slams her head on the back of the couch.

"Du-uuh, you said that like fifteen hundred and eighty times already and I'm actually sick of it. I want to go outside."

"How about a lollipop?"

The phone shrills. I hand Gabby a grape Tootsie Pop and wait for the answering machine. Lately every time the phone rings it's a reporter calling for an exclusive. This time it's Hilda, the Teutonic owner of the board and care where my mom lives. She speaks in her clipped officious German accent.

"Your mussa iss out of diapers. As part of ze agreement you signed, *you,* not ze board and care, are required to provide diapers for your mussa. Vee are not in ze diaper business. Please come over and remedy zis situation ASAP."

I haven't visited mom since Alex left. I haven't gone to work or taken a shower. I haven't eaten. I haven't fed my daughter anything today except for the purple Tootsie Pop.

I look over at Gabby. Her narrow back is facing me. She's clicked the TV back on and is immersed in the animated world of stupids, duhs, and whatevers. Angelica's probably about to go on The Pill. Gabby's thick, shoulder-length, honey-colored hair is a tangle of knots and grease. Her Cinderella dress is stained with spaghetti sauce and milk. Two miles away, Mom is festering in feces.

I've got to get it together. One person's needs depend on me. Another person needs Depends.

I click off the TV again. "You're taking a shower with Mommy," I say.

"Tartar sauce! I hate showers."

Somehow we manage. I find coconut and lavender swirl soap.

"Look, this is special secret princess soap."

She perks up. "Will this turn me into a princess?"

"It might. It's the soap all the princesses use."

"Even Ariel?"

"Sure."

She thinks about this. "Actually, how does Ariel take a shower if she lives under water? You're making this up."

We stay in the shower for nearly a half hour. I keep my head under the hot water and feel the stress oozing out of me while Gabby soaps up every inch of her body until she is covered in a layer of foam and resembles a snow tot. We get out and dress. Miraculously, Gabby doesn't protest when I tell her the Cinderella gown is too filthy to wear. I manage to shove my contacts into bloodshot eyes. I comb out Gabby's hair.

"What are we gonna do?"

"We're visiting Grandma." Again, I sound as chipper as possible.

"Oh no. I hate that place. It always smells like poo-poo and pee-pee. I want to do something fun. Let's go to Disneyland. Please! Please!"

"Sure, honey."

"Yay!"

"Just not today, okay? Soon."

Gabby balls her hands into fists and punches the air. "Soon means never, never, never. We never do anything fun. I want a new mommy."

I look out the front door window. There are about ten of them, talking, laughing, flirting. Their cameras dangle from their necks like an afterthought. This has become a party. They figure I'm holed up here for good, so why not make the best of it? There are six empty Domino's pizza boxes on the sidewalk. Next they'll bring a keg, a boom box, and a limbo stick. My misery is a cause for celebration. A day out of the office, soaking up some rays, enjoying another perfect early September Los Angeles day. Temperatures in the low eighties with absolutely no chance of precipitation. Ever.

I'm sure the neighbors are enraged. I've only lived in this house Alex and I built from scratch for a few months now. I don't know the neighbors yet. The association is probably convening right now to discuss this latest problem. That woman with the paparazzi staked out in front of her house. No welcome wagon for me.

Welcome wagons? Whatever happened to them? When I was a kid, my parents moved us out of our Bronx apartment to a colonial house in Larchmont, New York. All the neighbors stopped by to meet us with pies, casseroles, and wine. It was mandatory that your neighbors become your best friends, for better or worse. When Alex and I moved here, the neighbor next door grunted a hello. No cookies. No cake. No wine. Everyone says Los Angelinos are so much friendlier than New Yorkers. It's not true. They're only friendly if they think you can help them move up the Hollywood food chain.

I must get out. I look in the mirror in the hall by the front door. Sunlight pours in, denying me any illusion. They say some women one day look in the mirror and think, What's my mother doing here? But how could she be here when she's wallowing in her own excrement at Hilda's House of Horrors? When did I start to age? Just the other day I was twenty-eight and now I'm thirty-eight. My skin has lost its softness. My hair looks flat and dull. I haven't slept for days and it shows. There are dark circles and puffiness under my eyes. A few years ago I could pull all-nighters and sparkle the next day. Now I just look like, well, my mother.

I can't go out like this—not with them waiting for me. I think of a strategy. I remember that I parked the car in the driveway. When Alex was here, the cars were always parked in the garage. He was meticulous about it. "I don't want olives from the tree dinging the hoods," he said. But I'm lazy. I left the glinting white Volkswagen Passat outside for three days and now I must be punished. Instead of sneaking into the garage from the house, Gabby and I will have to walk out the front door and make a run to the car. I'll have to wear big sunglasses and a baseball cap.

I can't do it.

I scan my head for someone to call to pick up a box of Depends Super Absorbent Protective Underwear. But I know no one in the Valley. The meager friends I have made since we moved to L.A. three years ago all live on the other side of The Hill in places like Santa Monica, Brentwood, and Laurel Canyon. We lived in Laurel Canyon, too, before trekking to the Valley for the schools, space, and domestic bliss.

I take a deep breath and search my bedroom closet for a baseball cap when I hear commotion outside. A murmur of excited voices. Maybe Alex is back? Begging for forgiveness? I rush to the window as my heart skitters.

The paparazzi have multiplied and are scuttling along the lawn, cameras in front of their faces, hands pressing buttons and massaging lenses into focus, mouths pinched in concentration. I scan the lawn for their subject. Whoever it is must be obscured by the portico. Is it Alex? Maybe he parked up the street and tried to sneak back? Maybe he took a cab? Most likely it's Claire, a coworker of mine. Claire's been threatening to check up on me. She's one of those people who'll stop by with a casserole and act all concerned. But the truth is, she's real big on schadenfreude. She'll run back to the office to tell everyone how horrible I look, how devastated I am, what a mess the house is.

"Gabby. Come here. Gabby? *Gabby!*"

I check the living room. *SpongeBob*—Gabby's favorite cartoon—is on, but she's not there.

"Gabby?"

I hear muffled applause and whistles. That's when it hits me. I run to the front door. It's slightly ajar. I open it wider. There's Gabby on the front steps wearing a tiara, a pink boa, and her filthy Cinderella dress. She's singing "Once Upon a Dream," a song from *Sleeping Beauty*, or is it *Cinderella*? Photographers click away and videotape.

Without thinking, I pull open the door.

"It's Alice! Alice! Over here!"

"Gabby!"

"Alice! Alice!"

Gabby's voice gets louder as she trills. " 'I know you, I walked with you once upon a dream. Oh-oh, I know you!' "

"Gabby! In! The! House!"

She waves her magic wand through the air.

"Gabby. Right now!"

She turns toward me, her mouth open wide. Then she turns back, jumps down the steps, and races across the lawn, closer to the paparazzi. Her voice gets louder and louder. She twirls and leaps like a drunken ballerina.

" 'You'll love me at once, the way you did once upon a *dree-eaaam!'* "

She dramatically swirls her wand through the air and bows. She waits for the photographers to applaud, but they don't. They're too busy snapping away at me as I grab Gabby. She kicks and flails.

"Stop it right now," I say.

"No! You ruin everything. I'm performing."

I can feel them right behind me, clicking away. My face is on fire. My chest burns. Could I be having a heart attack?

"Get in the car right now."

"No!"

"Okay, Gabrielle." I speak through clenched teeth. "No ice cream for the rest of your life. *Ever!* And no more cartoons. *Ever!* I mean it."

She rolls her eyes at me. "I don't care."

Gabby wriggles away from me. She darts across the lawn. I chase after her.

Clickclickclickclickclickclickclickclick . . .

I am giving them so much. An insane mother. No sunglasses. No baseball cap. Eyes swollen from crying. Gray streaks. A little left-over paunch from the pregnancy gone bad. An unruly, undisciplined brat. What will happen next?

No wonder he dumped her. What a shrew! What a brat!

Clickclickclick . . . The shutters capture every millisecond. I keep my head down as I leap at Gabby. I grab hold of her Cinderella gown. Gabby keeps running, and the gown rips. Gabby is propelled right into the leg of a photographer who has been snapping away.

She crashes into his knee and falls to the ground, her gown now a miniskirt as I hold part of it in my hand.

The paparazzo lets the camera dangle at his chest. He bends down and sticks out his hand to Gabby. "Are you okay?"

She stares blankly ahead. "You okay," the photographer says again, waving a hand in front of Gabby's face.

"Who are you supposed to be," she asks him.

She grabs his hand and he hoists her up. The pack of wild cameramen closes in on us, pushing each other to take this photo of me holding half a Cinderella gown. I can see the headline: THE BALL'S OVER.

"Let go of her," I growl. My voice again sounds foreign to me. It's so ferocious, so nearly primitive, that Gabby understands she's in the presence of the enemy, a vicious predator. I am her protector. She drops her hand and hides behind my leg, squeezing it tightly. Dragging her along, I limp towards the car.

Clickclickclick . . .

"Here's your crown, Gabby," the photographer says.

I pull it out of his hand. "Leave her alone."

"Alice, I'm sorry. It's just—"

I turn around, whipping Gabby along with me.

"You're sorry? *You're sorry?* How dare you tell me you're sorry! If you're so sorry, don't publish those photos. If you're so sorry, destroy the pictures you just took."

I turn towards the car.

"Really. I'm not such a bad guy. I'm just trying to make a living."

I stop in my tracks and turn toward him. I am no longer in my body.

"I love that one," I say, my voice hoarse as I let out a raspy laugh. "Love it. There's millions and millions of ways to make a living. You chose this. No one forced you. And you know what? I know exactly what you're going to do. There will be a picture of me, looking disheveled and frenzied and just horrible. Right? You'll run some caption. 'The Woman Scorned.' And next to it will be a picture of her, wearing a Versace gown at the Oscars. She'll look exceptionally elegant. I'll look especially frazzled and frumpy. And Gabby will look like a brat having a temper tantrum. Then the entire world will think, well, who can blame him? I'd leave her and that kid, too. And that's the end of it. The story's over for everyone but me."

"What?" A scared, tinny voice comes from my leg. In my rage I'd forgotten about Gabby. I hear tiny sobs bubbling out of her. I bend down and she throws her arms around my neck. Her body shakes.

"Baby. It's okay. It's okay . . ."

"No, Mommy. No."

She looks up at me, her enormous hazel eyes welling with tears.

"Daddy's gone?" Her voice sputters and chokes. "Daddy left us? Mommy, Daddy left *me?* Doesn't he love me anymore? I'll be better. I won't throw my toys. I'll clean my room. I won't have meltdowns anymore. I promise. I know I'm a really bad, bad girl, but I'll be good."

She starts sobbing so hard I pick her up. Her hot tears race down my neck.

"Shhh, you're the best girl. You didn't do anything, baby. You didn't do anything. Daddy loves you."

A video camera whirls. Cameras click away. A reporter holds out a tape recorder. I don't care. I close my eyes and squeeze my daughter tight as her tiny body convulses in sobs. My car keys drop. I feel a hand on my back. The photographer Gabby barreled into slowly turns me and guides me toward my car. I don't resist. I'm not even there anymore.

"Johnny, move. You're blocking our view," someone yells.

"What are you doing? Getting an exclusive? We're onto you. Move your ass, John."

"He's sabotaging our photos! Move it."

He ignores them. I feel his hand leave my back for a second. I imagine he's flashed the finger. He opens the car doors for us and straps Gabby in her car seat. Even though I hate him, I let him. Every drop of energy has been sucked out of me. He hands me the keys. I stare at them as if trying to figure out what they're for. As my hand shakes, I fit the key into the ignition. I try to remember how to drive. The window is filthy with tree sap. Alex would never have let that happen.

Johnny slams Gabby's door and moves toward mine. "I'll shut your front door. Just drive out of here and don't make eye contact with any of them. Okay? And as for what you said before, you're more beautiful than she is, even in jeans and a T-shirt. Okay? I'm really sorry."

"Yeah, sure," I snarl. Johnny actually winces as if my words have punched him in the jaw. I guess everyone else he's said this to has believed him. I shut my eyes and pull at the door. Tomorrow he'll get his check and move on to the next pathetic subject.

My eyes well up again. I can barely see out of the window. I hit the wiper fluid button and am surprised to find that some water trickles out. I turn on the windshield wipers.

Rainbow makers. That's what Gabby calls them. Every time I turn them on she claps her hands as if it's a magic trick. Today she is silent as the wipers smear sludgy sap across the window.

I slowly back out of the driveway. I can sense them on either side of me, snapping away, but I refuse to turn. I hear them calling for me.

"Alice! Alice! Alice!"

I look straight ahead. My eyes land right on Johnny. For a second I forget what he's done and I think they might be the kindest eyes I have ever seen. Deep blue with little wrinkles underneath, probably from squinting through a lens for so many years. Then he pulls his Nikon up like he's about to take my photo. Asshole! But instead of clicking away, he turns it around so its back is facing me. Then he presses what I imagine is the delete button. He pounds away with his thumb, throwing out all the photos of Gabby and me.

I nod. But I don't really believe him. It's for show. Maybe he just deleted a bunch, but there's probably hundreds more. Maybe later he'll pull the photos out of the trash bin. I'm a publicist. I know the game. He's playing good cop so tomorrow or the next day he can ring the bell and get the exclusive.

"Remember me? I'm not like the others. I'm a good guy. So, you think I can have some photos of you and Alex in happier times? Maybe from your wedding? Your honeymoon? The birth of Gabby?"

After all, if you can't even trust the man you thought you loved more than anything, how can you trust anyone?

2

Try to Remember

Sometimes I call my mother by her first name, Mary, because it's easier. This woman with the expressionless eyes and the clamped dry lips and the disheveled hair doesn't resemble my mother in the least. My mother died about three years ago. The gods shut down her brain but forgot the heart switch, so it beats on, oblivious.

For a while I would try to force her to remember. I'd show her pictures of Dad, her sisters, Madeline and Margaret, her house in Larchmont, Gracie, our black Lab, vacations at the Cape or the Jersey Shore or Montauk.

"Remember? Remember?" I'd plead. "Of course you remember Dad, right? Remember? Look how handsome he was. That's you, me, and Dad when we took the cruise to Bermuda. Remember how seasick you were? I won one hundred fifty-nine dollars at bingo. Remember?"

She'd smile and nod her head, but her cloudy gray eyes remained unfocused. Still, I'd convince myself that it was all coming back, that any day Mom would return to me. Despite what the doctors had said, it wasn't really Alzheimer's. Only an autopsy can diagnose Alzheimer's.

Every day Mom's memory was improving. Even Hilda, the Teutonic caregiver, would agree. "Yes, your mother hass more clarity."

Only Trinity, one of Hilda's employees, was honest with me. She was in her mid-forties, but sometimes she looked like she was barely twenty and other times she looked sixty. She's from Manila, where Filipinos leave their mothers and fathers and sons and daughters and husbands to come to America to care for our mothers and fathers and sons and daughters and husbands.

Trinity met me outside one day before my visit.

"If you don' mind, you visiting with the mommy of yours is berry much upsetting. When you leave, he cries," she said, bungling pronouns as usual. "If you don' mind me tell you this, he will never be better. It is berry much frustrating for him."

She looked at me, nervously, her eyes brimming with tears, and I knew she loved my mother. She was the only one I could trust.

"Thank you," I said weakly.

"If you just sit with your mommy and hold his hand, he would be berry much liking that. Or talking, too, but not force, force, forcing to remember what's forgotten forever. That mommy of yours is dead, I'm berry sorry to say. You must be accepting of that."

So that's what I do now. I sit and hold her hand and tell her about my life and imagine what she would have said just a few years ago. I force myself not to use the word *remember*.

When I arrived earlier, Hilda met me at the door.

"Your mother's language iss very bad. It iss very upsetting to zee other boarders. You must do something ASAP. I cannot subject my boarders to such vulgarities. Zey are very sensitive."

Trinity had mentioned a few weeks ago that my mother had started cursing.

"He has been saying cockasucka and muddafooker," she whispered, her eyes staring at the floor.

I laughed. "What?" Surely I heard her wrong. This is a woman who said "heck" for hell, and "cripes" for everything else when she felt naughty. I must be naïve, but it's hard for me to believe that my mother even knows these words or what they mean.

"He has been using berry bad words."

"It's a mistake. You must have heard wrong."

Today Mary and I have the drab living room with the pilled and stained beige carpeting practically to ourselves. Trinity is outside playing catch with Gabby. Hilda went to Costco with her son, Hans, who helps run the place. Dorothy is napping in her bedroom. DeeDee, the other caregiver, is changing Hal's diaper. Agnes went to lunch with her daughter. Only The Laugher sits near us on the other beige floral couch. Her eyes stare at Dr. Phil on the television. Every few minutes, she'll break out into a fit of hysterical laughter that ends as abruptly as it began. And The Satellite walks in and out every few minutes. All day long she slogs through the house as if searching for the mother planet.

"Alex is gone," I say. I can't help but study Mom's face for a moment to see if it registers. Her milky eyes stare at something ahead only she sees.

"Alex is my husband. We've been married for six years. Rem—" I stop myself. "I really thought it was forever. I never ever imagined this would be my life. I know it's probably naïve of me, but divorce is something for other people. I mean, look how happy you and Dad seemed to be. Re—I know Alex and I could fight, but every couple has problems. I always figured we'd work everything out."

I pause and take a deep breath as The Laugher guffaws for a moment. The Satellite does a lap through the living room and heads toward the back bedrooms. I see a Waxie, those paper toilet seat covers, hanging out of her faded elastic-top polyester pants. The Satellite was once a headline singer with the Tommy Dorsey Band.

Frank Sinatra hit on her, her son once told me. Maybe she believes if she walks long enough, she can reenter that world.

"And even now I think it's somehow going to work itself out. I never thought I'd be one of those people, but part of me thinks I could forgive him. Well, he'd have to come crawling back, admit he was a fool, tell me he always loved me, what a mistake it was, how he was going through a crisis. Of course, I'd say I need some time to think about it. But he'll probably be persistent. He'd beg and beg. He'd leave me bouquets of flowers. He'd write me poetry. He'd send me romantic homemade CDs. Then when I couldn't resist anymore, I'd take him back, but I'd insist on serious couple's therapy before he could live in the house again."

As if on cue, The Laugher erupts into hysterics. She clutches her stomach and wheezes. She curls her head into her lap and her body shakes. Then it abruptly stops. Dr. Phil chastises some woman about her weight. Dr. Phil, a paunchy guy who reeks lethargy, has somehow become a weight loss guru. Am I the only one who doesn't get it?

Mom would have understood. She would have loathed Dr. Phil. *"That fraud,"* she would have said. *"Why are people so stupid? He's fat and he's telling them to diet? And they're eating it all up. See the way they look at him? Like he's their god."*

Mom would have been the one I'd talk to about this. The infidelity part would have been hard, though. Mom would have said don't ever take him back. But right now, in order to get through the day, I have to believe I could eventually forgive. Just like we all must believe we'll always be the same person we are right now, never some old lady shuffling around wearing a Waxie like a tail.

I would have told Mom everything. This is where I would have begun.

Alex is an entertainment lawyer. He works for a big firm that handles actors, singers, directors, producers, screenwriters. For the most part, Alex negotiates contracts for the behind-the-scenes people, like set designers and costumers. It wasn't the most glamorous job at the firm, but he seemed happy. Then, a few months ago, he was hand-picked by Rose Maris to represent her in a breach of contract suit. It turns out the woman who designed her costume for some period piece raved about Alex, so of course she had to have him represent her. Although she's the biggest movie star out there, Alex was blasé about handling her, even if he was slightly giddy about the publicity the case would receive. He was on his way to big times, we thought.

At first we made fun of her. He'd come home from the office, pop open a bottle of Sierra Nevada, and tell Gabby and me stories.

"Today she showed up with Taquito, her Chihuahua. She was dressed in a plaid pea cap, a matching scarf, and her nails were painted red."

"So?"

"So? I'm not talking about Rose, Al. I'm talking about the dog. It's crazy. She talks to the thing like it's a person. She kept feeding it these little macrobiotic dog bone treats she had specially baked. She's making twenty mill a picture and she's completely insane."

"I want a Chihuahua with red nails," Gabby said. "Can I? Can I?"

The case consumed him. Rose had signed on to star in a thriller called *Calm Storm*. Three days into production she decided it was a mistake and she just didn't show. Because of it, the producers lost millions and sued her. She says they reneged on many of the con-tractual agreements, including creative control and final script ap-proval.

"This is great for my career, but stop me if I ever take on another celebrity, please. She's nuts," Alex would say.

All the women at the office I worked in thought *I* was nuts.

"You've gotta be kidding me. I would never allow my husband to take on that case," Judy said. "I mean, I trust my husband up to a point, but come on, they're only human."

"You know her reputation. She'd sleep with her dog if its cock were big enough," Claire said.

"Her dog's female," I said. "Besides, I completely trust Alex."

"There's no such beast in Hollywood. Trust is something you can have when you're a beauty queen living in the Ozarks."

But I laughed it off. Alex and I were soulmates. Yes, he started working later and later, but I supported it. He needed a big high-profile case like this to get him in the spotlight. We'd just built a 3,500-square-foot ranch house and dumped most of our savings into it. The bulldozers had started digging up our property for the infinity pool. We were hemorrhaging money. And while I questioned the need for a state-of-the-art entertainment center, an infinity pool, and a Jacuzzi with jets that could blow you to another planet, Alex said I needed to relax. He was on his way to partner. Soon we'd be having lots of parties.

"So? I hate big TVs. You used to hate them, too. You'd say the bigger the TV, the smaller the IQ."

"I'm an entertainment lawyer. I need an entertainment center. And I need a big HDTV. I'm going blind from reading fine print all day. Stop being such a downer."

Yes. It's true. Alex was working longer hours and we were fighting more. And one day I realized he'd stopped telling horror stories about Rose. I think it dawned on me the day he came home with an enormous box of Krispy Kremes.

"We don't eat this junk," I said. "One of those and Gabby will be jumping on the ceiling for days."

"Rose brought about five hundred donuts in for the office. She gave me this box to take home for you and Gabby. She said to tell you thanks for sharing me with her."

"What the hell does that mean?"

"Jeez, Ally, she was just being nice. She's not so bad. She knows I haven't been home as much as you'd like. This was a kind of peace offering."

"Yeah, a peace offering designed to turn me into a blimp. I bet she's never eaten a donut."

Alex smiled at some private thought. "Actually, I saw her eat two enormous chocolate ones right in my office. Really, she's not obsessed with her weight."

I suddenly flashed to the movie *Vegas Charade,* where she plays a stripper who suggestively devours a box of Godiva. She licks the chocolate off with more passion than most of us have for our husbands. God knows what kind of head she gave a Krispy Kreme.

"And then she probably left to puke."

"You know what? She's pretty down to earth. I bet the two of you would hit it off. Actually, she really wants to meet you. Well, listen, I'm going to run to the gym."

That's another thing. The gym. Alex, who'd usually come home from work, eat dinner, scoop out a bowl of Cherry Garcia, and stretch out on the couch in front of the steroid-laden TV, started heading for the gym. His beer gut melted away.

"Daddy, your arms look just like Popeye's," Gabby would say.

He'd flex for her. Then hoist her into the air until she'd scream with glee.

"I love you, Daddy. You're the best daddy in the whole world. And I love this," Gabby said, pulling at the tuft of hair growing on Alex's chin. "Even though Mommy doesn't."

That would be his new goatee. Another sign I ignored. Alex had just turned thirty-nine. I chalked it up to a midlife crisis.

And then came the baby issue. We'd wanted a playmate for Gabby for a long time, but kept procrastinating. We decided our Laurel Canyon bungalow was too small for another child. We'd wait until we could afford to move. Then we bought property. We'd wait until the house was built. Then we'd wait until Alex got a bonus, a promotion. We'd wait until I had enough clients to freelance.

Wait. Wait. Wait.

Tick. Tick Tick.

One day I was thirty-eight.

We finally had the house. Alex was close to a promotion. I had a lot of clients. There was no reason to wait.

"Just let's see how this case unravels."

"*What?* You can have an entertainment center and an infinity pool, but not another child? What are we waiting for? This is what we always wanted."

"It's just . . ."

"It's just what?"

"No, you're right. It's what we always wanted."

"Gee, that's convincing."

"I've just been so tired lately."

"Then don't go to the gym every night."

"What do you want, Alice? A few months ago you told me I had a gut. Well, look, I got rid of it."

"Okay. Okay."

"*Mommy*, stop yelling at Daddy."

"I'm not yelling at Daddy. I'm discussing."

"Why does dis-custing sound just like yelling?"

A few weeks later, Alex took me to dinner at Koi, an oh-so-trendy Japanese restaurant in West Hollywood frequented by the people Alex and I used to loathe. We were having a night out with Rose and her boyfriend, a musician I'd never heard of named Finn.

"I can't believe you're having dinner with her. I mean, you know what her motives are," Judy had said earlier that day.

"Motives?"

"She wants to check you out before she swoops in for the kill. She wants to meet the enemy."

"I don't consider her competition."

"No offense, but she doesn't consider you competition either."

"Gee, thanks for the support."

"Come on, Al, she's a multimillionaire hot mega star. She gets what she wants. And it sounds like she wants your husband."

That's the part that still baffles me. Alex is cute. He's got dark, liquid brown eyes and thick brown hair that hasn't shown any signs of receding. He's got an angular jaw. But sometimes his eyes seem to pop out of his head when he's angry or excited, and it makes him look insane. Besides, Los Angeles is awash in beautiful people. Why Alex Hirsh?

"Judy, you need a hobby."

"Ally, you need a reality check."

I snuck out of work early, had my hair highlighted and cut, my nails and toes manicured. I wore the hottest outfit I owned—a tight black dress with a plunging neckline and a pair of black three-inch Jimmy Choos. I looked great.

I was whisked to a table by an obsequious host as soon as I mentioned the reservation was under Rose's name. Ben, a partner at the firm, and Ben's wife, Aurora, were already at the table with Alex when I got there. Two empty seats remained for Rose and Finn.

"Isn't this exciting?" Aurora giggled. Aurora was about forty years old with enormous fake boobs and a body toned from hours and hours of kickboxing and pilates. She was one of those women who did nothing all day but exercise and drive around in her Lincoln Navigator while chatting on her cell phone and depositing her kids at private schools and soccer practices.

"I just love everything Rose is in. I am so nervous. I have no idea what I'm going to say to her. Ben says she's really down to earth. Did you hear how she brought in like one thousand Krispy Kremes? And she even ate a few? Can you believe it? If I ate just one of them I'd be a blimp. She probably is one of those people with an incredible metabolism, too."

Alex stood up, kissed me, and told me I looked beautiful. I felt giddy, too. Not because I was meeting Rose, but because I felt like I was on a date with my husband. He looked so handsome in his black Armani blazer, dark blue button down shirt, and tan linen pants. Even his goatee looked great. He smiled as he poured me some Pellegrino. A wave of relief washed over me. I had nothing to worry about.

"Isn't this place great," he said.

It quickly crossed my mind that a few years ago he would have made fun of this overly feng-shuied, forced Zen kind of place. But maybe it wasn't so bad. Maybe I was too judgmental. *Lighten up, Alice,* I told myself. *Learn to have a good time.*

"Sure. It's really great," I said. "And you look great." I squeezed his six-pack.

About a half hour later a murmur raced through the restaurant. Even here, where celebrity sightings were as common as sushi, Rose's entrance commanded attention. She pretended not to notice any of it as she headed directly for me. She wrapped her slinky but toned and buffed arms around me. Finn stood behind her, grinning. Alex got up and shook his hand.

"Ally, it's so nice to finally meet you," she said, ignoring everyone else, including poor Aurora, who had jumped out of her seat.

Rose turned toward Alex. "Now move your butt over a seat. I'm sitting next to your beautiful wife and there's nothing you can do about it. And if you or Ben bring up the word lawsuit, I'm walking out. Right, Ally? I've had enough legal talk for a lifetime. I'm sure you have, too."

Throughout dinner, Rose touched my leg and my arm. "You're so wonderful for sharing Alex with me. He's really talented and dedicated. Before I met him, lawyers were all these horrible stereotypes. But he's so much more than that. He really seems to care about what he does. You're so lucky, Alice. He seems so devoted to Gabby. Now tell me more about that beautiful daughter of yours. I hear she's quite precocious."

"She is, but every mother probably believes that about their kids."

"One day I want to have children. I'd love a girl and a boy. I have their names picked out and everything—Avalon for the girl and Paz for the boy. But I hate the thought of pain. I can't imagine pushing out a baby. Drugs. Did you have drugs? I know it's trendy to say you want to do it naturally, but I can't imagine it. Drug me up, baby. Knock me out. That's how I was born. My mother was unconscious from all the drugs they pumped into her. Maybe that's why I'm so insane. Anyway, you'll have to give me advice. Okay? A friend of mine did the whole hypnotherapy thing, but I think I'm too strong-willed for that. I don't think anyone could convince me I'm not in pain when I'm in fucking pain."

Throughout dinner, she talked and talked and asked questions but never waited for answers. Actually, I didn't mind. It was effortless for me. I sat there, nodded my head and everyone around wondered what I was saying that had the biggest actress in the world so enthralled. Poor Aurora desperately tried to become part of the conversation.

"Pain? I have two boys with enormous heads, just like their father. I tore my vagina so bad."

Rose scrunched up her face. "*Gross.* You poor thing," she said to Aurora. Then she turned toward me and rolled her eyes. "Too much information, thank you very much. Like I need to know how enormous your pussy is."

Afterwards Rose invited us to a private party at Dolce, but Alex declined. He swung his arm around me. "I think we'll just head home. We've got a babysitter with a curfew." Then he whispered into my ear. "Plus, we should try out our new Jacuzzi."

"That's so cute," Rose said. "A babysitter. Hell, I feel I still need a babysitter."

"Hey, I just realized something—you're Alex and Alice. Al and Al. Al Squared," Aurora said. "How adorable. It's like you two were meant to be together."

"Very adorable," Rose said flatly.

I barely heard any of them. The innuendo of sex lingered in my mind. Alex had been so tired lately it had been nearly a month. But when he mentioned the hot tub, I knew what he really meant. It's funny what happened to us once we were married people with children. Suddenly, there's this shyness about sex. When we were single or married without kids we'd just say things like, "Let's get home and tear each other's clothes off." Now it's, "*Let's take a hot tub.*"

Rose's black Maserati pulled up, followed by Alex's white Lexus and Ben's bright red Hummer. We all exchanged air kisses and promises of future get-togethers. Rose hugged me hard, said it was great to finally meet me and that we should get together for lunch and shopping real soon. Then Alex and I drove the twenty miles back to the Valley.

"See, she wasn't so bad," Alex said.

No, she really isn't, I thought, silently thinking how wrong my friends had been. Alex barely looked at Rose throughout dinner. *Alex is in love with you, Alice. Al and Al. Al Squared. You were meant to be together.* Even Rose had to notice that.

Alex lit votives around the Jacuzzi. He poured us Grand Marniers. We sat in the hot tub with its waterfall illuminated by rotating colored lights, sipping our drinks and looking out at the dazzling lights of the valley in front of us.

"So did you have fun tonight?"

"Sure. I'm having fun right now."

We leaned in and kissed. Soon we were right on the deck, atop a towel, having sex and keeping one ear open for Gabby.

A month later, I discovered I was pregnant.

Gabby followed me into the bathroom when I checked the stick. Her big eyes stared hard at it. "What's that?"

I blurted it out. "Mommy's going to have a baby."

I should have waited. She's only five, but sometimes I forget. She seems like such an old little soul. That night when Alex walked into the foyer, she jumped on him.

"I'm getting a sister. I'm getting a sister. Mommy's having a baby."

He squinted at me. "Is that true?"

I smiled so hard my cheeks hurt.

He smiled, kissed me lightly on the cheek, and went into the bedroom to change into his gym clothes.

"Aren't you happy about it?" I asked when I followed him in.

"Well, you could have told me before you told our child. Who else did you tell?"

"No one."

"Yeah, sure. I'm sure you told Judy already. You tell her everything."

"I didn't tell anyone. Gabby happened to see the stick."

"And you couldn't have bullshitted her? I mean, come on, Al, it's kinda weird hearing this from your kid." He shook his head and tied his sneakers. "I just gotta get a workout to clear my head. I'll be back soon."

That night I lay in bed thinking how different it was when I told him I was pregnant with Gabby. We hugged and kissed and went out to our favorite restaurant and came back and had crazy sex. Now he slept with his back toward me. What did this mean?

A few weeks later, Alex was working late when a searing pain shot through my left side. I curled on the couch imagining there could be a positive explanation for this. My stomach was expanding. It was muscle cramps. The fetus was attaching itself to the wall of the uterus. Normal pregnancy stuff, I told myself. There was even an explanation for the drops of blood in my underwear. Implantation, the pregnancy book said.

The pain didn't subside. It got worse. I started vomiting. I called Alex at work. Nothing. I called his cell phone. Nothing. I called my doctor, who said to go to the emergency room. I called Celia, Gabby's babysitter. Gabby was already asleep. When Celia arrived, I could barely stand, but I forced myself upright.

"I've got to go to the emergency room," I said through clenched teeth.

She looked at me like I was insane. "Gee, Alice, should I call someone?"

"I'm fine. It's probably nothing," I said as I walked doubled over to the car.

I drove to the Tarzana hospital, only a few miles from my house. My fingers shook as I dialed Alex's number over and over. When I got to the hospital, I had to take a ticket for parking. As I stuck my hand out the window for the ticket, the pain coursed through me and I squeezed myself into a ball. I sat there for a moment, breathing heavily as a few cars lined up behind me. I vomited out the window. I wondered why a hospital would have this. Isn't it the most horrible thing in the world? You can be dying, bleeding to death, yet you must stop to take a ticket to park your car. Nothing is free. Hopefully you won't take too long to die, because then you'll owe a lot of money.

A car behind me honked.

I took my ticket and the gate opened.

Inside, the emergency room was empty and quiet. The admitting nurse was a fifty-year-old man who looked like he should be doing something else, like swabbing a deck. He grilled me.

"What are your symptoms?"

"I think I'm having a miscarriage," I said, trying not to cry.

He impatiently shook his head, scribbled something into his admissions books and spit out, "That's not a symptom. That's a diagnosis."

I wanted to scream and curse at him, but I knew I'd be stuck in the waiting room for hours. "Well, I'm in a lot of pain," I said, gritting my teeth.

The nurses took my blood and urine. They hooked me up to a painkiller that instantly numbed me.

"Am I having a miscarriage," I asked.

"You'll have to wait for the doctor."

"Can't someone tell me something?"

Dr. Ryder raced into the emergency room at the same time as Alex. Alex held my hand as the doctor examined me. He stuck a wand up me and gave me an internal ultrasound.

"Am I having a miscarriage?"

"I don't think so," Dr. Ryder said.

"Really?" A wave of relief washed over me. "I guess I have a low pain threshold. It's just implantation, right? I'm so embarrassed. Because I was convinced that—"

Dr. Ryder coughed softly as he stared straight ahead at the monitor. I watched the grainy image of my womb. It looked like images being transmitted from the moon.

Dr. Ryder squinted. "See, there's no rice."

"What?"

"That's what the fertilized egg should look like. A pulsating piece of rice, but it's not there."

"So she's not pregnant?" Alex asked.

"I imagined it?"

"No. It's what's called an ectopic pregnancy. The fertilized egg is most likely lodged in your tube. We have to operate right away. It's a simple procedure, actually. Laparoscopy. We have to locate the pregnancy. It could be in the tubes. It could be in the ovaries. I'm hoping it's in the tubes. If it's in the ovaries we face the risk of it exploding and possibly damaging—"

I turned to Alex, who was suddenly pale. His eyes rolled back. Dr. Ryder and a nurse helped him to a chair while someone else raced to get him water.

I felt numb. "I don't want to be operated on. Can't I just go home and see how I feel tomorrow? Can't I get a second opinion? Isn't there a pill I can take?"

Dr. Ryder ignored me. "There are a few things you must know."

He started rattling off everything. How they'd pump my stomach with gas. Then he'd search around my tubes for this wayward baby. He explained worst case scenerios, something about never being able to reproduce again. Alex and I started crying.

A nurse breezed in with forms to fill out. "Would you like more information about a living will?"

"A what?"

"It's just a formality, in case you . . . well . . . can no longer take care of yourself."

"Shit," Alex said, his hands trembling.

"I don't want to be a vegetable."

"It's just routine. It won't happen. So, do you want more information?"

"No."

"Sign here then."

As I signed away my life, Alex bent down close to me. He held my face.

"I love you, Al. I'm so, so sorry. Please, please, please forgive me."

"For what?"

"Everything. I'm sorry I wasn't more excited when you told me. I'm so sorry. We'll try again real soon. I promise. As soon as you're better."

He held my hand as they wheeled me down the fluorescent-lit corridor. Then our hands parted as the doors to the emergency room swung open. *God, he really loves me,* I thought as they put the gas mask on my face and told me to count backwards.

When I woke up, Alex's face was staring down at me. "You're okay," he said, rubbing my head. "They got it out. Your tubes are fine. You can have lots more children. The doctor said you could go home in about two hours. Can you believe that? I thought you'd at least have to stay overnight. And in a month or so, we can even start trying again."

"I'd like that," I said drowsily.

He put his head on my chest and heaved with sobs. I stroked the back of his head. I'd known him for eight years and I'd never seen him cry like this. It was actually starting to scare me a bit.

I spent the next three days in bed, with the blinds shut. Alex worked out of the house on Thursday and Friday to take care of Gabby and me.

"Was it my fault the baby went away," Gabby asked when I tried to explain what had happened.

"Of course not. That's crazy."

"Maybe it didn't want to have me as a sister so it went away. Maybe I shouldn't have screamed so much. Maybe I scared the baby. I'm sorry. I'll be better."

I started to cry. "No. The baby was in the wrong place. It was so small. The size of a piece of rice. But we'll get it to come back. I promise. We'll give you a little brother or sister."

"I don't think I want a brother."

I slept a lot. I'd never felt so tired in my life. I didn't dream. I'd sleep, wake up, get out of bed, take a shower, and feel totally depleted. So I'd go back to bed and fall back into a thick, dreamless sleep.

Little did I know it would be the last dreamless sleep I'd have for a long, long time.

On Saturday, I slept most of the day while Alex took Gabby to a park. When I woke up, I had some energy for the first time. I took a shower, brewed some tea, and sat outside on a teak chaise lounge. I looked out at our incredible view of the valley with its chaparral-covered mountains and hills, its perfect grid of streets, the manicured lawns, each with a backyard pool. Maybe the Valley wasn't as soulless as I had thought. At least it wasn't Calabasas, a few towns over, where every house looked exactly the same.

Maybe I could even start liking the place.

I was suddenly overwhelmed with happiness. I had a husband who loved me, a wonderful little girl, and in about a month, we could start trying to expand our family again.

The door clicked opened and Gabby bounded into the house.

"Mommy, Mommy, Mommy," she screamed.

"Shhh, let Mommy sleep," Alex said.

When she saw me on the deck, she squealed, raced toward me, and jumped onto my lap.

"Oww," I groaned. "Be careful. Mommy's a little sore."

"But you're awake. Yay." She slathered me with kisses.

"How was the playground?"

"We had fun. Daddy and I did spider on the swing for the longest time. He's really good, you know. He can go very high high high. Much higher than you."

"That's good."

"Gabby," Alex said. "Let Mommy rest."

"Then we played tag, but Daddy couldn't catch me. And then we got ice cream. Daddy let me get two scoops and I got gummy worms on top. And you know what—"

"Gabby," Alex said sternly. "Let's let Mommy rest."

"Daddy's famous."

"Really? Well, that's nice," I said.

Alex coughed. "So how are you feeling?"

"A lot bett—"

"It's really, really, really true. There was a picture of him on the front of a magazine at the ice cream store. Even the man at the counter knew it was Daddy. He said 'way to go' and he gave Daddy a thumbs up."

I looked quizzically at Alex and shook my head in confusion. When she was younger, Gabby would always mistake people on the covers of magazines for Mommy or Daddy. She'd point to a picture of Brad Pitt or Bill Gates and say, "Dada."

"It's really, really true. Tell Mommy, Daddy."

I giggled and rolled my eyes at Alex. But he looked absolutely petrified. His face was bright red. His eyes bulged. He tried to casually shrug.

"You know how it is. You take on a high-profile client. The *Enquirer* sees you out in public and assumes things. It was bound to happen."

"The *Enquirer*?" I said.

The tea I sipped got stuck in my throat and I coughed. One thing I had learned over the years about the *Enquirer* was that no matter how sleazy it was, it was almost always right. If it said someone was on their deathbed, they'd be dead in a month. If it said a celebrity was cheating on his wife, in a week they'd be filing for divorce, announcing it had nothing to do with the horrible tabloid reports, and that they were still the best of friends with mutual respect and love for one another and to please honor their need for privacy at this most sensitive time.

"Ally, it's crazy." Alex checked his watch as if trying to decipher something. "Well, it's good to see you up again. I'm just going to read some e-mails."

Gabby brought out her Barbies. "Let's talk dolls," she said. "My Barbie is Cinderella. You can be Ariel. But you're not still living in the sea. You already have legs, okay? If you try to go back, you'll drown."

Later, I checked the phone messages. The phone had been ringing nonstop all day but I'd been too tired to answer. I figured everyone was checking up on me. Now, I realized that they had seen the *Enquirer* and wanted to know what was going on. There was a message from my Aunt Maddy, Claire, and Judy. I decided to call Judy. She'd have the story right next to her and be waiting for my call.

"It says here they were seen canoodling. God, I hate that word. Anyway, witnesses say they were canoodling at a remote table . . . Wednesday night at Spago's."

Wednesday night I drove myself to the hospital. Were they snuggling at Spago's while I was struggling with a toll machine at the hospital?

"So are they canoodling? Is there a picture of them canoodling?"

"No. There's just a picture of Alex holding open a car door for her. But I mean, come on. Alex would do that for anyone. It could have been just a confab about the case."

"Sure. You're probably right," I said, while thinking, why did he tell me it was a staff meeting? And why would Judy suddenly pretend everything's okay when for weeks she's been warning me that everything wasn't?

"You okay?"

"Sure," I said, trying to smile into the phone. "No. I mean, I really don't know what I am."

That night I waited on the sofa for Alex as he read *Cinderella* to Gabby. He seemed to take longer than usual, nearly an hour. Afterwards, he grabbed a Red Trolley Ale out of the refrigerator and headed towards his office. I grabbed my stomach—the pain was like a few quick stabs with a knife.

"I gotta shitload of work," he mumbled.

"We need to talk."

"Can it wait? I'm so behind, what with taking the last few days off and all."

"Alex, what's going on?"

My head pounded. I felt sick. *Please say the right thing*, I begged. *Please, make this easy and we can just move on.*

"Shit, Alice, it's horrible, isn't it? It was an innocent dinner. We needed to discuss some aspects of the case. We were both hungry. I probably should have kept it at the office, that was stupid of me, but I wasn't thinking. I'm not used to the press. I mean, I go out to dinner with lots of clients. But canoodling, come on. We were hardly canoodling. It was a lawyer-client meeting. You know you're the only one for me. But if this has upset you, I'll tell Rose someone else at the firm will be handling the case from now on. I'm not going to risk my marriage for some stupid breach of contract bullshit, which by the way, she is completely guilty of. God, she's just a vapid idiot."

If only he would say it. My whole body was on the brink of convulsing. I swallowed hard. A few knives stabbed my sides.

Alex stood there for hours, it seemed. He took a long, slow slug of his Red Trolley and wiped his mouth with a hand. He took a deep breath and shifted his eyes towards the floor. Everything was in slow motion.

"I don't know."

I don't know. What did that even mean?

"You don't know what?"

"I'm really sorry. I didn't mean for any of this to happen. Honest, I didn't. And I feel like a complete shit, especially with what happened to you the other day. I should have been there for you."

I couldn't see. Everything was suddenly blurry. My stomach felt turned inside out. Maybe I wasn't hearing right.

"You didn't mean for any of *what* to happen?" My voice was loud and unsteady. "You mean you should have told me you were having a business dinner with Rose, right? You forgot to tell me and you feel bad. No big deal, right? A client-lawyer thing. Right? Right?" *Just. Say. It. Even if it's a lie, just say it.*

My voice throbbed in my ears. I was screaming. Alex's Adam's apple bobbed up and down, up and down. It looked like it was having some weird seizure. My head felt like it would implode. I braced for what I imagined would be the worst, but still hoped for a miracle.

Say this, Alex, please say, "Things got a little out of hand. I'm sorry. I didn't mean for anything to happen, but she was so persistent. It really was not a big deal. It will never happen again, Alice. I promise. I love you. Can we get past this? I'll do anything not to lose you."

I waited and imagined that I could eventually live with this. I never thought I could be one of those forgiving wives. Maybe it wouldn't be so bad. I remembered Greg, my personal trainer. I had some impure thoughts about him. He had the best body I'd ever seen, with those crazy ripples of muscle everywhere. Maybe if he hadn't been gay, I would have cheated . . . *No, Alice, who are you kidding? You're not the cheating type. No one in your family's the cheating type. You hate cheaters. You said you'd never ever put up with a cheater.*

The thoughts churned in my head. It had been minutes since Alex had spoken. I looked over. He held onto the back of the sofa and his eyes were shut. I wondered if he was about to faint.

"Alex . . ."

"I really don't want to talk about this."

"Well, I do."

"Can't we talk about this later? I have to sort through things before I put them in words."

"Sort through what?"

He squeezed his eyes tighter and inhaled. Suddenly cheating seemed innocuous. Suddenly I had the most horrible thought in the entire world. My heart pummeled at my ribs.

"Are you . . . are you . . . in love with her?"

I felt like I was reciting cheesy dialogue from a bad rom-com starring Kate Hudson. The word *love* got caught in my throat as if I had swallowed it the wrong way.

Cue the laughter. Hysterical laughter. "With who? Rose? You've gotta be kidding me. Alice, I love you. I don't love Rose. I told her you were the only one for me. Oh, Ally, you and that imagination of yours."

But instead there was silence. The loudest silence I've ever heard. The refrigerator hummed. A fly buzzed somewhere. Air molecules crashed into each other. A clock in the kitchen ticked off each incredibly endless second of silence.

"Are you in love with her? Alex? Alex?"

He stared at the floor while holding the couch as if it would somehow protect him.

"Alex?"

Come on, you moron. How could you be in love with her? Sure, she's beautiful, rich, and a movie star. But it's Rose Maris. She's not someone you fall in love with. You might want to sleep with her. I can't blame you for that. But come on, you have a wife and a child. She has a new boyfriend every week. When we went out to dinner it was Finn. Since then, she's been linked to someone named Cory and someone named Marlon. You're willing to give up all this for a week with a flaky movie star with a Chihuahua with painted nails? Come on! Where's Alex Hirsh? The man I married? Who is this alien standing in front of me?

He looked up at me, tears streaming down his face. And everything became clear. But as if I needed the words, he spoke in the smallest voice I'd ever heard.

"I don't know."

"You don't know? *You don't know? What don't you know?*"

"Mommy? Mommy, I want water," Gabby screamed from her bedroom. Gabby always has impeccable timing. It's like some unconscious part of her detects stress in the house.

"Mommy! Mommy!"

I was paralyzed. Alex didn't move. He gripped the couch even tighter.

"Get out," I growled in a voice I'd never heard before just as Gabby shuffled into the room in her Ariel nightgown. She clutched Lambie Pie, her stuffed wooly lamb that plays "Jesus Loves Me" when you wind it. She was sleepy and beautiful and disheveled and the most innocent thing in the world. I felt all her innocence slipping away and she was too innocent to even know it. As she stood there, she was losing all the things I took for granted as a child. And I started bawling right there, uncontrollably.

"Mommy? Mommy . . ."

"Mommy's just a little sad about the baby," I said. "But it's okay."

So that's what I would have told my mom. Just a few days ago, I was sipping tea, looking out into the Valley and believing life couldn't be better. Now I want to cry. My husband is living in a condo in Marina del Rey while trying to decide whether or not he's in love with Rose Maris, whether or not he loves me. What to do next. Gabby and I are in limbo, holed up in a still mostly unfurnished, undecorated house, trapped by paparazzi vultures feeding on the entrails of our marriage.

The Laugher chortles. Dr. Phil chastises another chubbo who doesn't look nearly as large as good ol' Phil. "You must take control of your life." The Satellite shuffles through minus the Waxie. I wipe away tears as I stroke Mom's hand.

"I wish you could understand," I whisper.

She squeezes my hand hard and I imagine she's saying, *"I do un-*

derstand. I just don't have the words to tell you. I'm still here, right next to you. It's me, Mommy. The same person who sang you to sleep with 'Puff the Magic Dragon,' who cooked you chicken soup when you were sick, who told you bedtime stories, who took you shopping for prom dresses and a wedding gown, who rocked the infant Gabby to sleep while singing 'Puff the Magic Dragon.' Don't listen to what they tell you. I could never really leave you. I'm still here."

But I look into her eyes and see nothing, just emptiness and distance. Does she even know who I am?

No, Mommy doesn't understand. I stare out the window. Trinity is trying to help Gabby cartwheel. Her Cinderella gown hangs over her head.

I turn back toward my mother. I notice her lip is trembling. It's as if she's trying to say something.

"What is it, Mommy? What is it? It's me, Ally. Remember me? Tell me something. Anything. Help me, please."

She squeezes her eyes shut as she bites her lip. Then she slowly opens her mouth, looks straight ahead, and whispers in a voice almost as quiet as silence. I lean in to hear.

"Cocksucker," she says. "Cocksuckercocksuckercocksucker."

Despite what Trinity says, I can't help feeling that somehow, somewhere in the depths of her being, my mother understands. Some part of her is still there.

"Cocksucker," she whispers again.

3

School Friends

It is the first day of kindergarten. Gabby sits in the back of the Toyota singing along to a Disney princess CD. Ariel is trilling about the futility of life under the sea. I sip my grande nonfat latte as we head into the parking lot of Gabby's school.

It is overwhelming. A sea of mostly white and black and a few red SUVs, minivans, and even one enormous, bright mustard-colored Hummer cram into the parking lot. I search for a spot. The SUVs have hoarded them all; the Hummer pulls into a spot marked "compact."

Ariel, believe me, stay under the sea.

As I wait for somewhere to park, I search for future friends. There are buffed women with well-manicured nails and perfectly made-up faces, wearing low-riding velour sweatsuits with lettering that reads "Juicy" or "Hello! Kitty" or "Angel" on their perfectly Pi-latisized butts. They stand back as the nannies unbuckle screaming children. There are pony-tailed women in baseball caps, T-shirts, and stained Gap sweats cajoling kids from the backseat. There are harried businesswomen in suits, their makeup half done, their hair still wet, pulling tots to the front door of this primary-colored building while juggling cell phone conversations. Where do I fit in all of this?

I am going to be positive. I am going to open myself up to these women. I will not be judgmental because they have boob jobs, colla-gen lips, and always look like they're on the way to the gym. I will not judge the ones who look dowdy and stained. We are mothers. Maybe if I get to know some of them, I won't find them all so boring and one-dimensional. We are in the same club. Maybe we can forge friend-ship. And I have no friends in the Valley, so I will make an effort. I can do this.

I find a spot. Gabby unbuckles her car seat and checks herself in the dashboard mirror. She pats her pigtailed hair and smiles at the reflection. She's a beautiful honey-blonde girl with thick red lips, big almond-shaped eyes, and chubby cheeks. I check myself in the mirror, too. My eyes are still red, puffy, and swollen from nights of endless sobbing. I look one thousand years old. The teacher will say, "Oh, you must be Gabby's granny. Nice to meet you."

"Mommy, can I borrow your lipstick?

"No."

"Darnicles. Why not?"

"You can't wear lipstick to kindergarten."

"That's ridicleus. You wear lipstick when you're going out. I should be able to! Mommy, do you think I'll make school friends? Do you think my teacher will be beautiful?"

"We'll see."

"I hope so."

We head into the building. I search for Mrs. Waring's room. It's the name of the teacher listed on a note I received about a week ago. According to the note, I was supposed to schedule a quick meeting for Gabby, since "this will help transition them into kindergarten." I wanted to send the note back and write in big red block letters:

TRANSITION IS NOT A VERB. But I stopped myself. And instead forgot about the meeting altogether. Besides, Gabby is the most self-confident person I have ever met. She doesn't need to help *transitioning*, unlike her mother, who has no clue.

I open the door to Gabby's classroom. Mothers and a few fathers sit in a circle with their children on their laps or next to them, waiting for the teacher. We walk in and I can feel the looks of recognition on some of the parents' faces. They have seen my photograph in the tabloids, I'm sure. Or maybe I'm just being paranoid. Some smile. Some just allow their eyes to graze over me.

"Hi," I mumble as I crouch toward the floor. My joints crack.

Gabby stands next to me. "Hello, everybody! My name's Gabby. This is my mother. Her name's Alice or you can call her Ally. People call her both. Mom, say hello."

The moms laugh.

"Well, good morning, Gabby and Alice," someone says from behind us. I turn. It's a morbidly obese woman wearing a bright purple muumuu decorated with gold flowers.

"My name is Mrs. Waring. I'll be your teacher this whole year. I promise we'll have lots of fun together. And we're going to do a lot of learning."

"Hello," I say, sounding as pleasant as possible while my heart gallops. Gabby has become so obsessed with beauty and princesses that I'm afraid she'll run out of this classroom right now because her teacher hardly has Cinderella or Jasmine or Ariel's body type. Hell, even Ursula the Sea Witch is more svelte.

I watch Gabby. Her mouth is wide open and her eyes are huge. I watch her study Mrs. Waring. *Please, Gabby, please,* I silently beg. I've got to wean her off princesses and Barbies. I never encouraged it. As a kid, I was a tomboy. When I became pregnant, I swore we'd never have a Barbie doll in the house. Now she has at least thirty.

There are Swan Lake Barbie, Happy Family Barbie, Pink Sparkle Fairy Barbie, Lavender Sparkle Fairy Barbie, the Princess and the Pauper Barbie, Pet Doctor Barbie, Barbie Loves SpongeBob, Barbie Loves Patrick Star, Holiday Barbie, Totally Spring Barbie, Magical Mermaid Barbie, My Scene Barbie Styling Head, Beautiful Bride Barbie . . .

"Oh, that's the mother who conditioned her child to be completely superficial. Alice Hirsh. You know who she is, right? Her picture was plastered all over the tabloids the other day. She looked insane. And she's one to talk about appearances—her hair was horrible, all split ends and disheveled. I don't think she had any makeup on, either. I don't blame her husband for leaving her."

Gabby squints her eyes and scrunches her face. She's about to make a declaration, I can feel it. I quickly try to distract her.

"Isn't this classroom nice?" I whisper to her.

"Shh, Mommy. I have to talk to the teacher about something."

"Gabby! Stay here!"

She ignores me as she heads toward Mrs. Waring.

"Is it okay if I tell you something?" She cranes her neck up.

Mrs. Waring smiles down at her. I imagine it is the last smile Gabby will receive from this woman.

"Yes, Gabby, what is it?"

"Well . . . well . . . it's just that dress you have on," Gabby starts.

"Gabby," I say, again in the weird sing-songy voice. "Don't bother Mrs. Waring."

Gabby rolls her eyes at me as Mrs. Waring smiles too hard at her. I feel even she's bracing for what's next. I'm sure she's been battling insensitive comments about her weight from kids who don't know any better most of her life.

"Anyway, that's the most beautiful dress I've ever seen. You look just like a princess." Gabby looks over at me. "I wish my mommy wore dresses like that. But everything is jeans, jeans, jeans. She must have one hundred pairs of jeans and one dress and it's black. Why would you just wear a black dress when there are so many beautiful colors in the world?"

Mrs. Waring chortles as the rest of the moms look at me and laugh. I relax and smile. Gabby has instantly become the teacher's pet.

"What a wonderful little girl. Her mother must have really instilled her with good values. You know who her mother is, right? Her picture was plastered all over the tabloids the other day. She looked great, even without a drop of makeup on. Her husband, the cad, is having an affair with Rose Maris. Can you imagine? We should invite her over for dinner. Maybe our cute single doctor friend is available?"

Mrs. Waring reads a story about a rabbit named Max and his first day of school. He's scared, but he has a lot of fun and everything works out for the best. After that, she says it's time for the mommies and daddies to leave. I haven't felt this relaxed in months. My body is rubbery. I could stay here all day, fingerpainting, singing songs, and learning how to spell. I want naptime and storytime and recess and cookies and milk. I want to be five again.

Some of the children cry and cling to their moms or dads. I search for Gabby. She's in the back of the classroom rummaging through a trunk of dress-up clothes. She pulls out a tiara and affixes it to her head. I try to make eye contact with her, but she's too engrossed. I go over to her.

"Good-bye, sweetie, I love you."

I bend down to kiss her, but she moves her cheek away.

"Mom, that's too embarrassing."

Only five and already I embarrass her. I didn't expect to hear this until she was at least thirteen. I watch her for a few seconds. My baby's already in kindergarten. Tears well up in my eyes. I think of how fast the last five years have gone. How each age is like a little death. Where is my infant? My baby? My toddler? What happened to Tickle Me Elmo? Minnie Mouse? Unicorns? I silently command myself to play Barbies with her the next time she asks, before that phase gives way to the next.

"I love you very much," I say, hugging her. She squirms.

"Mommy, I think I saw a magic wand in here. I have to get it fast before some other girl wants it."

"Remember to share," I say.

She smiles at me and whispers, "I don't like to share. But if the teacher's looking, I'll share."

Another mom heads out at the same time I do. She wipes tears from her eyes. We smile at each other.

"This is harder than I thought," she says.

"I know. If I'm crying over kindergarten, what will I be doing when she's in high school?"

She hands me a tissue. "Hi. I'm Nancy Potter. My son's Ethan." She sticks out her hand and I shake it.

"I'm Alice. My daughter's Gabby."

"What a sweetie she is. We'll have to have a playdate one of these days."

Nancy keeps talking. She seems nice but I can't get past her sweatshirt. It's got a picture of Winnie the Pooh sticking his paw into a beehive. "I love my honeys," it reads. Underneath it reads "Ethan and Sarah." I know it sounds incredibly superficial of me but I can't imagine becoming friends with a woman who wears a Winnie the Pooh sweatshirt. *Come on, Alice,* you're probably thinking. *Maybe it was a gift.* But it doesn't matter. This could be the most wonderful person in the Valley but all I see is the sweatshirt. What kind of person wears a Winnie the Pooh sweatshirt? What kind of person judges someone who wears a Winnie the Pooh sweatshirt?

"Sure. A playdate would be great," I say as I head to my car. I wonder where to go. For the first time in years I have no responsibility. I have taken a few weeks off from my public relations job.

Actually, I can't imagine working ever again. I thought my boss would be devastated, but he sounded relieved.

"We're not supposed to make news. We're supposed to get our clients news. I just think right now your presence might be too disruptive," my boss said.

Dr. Phil would yell and say I should jump right back in, forget about that cad and get on with my life. That's what Judy said, too.

"You have to come back," she said. "I can't imagine being in this place without you here. And you'll be bored silly just being a mom."

But I don't want to go back yet. I want to wallow in self-pity. I want to cry. I want to figure out what I should do next. Public relations was never for me. I hate being fake and upbeat and perky. I'd rather be real and pessimistic and cantankerous. I had always wanted to be a writer. When I graduated from college, I was brainwashed by some headhunters into thinking that public relations would be a good stepping stone.

"You'll make a lot of contacts at newspapers and magazines. You'll be writing blurbs that will run nearly verbatim in the press." But it's not a stepping stone. No one believes a publicist can write anything but blurbs. By the time I figured this out, I felt stuck. I had a house, a baby on the way, and lots of expenses. I played by the rules. But now there are no rules. Alex can do what he wants. So can I.

Alex stopped by yesterday to take Gabby to the zoo. Gabby ran to the door screaming, "Daddy's here! Daddy's here." I snuck peeks from the bedroom window. She grabbed Alex's hand and pulled him towards the car. He looked different. His hair was shorter and the front was cut in a trendy faux hawk. No more weekend Hawaiian shirts. He had on a tight white T-shirt with something written on the front that I couldn't read. Gabby beamed at him. She thinks this is all some great adventure.

"Daddy's living somewhere else—for now—and when I see him, I

get him all to myself. We always do really fun things. He lets me eat whatever I want."

"Are you okay," I asked Gabby after Alex dropped her off last night.

"Sure. Great. The elephant ate peanuts right out of my hand. Daddy said when he was a little boy, he didn't keep his hand out flat and the elephant sucked up Daddy's hand in his trunk. When he pulled it out, it was covered in boogies. Isn't that disgusting?"

I looked hard at her. "I mean, are you okay with Daddy not being here all the time?"

"Sure." She eyed me suspiciously.

"Really?"

"Sure, why not? It's nice and quiet here."

"Oh, Daddy was too noisy?"

"No, *you* were. You were always yelling at Daddy."

"I was not."

"Yes, you were. And then he'd yell back. Then you'd yell. Then he'd yell. It was loud. It really damaged my cochlea."

Cochlea. I had read Gabby a book on her body. I explained to her when she screamed, she could damage her cochlea, or inner ear. Now she was using it against me.

"I don't think I yelled that much at Daddy."

"Okay, Mommy, I could be wrong," she said, rolling her eyes. "Anyway, now I get to go to all these fun places and Daddy buys me tons of ice cream. If you were there you'd say I'd get cavities, blah, blah, blah. You're really mean sometimes."

I have already become the enemy. The nagging fishwife. Moms don't stand a chance in separation's ugly battlefield.

I don't know what's going on with Alex. He said he was taking time to think, to be on his own. Judy says it's a midlife crisis and he'll come to his senses. She's probably right, but every day I Google his name and Rose's to see if there have been any sightings around town.

So far nothing. According to E! Online, Rose is in Toronto shooting a movie opposite Colin Farrell.

Fall in love with your costar, just like you always do, I silently pray. *Colin is cute and charismatic and much better looking than Alex. Come on, Rose, fall in love with him. Let Alex remember how good he had it. Make him beg for me back. I will make him work for it. But please, let us live happily ever after.*

Every day I read Page Six, hoping for a mention of Colin and Rose. I even scan the Toronto papers online—nothing. Defamer .com and Thesuperficial.com have photos of Colin and Rose embracing, but it's just from a scene in the movie.

If I had been born in another time—even just fifty years ago—I'd be dead right now, I realized the other day when I sat with my mom. The baby in my tube would have kept growing until the tube burst and I hemorrhaged to death. Matricide. I can't stop thinking about it. Modern technology saved me. But the truth is, I've worn out my welcome. I'm living on borrowed time.

Maybe things happen for a reason. I should have died, just like my pioneer foremothers would have. Alex could have played the grieving widower for a few months. Then Rose, the eccentric neighbor in the township who performs at the local theater, would have stopped by to mend his overalls and fix him some home cooking. They would have married. A marriage based on grief, everyone would think. Someone to be a mother to Gabby. There would be a picture of me on the mantel. They'd plant flowers at my grave. No one could really ever take my place.

I pull into my driveway. The paparazzi left over a week ago, and strangely, I miss them. I didn't expect to feel this way. My story is over. They've moved on. I'm a footnote in tabloid history.

"Rose Maris broke up another marriage. This is the woman scorned. End of story. But now Rose is in love with Colin Farrell. Maybe in ten

years we'll check back on Alice Hirsh to see if she's addicted to crack or fat as a house."

The other day, I scanned the photos that ran in the tabloids and newspapers. I even looked for Johnny's name, but it just listed the wire services. I'll never know if he really did toss his pictures. He never did come back looking for a favor.

I settle in front of the computer to check my e-mails. Judy tells me how much she misses me. How boring things are there without me. Then she asks questions about one of my accounts that she's now handling. "Just until you come back." Claire says she's stopping by with a casserole. Lauren, my best friend from college who's an acupuncturist in Rochester, New York, says she's inserting needles into the balls of the voodoo doll she's made of Alex. I start deleting spam. I am about to delete what I think is spam when the subject matter makes my heart race: GeorgeK77@aol.com Re: SCHOOL FRIEND.

I hit the open button and leave a trace of sweat on the mouse. There's only one person I think it could be. George Keller, my boyfriend for the last two years of college. I haven't heard from him since we graduated in 1993. Could he be George K? The e-mail seems to take forever to open. I hit the open button again and again. Finally, the screen blinks alive. I begin to read.

Dear Ally,

I've been feeling very nostalgic lately. I thought I'd be bold and drop you a line from the safety of the Internet. You can stop here and throw me into the recycle bin right now.

Hello! If you're still reading. I live in Arlington, Virginia, and am a reporter for the *Washington Post*. I cover the transportation beat. I know that probably sounds horribly boring to you and guess what? It is horribly boring! I know what you're thinking, too. I was supposed to be exposing Watergate-type scandals. But alas, I'm a glorified traffic reporter. I have two children—Frankie,

7, and Gabrielle, 4. I remember we said if we had a girl, we'd call her Gabrielle. I guess I could never get the name out of my head.

Yes, I heard about what happened to you so I Googled your name. Your company's name came up with a phone number. I was able to cajole an e-mail address from Samantha, your secretary. By the way, she's not really from England is she? That sounded like a fake accent to me.

I also saw your picture in the *Enquirer*. Our office always gets a copy. It's one of my guilty pleasures—when no one is looking—to thumb through it while feigning indifference. But who can resist the sordid stories? Then I saw you. You in the midst of all this. I was stunned. I hope you're doing okay. It sounds like you're going through a tough time. I want you to know that while it may sound clichéd, I am here for you. It probably doesn't sound like much since we haven't talked in— what?—fifteen years, three months, and two weeks.

If you feel like updating me on your life, I'd love to hear from you. I think I'm going to be crazy and get to our reunion this June. Maybe I'll see you there?

Love,

George

Love, George. I read it again and again. Is it filled with innuendos or am I just an abandoned, bored housewife imagining drama? Does George still love me or am I losing my mind? Why didn't he mention a wife? I want to write him immediately and tell him that I, too, have a daughter named Gabrielle, but I stop myself. I need to think about this first. After all, I am vulnerable right now, Dr. Phil would tell me. I need to be careful.

"Alice, what were you thinking? Internet relationships are so clichéd. What you need right now is a gym membership! Exorcise the demons with exercise!"

Speaking of demons, Claire's red Matrix pulls up into the driveway. I want to hide, but my car's in the driveway. She'll know I'm home. Claire's one of those people you have to be friends with when you work together because it's too dangerous not to be. She'll stab you in the back. She'll talk about you to other colleagues. She comes across all sweet and caring with her pudgy freckled face and her intense brown eyes and her homemade brownies and cookies with M&Ms instead of chocolate chips. But I've learned over the years that people who bake are dangerous. They spend too much time in the kitchen trying to make sweet things to compensate for the bile churning inside of them. Think about bakers you know and you'll see I'm right. Betty Crocker was probably filled with rage. And if Duncan Hines was a real person, he or she was probably mean as hell.

She lives for moments like this, reveling in someone else's misery. She's heading to the door with an enormous smile plastered on her face and a big vat of something fattening in her arms. Comfort food, I'm sure. And a plate of cookies to wash it all down.

I open the door and she pinches her face with concern.

"Oh, honey, how are you doing," she says, her voice verging on collapse. Then she hugs me tightly with one arm, while balancing her casserole with the other. I hug her back. Until I know I'm leaving the firm for good, I must play the game.

"I'm okay."

"Well, I don't want to keep you."

Translation: *"I'll be here as long as it takes you to tell me everything. Then I'll head back to the office and tell them everything."*

"No, come in, sit down a while. Do you want something to drink?"

"Just some water."

I will not cry in front of her. I will not cry in front of her. I will not cry in front of her.

I grab the casserole, thank her, head to the kitchen, and take a deep breath. Claire's right behind me, her eyes leaping over counters and stoves and settling on the oversized Subzero refrigerator.

"*A Subzero. Viking appliances.*"

"So, how are you doing?"

"I'm okay," I say as if she asked me about a common cold.

She puts her arms on my shoulders and looks hard into my eyes. "Really, Ally, how are you doing?"

"Seriously, it's all going to be fine."

I fill glasses with water from the refrigerator and plop down on the sofa in the living room. I follow Claire's eyes as she scans the photos of Alex, Gabby, and me. We all look so happy. The perfect family. There's Alex and me beaming on our wedding day. Alex and me snorkeling on our Hawaiian honeymoon. Alex and me with the newborn Gabby.

My eyes cloud. *Please don't do this in front of Claire,* I beg. But the tears slide down my face and before I can stop any of this, I am sobbing. I put my face into my hands and feel my body convulse.

Claire rubs my back.

"There, there," she says. "Come on, Ally. *People* magazine is a complete rag. They probably got all their facts wrong anyway."

I suck in my tears and breathe. "*People* magazine? What are you talking about?"

Even though I can barely see, I can feel Claire's eyes as they pop out of her skull.

"Oh, I thought you knew. I thought that's why . . ."

"Knew what?"

"Nothing, really."

"Claire."

"*People* magazine just came out with an article on Alex and Rose."

"*What?*"

4

Sexiest Lawyer Alive

Xander Hirsh is one of the sexiest men alive."

No! I want to scream to the *People* magazine editors. Xander isn't sexy at all. He used to have a beer gut that he'd hide behind oversized Hawaiian shirts. He never picks up after himself. He never cleans out the toilet bowl. He wakes up in the morning with horrific breath.

And most important, Xander doesn't exist. He's *Alex*. Alexander Stephen Hirsh.

Xander is my husband's reinvention of himself. Or it's Rose's creation. He's this guy with no beer gut, a goatee, gelled hair, and tight T-shirts that show off his newly rippled biceps.

No more Al and Al. Al Squared.

Rose and Xander. "Rx for love," was the caption under a photo of the two of them walking towards a parked Porsche. According to sources close to the couple, Rose calls him her "Hirshey" bar. She's never felt like this before. This is the real thing. "They seem really good for each other." "They're a fairy tale couple."

My daughter, who practically holds a doctorate in fairy tales, would know this one is severely flawed. The prince doesn't tell

Cinderella you can move into the castle once I kick my wife and kid out. The prince doesn't wake Snow White with a kiss and then mention he's still married. *What about me,* I want to scream. Does it matter that Rose is a homewrecker? Alex is a cad? No, it's a beautiful love story with just an oh-so-minor inconvenience.

"Hirsh had recently separated from Alice, his wife of six years. "They've been drifting apart for years," says a source close to the couple. "[Xander] hasn't been happy for some time. They don't have much in common. He adores his daughter, so this has been a rough time for him. But I think Rose is the best thing that's happened to him in a long time. He seems so happy . . ."

What?

I scan our friendships for this traitor. It has to be one of Alex's friends. Ben? Tom? Carl? I thought they all loved me. I'm funloving Ally. Ally with the great appetizers—spinach dip, homemade guacamole, baked brie with caramelized walnuts wrapped in a puffed pastry. Ally who crushes mint with a mortar and pestle for Mojitos. Ally with the witty retorts. Ally who helped Carl decorate his apartment; who introduced Peter to her cute assistant. Alex not happy? Who could say such a thing?

"I'm sure it's someone you don't even know," Claire says. "That's what these magazines do. They'll talk to anybody. It's probably someone you've never even met. Or maybe the reporter made it up for the story. I've heard lots of the reporters at *People* do stuff like that."

I study Claire hard. Could she be the snitch?

"What? What?" she says.

No, she wouldn't stoop that low. Right now she feels like the best friend I've ever had.

Alex and Rose didn't talk to anyone for the story. Rose's publicist wouldn't even confirm the romance. "She's busy shooting in Toronto.

No comment." However, there were a few pictures of the "happy couple" having lattes at Coffee Bean on Sunset, standing in front of her red Porsche Roadster, walking down Melrose with shopping bags.

I'm a publicist. My job is to spin stories in my client's favor. I can do it for myself. The photographs prove nothing. Rose is in Toronto, so the photos are weeks old; and they're not even touching each other. Besides, she's got to be screwing Colin Farrell by now. Alex and Rose weren't quoted in the story. Even her publicist didn't confirm the romance. The sources close to the couple are typically people who don't know anything. Next week there'll be a correction.

"The story about an alleged relationship between Rose Maris and Alex Hirsh was false. Hirsh is madly in love with his wife, Alice. Maris was recently seen canoodling with Colin Farrell."

That night I can't sleep. Every time I drift off, I get smacked in the head with a *People* magazine. To put it out of my mind, I think about George. We'd gone out the last two years of college. We'd been friends since freshman year, ever since we took a class on William Blake together and spent hours interpreting such things as "the eye altering, alters all" and "the road to excess leads to the palace of wisdom."

Then the first week of junior year, George showed up at my off-campus apartment, tanned, newly buffed, and very nervous. He blurted out that he'd been in love with me since the first time he saw me at an orientation weekend before freshman year. He even remembered what I was wearing—jeans, a green Fair Isle sweater, and brown suede clogs. He said he saw me on line to sign up for the William Blake class, so he figured he would, too. He said he didn't want to be friends anymore. He wanted to be my boyfriend. And, after a weeklong dramatic soul-searching complete with confabs with college friends, I realized I loved him, too.

I thought this was the zenith of romance. There'd never been a more romantic couple in the history of romantic couples. No one could ever love me more than George. And we had a plan: After graduation, we'd work for newspapers in small towns. After we amassed some clips, we'd find work in the same town and get married. We'd name our daughter Gabrielle. Our son would be—time to cringe—William, or was it Blake? Don't judge me. I was only twenty.

I thought he was my soul mate. The love of my life. If we'd stuck to the plan, Gabby and William/Blake would be teenagers by now. We'd live in a Cape Cod–style house in the suburbs of Boston or New York or D.C. We'd have a black Labrador. I'd know nothing about celebrity. Rose Maris would just be another star of another movie we would never see. We'd work at the same paper. I'd be a general assignment reporter. George would cover politics. He'd always be faithful.

But what happened? We graduated from college and spent all of July backpacking through France. Then I went back to New York, rented an apartment with three college friends, and got a job in publicity. I was going to do it for a few months until I could find something in journalism. But the jobs at small newspapers paid less than half what I was making. And I couldn't imagine giving up the city life for some rural town. In short, I was having too much fun.

George wrote for the *Quincy Patriot Ledger* in Massachusetts. We had a long-distance relationship. We tried to see each other on weekends, but George never had weekends off. I'd go to Quincy and hang out in his apartment while he raced around town to car wrecks and board meetings. His editor was a sadist. It seemed whenever we had a few minutes to ourselves, the phone would ring with another assignment. After several weekends of this, I stopped visiting. We both figured that after a few months, George would start getting better assignments, along with weekends off.

Did I mention I was having a lot of fun? Lauren, Maura, Dawn, and I lived together in a two-bedroom, five-story walk-up on the Upper West Side. We'd come home from work, blend up some frozen drinks, and then head to the bars right down the street. We became regulars at O'Malleys, Insomnia's, and Hi Life. We drank too much. We stayed out too late. We met too many cute boys. And hey, I was only twenty-one.

I'd come home to messages from George. I'd call him back.

"I mish you."

"Ally, it's four in the morning."

"Shorry. I shust wanted to shay I luff you."

"You've been drinking again."

"Jush a little."

This continued for a while. Resentment escalated. George was annoyed that I wasn't chasing my dream. I was angry because George kept reminding me that I wasn't chasing my dream. He worked his butt off. I partied my brain out.

And then one night, he visited me, to talk things over, decide our future, I suppose. It was a surprise visit at 10 P.M. Of course I wasn't home. I didn't come home until noon the next day. I smelled of cigarettes, an annoying habit I'd picked up when I drank too much. George was asleep on my bed.

"Where were you?"

"I was out late. I stayed at a friend's."

"A friend's?"

"Mary Ann. You remember her from college? She lives in this great apartment in—"

"Yeah, right."

"You don't believe me?"

"Is Mary Ann the one who gave you a hickey, too?" George's eyes watered. "God, a hickey. You are pathetic."

George jumped out of bed, grabbed his duffel bag, and headed for the door. I put my hand on my throat.

I didn't know that Sean had given me a hickey. Actually, I didn't remember much at all of the night before. My head pounded and my stomach churned—a much too common state during the last few months. I ran after George.

"It didn't mean anything, George. I promise."

"This is over, Alice. I can't take it anymore. Who are you anyway?"

"George, George, I love you. Please. Don't go. I'll do anything. I can't lose you."

He was out the door. I chased after him, galloping down five flights of stairs. "George, George!"

I pounded on the windshield of his beat-up Saab as he revved the engine.

"You better move or I'll run over you," he spit out, his face bright red.

I threw my body on the hood. "Don't go," I screamed like a kid having a tantrum. Out of the corner of my eyes, I saw a small crowd gathering.

George pulled open the car door, picked me off the hood, and carried me to the apartment stoop. I held on tight, but he untangled me and dropped me to the ground. Then he got back in his car and floored it. I chased him for a block. I nearly reached his car—it was stopped at an interminable red light. But the combination of nicotine, alcohol, and this exertion was too much. I bent over and threw up to the soundtrack of honking horns. I always wondered if George saw that. If that was his last memory of me as he cruised on to a new life.

For weeks I called. Most of the time I got the answering machine. When George did pick up, he barely spoke. "I can't talk to you," he'd say.

"George, don't hang up," I'd plead. Then I'd talk and talk, until he'd say, "I've got to go now."

Click.

I drove to his apartment in Quincy. Someone else opened the door. George had moved on to another paper in Colorado, a mutual friend informed me.

I drowned my sorrows. I struggled to move on. I went on a ton of first dates, but lacked the follow-up skills. Most guys bored me. They'd talk too much about their tedious desk jobs, their cars, their football teams, their frat days, the money they were amassing. They'd call for second dates. I'd let the machine pick up and never call back. If I saw them at a bar, I'd grab my friends and we'd head down the street to another bar and another, until I'd lose them. Or I'd flirt a bit, let them buy us drinks, and then I'd head to another bar and lose them. Yes, I was a bitch. Sometimes, after many drinks, I'd call George, just to hear his groggy hello. Then I'd hang up. *Good boy*, I'd think. He'd been sleeping. He didn't have a social life, I imagined. All he did was work.

Yeah, right. About a year later, I read in the alumni newsletter that he was engaged. A year after that, I read that he got married. Two years later, I met Alex. I fell in love.

I never should have let George get away. That guy never would have cheated on me. Read the e-mail. After all these years, he still thinks about me. He's still in love with me.

I dream about George. We are backpacking through Europe. He tells me he loves me. We kiss by the Eiffel Tower. A director yells cut. We are on the set of a movie. The cameraman thanks me. His assistant grabs my arm and moves me off to the side.

"I want to stay," I say.

"You're only a stand-in," the cameraman says.

There's commotion and applause. George beams. Rose Maris stands where I was. George puts his arms around her. "I love you," he says. They kiss in front of the Eiffel Tower. I race over to it and knock it down. The Eiffel Tower is made of cardboard.

I am sitting next to Dr. Phil. We are watching the scene in front of a studio audience. They applaud when the Eiffel Tower collapses.

"Alice, these displays of violence are not healthy. You must look inside yourself for answers. You must take ownership of your problems."

I think about my dream as I sit at a coffee shop a few blocks from Gabby's kindergarten. I sip a nonfat latte and peruse the mail from Gabby's cubicle. She's only been in school a few days and already she's invited to three parties. There's a party for Nathan at a place called Chuck E. Cheese. There's a princess party for Sophia at a place called Princess For A Day. There's a Bob the Builder party for Beowulf at his home. *Beowulf?*

Gabby and I will attend all these parties. I will mingle with everyone and make friends. I will organize playdates and moms' nights out. I will acclimate to my new life. I will find the real mom behind the Winnie the Pooh sweatshirt. I will not judge. I will bake chocolate chip cookies with Gabby. I will keep every painting she creates.

I am finally getting to know my daughter. I haven't spent this much time with her since my three-month maternity leave. I had no idea she could sneak up on butterflies and they'd alight on her tiny index finger. I didn't know she had memorized all her fairy tales so if I used a wrong word or skipped words because I was preoccupied, she'd correct me. I just found out she could cartwheel and do handstands. She was learning all this while I was sitting behind a desk pretending to care about the opening of a client's restaurant.

I look up from my latte and Gabby's invites. My eyes settle on a black-and-white photograph on the wall in front of me. It's a sleeping newborn baby on its mother's chest. All you can see of the mother are her lips and chin. The lips are slightly parted, but you can feel the relief on the mother's face. It's clear this woman has just given birth to the child and is holding it for the first time. She was in labor for hours and hours and now is relaxed and euphoric. I read the caption: "Baby, Five Minutes Old."

The waitress comes over. She smiles at me.

"That's amazing," I say.

"Isn't it? It really says everything there is to say about giving birth and being a mother. It's painful and scary and wonderful all at once."

I order another latte and sit there looking at the other photographs on the wall. It's the first time in years that I've just lingered anywhere. There's a whole series of mothers with children. There are also a few landscapes. I stare into the photos. Even though my life is crumbling around me, I feel peaceful, something I haven't felt in a long time. I take a deep breath and savor the moment.

That is, until I notice a fellow coffee drinker staring at me. She's reading the latest *People* magazine.

5

Jingle Bells and Moans

I'm getting Gabby ready for Nathan's Chuck E. Cheese party when there's a knock at the front door. I peek out the window. It's my neighbor from just around the corner whose name I've forgotten. She's a fifty-year-old over-Botoxed realtor with sparkly spandex outfits. She has the look of someone who plays the slots at Vegas a lot. I take a deep breath, certain she's about to complain about the paparazzi, my unmowed lawn, my daughter's late-night temper tantrum yesterday, or just the general chaos surrounding my life. I'm shocked when she greets me with a big smile and an outstretched hand.

She shakes my hand. "Hello, Ally. Sherri Gold, from number 2804 Delacroix."

"Of course, Sherri. How are you?"

"Just peachy, Ally. Just peachy. I know it's been a crazy time for you," she says, smiling and running her eyes over me. She squeezes my hand. "I'd love to get together and chat over coffee one of these mornings. But today I'm going house to house with a reminder."

"A reminder?"

"Today is September tenth. You know what that means? It's never too early to start planning." She smiles hard, like she's about to burst with some kind of incredible information.

I quickly take inventory. A neighborhood association fee is due? A block party? Elections for a street president? Time to mow my lawn?

"Ummm, I really don't . . ."

"I'll give you a little hint," she says. Then she starts singing: " *'Jingle Bells. Jingle Bells. Jingle all the way-ay-ay.'* "

I'm baffled. This crazy woman has come over to hum Christmas carols in September? I stare at her blankly.

"You silly goose. It's three months and fifteen days 'til Christmas," she blurts out.

"Oh, right," I say, deciding that Sherri Gold is completely out of her mind.

Gabby comes to the door wearing her brand new Cinderella gown.

"Gabby, what happened to the dress you were wearing? You can't wear that to the party."

"That dress wasn't beautiful. It doesn't have any pink in it. And it definitely doesn't spin. I need a dress that spins." She twirls around.

Sherri smiles hard at her. "Aren't you adorable."

"Listen, Sherri, I have to drive my daughter to a birthday party. But thanks for reminding me. Does the neighborhood do Secret Santas or something?"

Sherri opens her mouth wide and guffaws. "Oh, honey, you don't know, do you?"

"Know? Know what?"

"About our neighborhood. I know your . . . your . . ." She looks panicked as she gropes for some word. "Well, your, um, husband? He knew. Your realtor had to disclose this information. I'm . . . Well, surprised you don't know."

Gabby stomps her feet. "Mommy, I am not changing my outfit and that's final."

Sherri smiles at Gabby as if she's the sweetest child she's ever seen. I know what she's thinking—*Make a good impression and when they have to liquidate their assets and sell this house, they'll use me.*

"You look just like a little princess, sweetie. Who are you? Snow White? Sleeping Beauty?" Sherri offers.

"Cinderella, duh," Gabby says, her voice lilting like Angelica Pickles'.

"Gabby!"

Sherri forces out a tight smile and clears her throat. "Anyway, at the holidays, this street, along with some streets to the north and south, is turned into North Pole Way. Everyone gets their homes all decked out. It's a tradition that's been going on for years and years. Everyone knows about it. People come from all over California to see it. The streets are backed up for miles with traffic."

I must have looked confused. She studies me and frowns.

"Are you Jewish? Because North Pole Way is nondenominational. You can do something that incorporates your faith, like blue lights and a Menorah. I know the Sussmans down the street are moving. You know, Tracy and Daniel? They've been doing a *Rugrats*-themed holiday for years. One of the Rugrats holds a dreidel and another has the Star of David. It's very tasteful. You could probably buy their display."

"Mommy hates the Rugrats," Gabby says, twirling in her dress. "She calls them Rug Brats."

"Oh." Sherri puts her hand on her chest and smiles. "Well, in that case, I'm sure there are other Hebrew characters."

"I'm not Jewish," I say. "Don't worry. We'll string some lights."

Sherri's eyes bulge. She nervously chortles.

"String some lights?" She spits this out like it's toxic. "You can't just string some lights. This is North Pole Way. It's over the top. Everyone must participate. If you, well, don't feel like decorating because of your, um . . . present situation? I can give you the name of

the company that does it for me. They're wonderful. Last year I had
an Aladdin Christmas. Jasmine floated on a magic carpet in between
my palm trees. I had fake snow covering my lawn." She smiles at
Gabby. "You would have loved it, sweetie. Anyway, we're going to
have a neighborhood meeting next Wednesday, just to make sure no
one overlaps. Last year there were three SpongeBob displays. It was
a disaster."

I promise to attend the meeting and Sherri finally leaves.

"God, that lady was so stupid," Gabby says.

"Gabby, don't use that word."

"You say it all the time when we're in the car."

"That's to cars, not people."

"Yeah, yeah," Gabby says, rolling her eyes. "But that lady *is* stupid. Doesn't she know Jasmine lives in the desert? There's no snow
there."

"Well, maybe the genie cast a spell and—"

"*Ohhhhhhh!*"

It's a moan from the mansion nestled right on the hill above us.
Gabby cocks her ear to the sound.

There's another moan. "Ohhhh. Ohhh, ohhhh!"

"Mommy, what should we do?"

I realize with the second burst of moans that it's not a call of dis-
tress. The woman is having some great sex.

Gabby is panicked. "Mommy, we have to get to that castle right
away. I think a wicked queen has trapped a beautiful princess in the
tower and she wants us to rescue her."

Ever since we've moved here, Gabby has been obsessed with this
house. With its mishmash architecture featuring a turreted roof,
stained-glass windows, Romanesque columns, and array of statues
of lions and Greek gods, she's convinced it's a castle filled with
princesses. Los Angelinos have a more derisive name for it: a Persian Palace.

There's another really, really long moan. That's when it hits me: I miss sex. I try to remember the last time I've had some. Hot tub night at least three months ago. I wonder if Alex was already doing Rose by then. Does Rose moan like this with Alex? Does he know she's acting?

"No. I think everything's okay," I say. "It's just . . . a TV."

"No, Mommy! It could be Rapunzel. We have to go there now and rescue her."

"Gabby, come on, it's okay. We have to get to the party."

"No! You're mean."

"I am not mean. That's not a princess."

"You just don't think there are any such things as princesses," Gabby shouts, her face turning red. "But there are. There's princesses all over the place. You just don't believe in anything anymore."

My daughter's face is balled up in anger. Her lips are pursed and her eyes blaze at me.

"I hate you. I hate you. I hate you. I want Daddy! Daddy! Daddy! Where's my daddy? Where's my daddy? I want my daddy back. He'd believe. First you made the baby go away and then you made Daddy go away. I hate you. I wish you'd go back to work already."

There's another long moan. Thanks so much for flaunting your pleasure in my face. I am overwhelmed with fury at The Moaner. No one needs to be this loud. It's like she's mocking me.

"Hahahaha, I'm getting some while your life is falling apart."

I squeeze my eyes shut. I can't believe this is my life. A mom in the Valley whose husband has left her, whose daughter hates her, whose mother can't speak to her, whose neighbor flaunts her sex life in front of her. I am a completely different person than I thought I was a few weeks ago, when I sat on the deck and contemplated my great life.

Yesterday while Gabby was at school, I met Judy for lunch at Ivy on the Shore. She asked me about some of my clients she was handling during my hiatus. Afterwards, she said she had a surprise for me. We drove in her silver BMW convertible to a high-rise along the Miracle Mile on Wilshire.

"Where are we going?"

"Just trust me."

"I really shouldn't."

She pressed the button in the elevator to the penthouse apartment.

"Is this your shrink? Because I'm really not ready to see a shrink," I said.

"It's not my shrink," Judy said. "But you really should think about seeing my shrink. She's great."

"Then who is it? You know, I'm totally not ready to date."

"Trust me. I know. Besides, you look like hell." She studied me and reached for a strand of my hair. She shook her head. "I should be taking you to my colorist."

The elevator tinged open. Judy led me to the door of the only apartment on the floor.

"Why am I following you?"

"Trust me. It's all good."

A maid in a crisp white uniform opened the door to a stark white apartment with sunlight bursting through the floor-to-ceiling windows.

"Hello, Tina," Judy said to her. "This is my friend Alice."

"Hello, Miss Judy. Hello, Miss Alice. Faye's expecting you."

Tina rapped on a door and opened it without waiting for a response. A diminutive sixty-year-old woman dressed in a flowing white gown and a white turban on her head greeted us. She kissed Judy on both cheeks. Then she grabbed my hands and smiled wide. I looked into her eyes—they were watery and gray and kind.

"This must be Alice."

"Yes," Judy said. "I guess I'll leave you two alone."

"Why," I asked. "Who are you?"

Faye laughed. "Naughty, naughty Judy. You didn't tell her."

"She would have resisted. Now that she's here and she's met you, she'll be too polite to leave."

"Maybe you should be the psychic," Faye said, laughing.

"Psychic," I said, horrified. "You're a psychic?"

"Judy thought it might be good for you. And I can tell by looking at you that your life's in turmoil."

"You probably read about it in *People* magazine," I said.

Faye huffed and closed her eyes, as if offended. "I don't read the tabloids. Besides, most of those celebrities are my clients, so if it's true, I know about it already."

I snorted.

Judy tsked. "See Faye, I told you. She's very cynical."

I wondered if she could tell when I'm going to die. My eyes blazed at Judy. "I can't believe you did this."

"Just try it. If you don't like it, you can leave. But Faye is magic, I swear. She's been a hundred percent accurate with me." Judy studied me and smiled. "And don't worry. She's not going to tell you if you're going to die."

Faye laughed. "That's right. If I see a car wreck, I'll tell you to buckle up. If I see cancer, I'll just tell you to get a body scan."

Judy left the room. Faye took out a deck of cards and asked me to cut them. I negotiated for a few seconds. The way I cut those cards might strangely predict my future or give Faye a clue to my life that I don't want her to have.

I cut the cards.

Faye told me, "I see a child lost. It is a child who didn't follow the right path."

I thought she was talking about Gabby. My heart thumped.

"Do you mean literally lost? Or do you mean lost, as in different? Because my daughter's a big dreamer. And she's headstrong. She doesn't follow directions."

I stopped myself. You're not supposed to give psychics too much ammunition.

"No, this not your daughter. It is your son."

I smiled. *Haha*, I thought. *This woman is a quack.* "I don't have a son," I said, sucking in my cheeks, while thinking, *I won!*

"This was a son you were to have, but it got lost. Maybe in your womb? Did you recently have a pregnancy?"

I narrowed my eyes at Faye. "Judy told you."

"I never discuss my clients or potential clients with anyone."

"I don't believe you."

She stared hard at me. "You must learn to stop being so skeptical, so judgmental. It will cost you plenty in life."

"I am not judgmental."

She reached out from across her table and squeezed my hand. "Yes, you are. We are all judgmental to a degree, but you are exceptionally judgmental. You must learn to be less so, or you will miss out on many of life's rich experiences."

I thought about the woman in the Winnie the Pooh sweatshirt. Maybe I should call her up for a playdate. But a Winnie the Pooh sweatshirt?

Then I thought, *At least Faye's not telling me to buckle up.*

"This son went the wrong way. Maybe you miscarried? Anyway, there was too much turmoil in your house. The baby didn't want to be born into a house of confusion, in a house of chaos."

I don't believe in this. How can a woman look at cards and see things? If I had cut the deck differently would she have told me I was going to run off with a Mambo King?

I suddenly saw an infant boy in a diaper floating around looking for a better house. I watched him flying over the mansions of Bel Air and Beverly Hills, searching for Rose Maris.

"Its soul went away for now. Does this make sense? Do you understand what I'm saying?"

"For now? What does that mean? Is it coming back?"

Faye breathed deeply. "I think it will be back. I don't know when. I believe it is waiting for a time when things are less complicated for you. Do you understand what that means? It is a very considerate little boy. You knew him in your last life. But it was interrupted. Maybe one of you died young. I don't know exactly. But in this life, I think the cycle will be complete and you will have this baby in your life. And it will be a very happy baby. You will be very happy. There is so much happiness, you will almost burst with it, but you must allow it to come in. You must accept certain things, move on, and then put aside your prejudices and let it in."

Haha, I think. *You are a quack. I will never be happy again for the rest of my life.*

Will I?

I didn't want to tell her anything more because that's their trick, isn't it? They come up with something that's pretty general and you tell them how it fits into the puzzle of your life. Like those people who say they can talk to the dead and really you're telling them everything they need to know about some dead relative. They repeat it to you and you're convinced that Aunt Estelle is right in the room, yammering away about the pot roast recipe she wants you to have.

I didn't mention Alex leaving me for Rose. I didn't mention that there's no way I could have a baby when I don't have a man. But then something dawned on me. Maybe Alex was coming back. Maybe we would have a baby together. Maybe this was just a phase he was going through. All eventually would be forgiven.

She told me to accept certain things and move on.

I was about to ask her about Alex, but I was too afraid.

Faye studied me. Her tiny gray eyes darted back and forth over my face. She caught the smile on my face and nodded her head. Then she told me more.

I would have a job change. She said Gabby would say something that everyone would repeat. I asked her to explain what that meant, but she didn't understand.

"That's all I know. Maybe it's a phrase that everyone picks up on. I'm not certain. She's some kind of trendsetter."

I tried not to laugh. I didn't hear much more. All I kept thinking was that Alex and I would get back together. This was just a phase. A midlife crisis. Rose was probably doing Colin right now. Alex would beg for my forgiveness. I would be apprehensive. He would be persistent. And slowly, after months of wooing me, I'd take him back. We'd go to couple's therapy. Our marriage would be stronger than ever. We'd have another baby. A considerate boy who had been waiting for the chaos to subside.

I forgot that about a half hour before, I didn't believe in psychics.

Judy waited for me in the stark white living room. She was tapping away on her iPhone.

"You look happy," she said.

"I'm okay."

"What did she tell you?"

I didn't say a word. Faye returned and walked us to the door. She kissed us on both cheeks. Then she stared at me hard. She grabbed my hands.

"Ally, make sure you buckle up, especially this Friday."

My eyes bugged out. My heart beat fast. She and Judy burst out in laughter.

Faye smiled. "A joke. Just a joke."

"Faye's a comedian," Judy said.

I laughed politely.

"No. Really. She's probably the only psychic-slash-comedian in the world. She's at the Improv on Wednesdays."

Faye smiled. "I only go when I can predict a lot of laughter."

"Ohhhhh, ohhhhh, ohhhhh."

Another moan. But nothing from the guy. How can he be going for so long? Is it tantra? A threesome? A foursome? Maybe I just don't remember how good sex can be.

Gabby stands there with her arms akimbo. A five-year-old who daydreams all the time and is obsessed with princesses has brought me back from the psychic's high. Alex is gone. The baby is gone. It's probably all my fault. Maybe I should have moaned louder. Maybe I never should have let him take Rose on as a client. That's what Judy would have done. She would have said absolutely no and then gone to Frederick's of Hollywood and spent a small fortune on sexy lingerie.

I am too weak to do anything, especially go to a kiddie party. So I head back to the house. When Gabby realizes we're not going, she will cry and scream, so I don't say a word. Instead, I think about a distraction. She was right the other day when she said I always tell her maybe when I really mean no. I'm always too busy, but what am I really doing? I head towards the pottery wheel that's still in the box even though she got it five months ago. I unwrap it. Today we'll talk Barbies, string beads, bake an Easy Bake cake, and mold clay into something that will somehow matter to Gabby.

6

Death in the Valley

There is a hearse in front of Hilda's. I sit in my car and watch as a body covered with a sheet is wheeled out of the beige stucco ranch house. Hilda stands at the door, looming, like the Grim Reaper, a strange half-smile plastered on her face. I look at the gurney and try to decipher who it is. The Laugher? The Satellite? Hal? Dorothy? It's impossible to tell. All old people become raisins of their former selves, except Jack LaLanne. I heard him on the news a while back saying that he can't die because it would be bad for his image.

The body is packed into the hearse. The doors are slammed and the car slowly drives off. It's a lonely sight, this hearse with no entourage, with no mourners gathered around, with no one but Hilda grimacing by the door. I nod to the driver, cross myself, and say a silent prayer for this anonymous person. I hope it's not The Laugher. I don't know what I'd do without her staccato guffaws every thirty seconds. A laugh track for this surreal place.

"It vas Hal," Hilda yells across the lawn as I get out of my car. "He vas moving hiss bowels. He died, right on zee toilet. Most of my clients die on zee toilet. It iss too much. Zey have heart attack and die."

A woman walking her dog pretends not to listen.

Hal, a big-time studio executive who worked with some of the hugest stars from the fifties, sixties, and seventies, died taking a crap.

When I approach the door, I give Hilda a quick smile, hoping that will be the end of our interaction. Instead she moves towards me. I smell bratwurst on her breath.

"Your mussa's language has not improved. This morning she called Hal a filthy, filthy word. It upset him very much."

She eyes me. Is she suggesting my mother killed Hal?

"It iss very disturbing to my clientele. I have tried to talk to her about it, but nothing iss working. You must figure something out or I vill have to ask you to find another place for her."

I cringe. Finding this place took months and months of searching. I don't want to put my mother in a nursing home, where they'll just keep her in bed all day. In Los Angeles, board and cares are regular homes in residential neighborhoods with about six residents, all of whom can presumably still take care of themselves but need a little extra help. It's kind of a way station between independence and incoherence. My mother is slipping into the next realm. She can't shower, eat, or go to the bathroom without help. If Hilda kicks her out, I don't know what I'll do.

"I'll work on it," I say, having no idea what that means. How do you tell your mother to stop saying cocksucker and motherfucker?

"Where's Trinity?"

Hilda shakes her head and frowns. "Vee had to let her go."

"What?"

Trinity loved my mother. She fed and bathed her. She'd check on her during the night to make sure she hadn't kicked off the covers. I don't think Trinity ever really slept.

"Some complaints."

"Complaints? Trinity was wonderful," I say, annoyed. "I can't believe you let her go."

Hilda leans in and whispers conspiratorially, "Vell, if you must know, she vas caught shoplifting at Sears."

"Trinity?" I laugh. This is something I can't imagine.

Hilda huffs as if I've offended her. "I cannot allow a member of my staff to engage in illegal activities. It was zee only choice. I haff a group of highly recommended people interviewing for zee job. I vill fill her space by zee end of zee day. And with Hal gone, vee have one less body to worry about."

How like Hilda to find the positive in death.

I sit with my mother. Dr. Phil is on the TV yammering away at some crying middle-aged women.

"Heave that baggage right out the window," he lectures in his homespun Texas twang. "Heal those painful feelings and get closure, or you will pollute your life. Anger is toxic."

The Laugher chortles. The Satellite orbits. Mom purrs and puts her head on my shoulder. I rub her hair. It is unkempt and greasy. When Trinity was here, she treated Mom like her very own Barbie doll. She'd put makeup and lipstick on my mother. She'd braid her hair. Now my mother looks frighteningly pale. Her hair is a swirl of white cotton candy atop her head.

"Cocksucker," Mom growls. I cough, just in case Hilda's eavesdropping.

Two years ago, I noticed it for the first time. Gabby and I had headed to New York to visit my mom. My Aunt Maddy said she'd been acting strange lately. Mrs. Marino, a next door neighbor, said my mom was becoming a recluse. She stopped gardening and going to church. She used to call me every day. Suddenly, she never called me. When I spoke to her, she barely said a word on the phone. I thought she was depressed since I had moved away. I wanted to convince her to move back with us. I imagined finding a cute little garden apartment on the lake in Calabasas for her. She could babysit Gabby. We'd take a yoga class together. Mom needed to exercise more.

Gabby and I took a cab to the house. I rang the doorbell. There was no answer. I rapped on the door; still nothing. Maybe Mom was visiting a neighbor? I had a spare key with me. I opened the door. Gabby ran in ahead of me.

"Gai-ma, Gai-ma," she squealed, running into the living room.

I stared in horror at the mess in the hall. My mother, who scrubbed, vacuumed, and dusted daily, would never allow her house to look like this. My feet stuck to the hardwood floor.

"Mom?" I said hesitantly. "Mom!" My heart throbbed. I couldn't breathe. When was the last time I'd been there? Five months ago? Could so much have changed since then?

I entered the kitchen. The counters were crammed with dirty dishes. I screamed when a roach scuttled from behind a utensil drawer. Another one followed.

"Mom?"

"Mommy! Mommy!" Gabby screamed from the living room. Her voice sounded high pitched and frightened.

I ran to her. She was staring at something, her mouth open wide. At first I thought my mother must be dead, but there she was, sitting naked on my dad's leather Barcalounger. She stared at Big Bird on the television screen.

"Mom?"

She didn't answer me. She watched Big Bird, Elmo, and Oscar sing about the ABCs as if it were a breaking news story.

"Mom! *Mom!*"

She ignored me. I walked to the TV and turned it off.

I bent down in front of my mother.

"Mommy. Mommy." I spoke in a whisper as tears flew out my eyes.

"What are you doing in my house," she screamed. "Get out or I'll call the police."

I decided the best thing to do was move my mother here, to sunny Los Angeles. I sold her house, moved the things I could move, and gave or threw the rest away. The years and years of acquisitions that Mom had meticulously and painstakingly gleaned from endless trips to antique stores and estate sales were distributed among relatives or sold to probably the same antique stores they were purchased at, or tossed in a big bin in front of her house. The beautiful dresses she never wore because she was saving them for a special occasion were donated to Goodwill.

For a while I believed Mom would get better. The sun and the fresh air would somehow cure her. Being around her daughter and granddaughter would waken her somnambulant brain. One day we could take yoga together.

As I brush the knots out of my mother's hair, it occurs to me how I accepted Alex's infrequent visits to Hilda's. He'd say, "What's the point, she doesn't even know I'm there. She doesn't even know she's there." He told me the place depressed him. Instead of saying, "Yeah, it depresses me, too, but that's no excuse not to be there for me," I said, "Okay, I understand." He'd come with us on Thanksgiving, Christmas, and Easter, but he'd act like he was doing me this big favor. He'd give Mom a kiss on the cheek, sit next to her for a few minutes, and then get antsy. He'd find a newspaper and read it or go outside and return phone calls or watch whatever was blasting on the TV. He'd barely look at Mom. I wonder if he believed that this was his future, too. After all, Alzheimer's runs in families. Maybe he thought he'd be changing my diapers one day.

Maybe with Rose he thinks he's found eternal youth.

When Alex met my mom she was still beautiful, with piercing blue eyes and her shiny gray hair pulled back in a bun. Mom and Dad invited us for dinner and Alex showed up with an enormous bouquet of flowers. He complimented my mother's cooking and talked law with my father, who had a private practice in New

Rochelle. After he left, I assumed my parents would heap effusive praise on my boyfriend. Instead, they were quiet.

"So? So?" I asked.

They looked at each other.

"He seems very ambitious," my father finally said.

"Ambitious? That's the best you can say?"

"Well, we just met him. We don't want to jump to conclusions."

My parents were always cautious, so I didn't think much of it, but maybe I should have. Maybe they saw something that in my hormonally charged state I couldn't see. I wish I could ask them now. I wish I had asked them then. Why are children so stupid? We never ask our parents the right questions when we have the chance. When we figure out how much we really need them, they're dead or brain dead.

I can tell Gabby will be the same way. I see the signs. The way she sometimes rolls her eyes at me. The way she walks out of the room when I'm telling her something. The way her eyes cloud over when she pretends to listen to me.

It breaks my heart, but I suppose it's unavoidable. You want your children to learn from your mistakes, but instead they dive right into them.

I read an article recently about how Alzheimer's often skips a generation and I felt a momentary sense of relief. So maybe I won't be wearing Depends and staring glassy-eyed at *Wheel of Fortune*. Then I glanced at Gabby. And I cried. Not only could my daughter get Alzheimer's, but I won't be there to take care of her. That's the hardest part about being a parent, knowing that your child will one day be out in the world without you. I want to wrap her in my arms and protect her forever, but every day she recedes a little farther away from me. I just hope I don't cause her sadness one day. But I suppose that's also unavoidable.

Alex should have visited my mom more. And I guess that's the best I can wish for Gabby. That she finds someone who will be there for her even if she laughs for no reason or has a Waxie dangling out of her pants. Someone who will come with her to visit me, even if I don't know who I am.

"Mommy!" Gabby screams at the top of her lungs when I pick her up from kindergarten. She hurls herself into my arms and I swoop her up and kiss her cheeks.

"Gabby's a wonderful girl," her teacher says, smiling. "So loving." Her eyes narrow a bit. "Myrna would like a word with you."

Myrna Shafley is the principal.

"Okay." I smile. "Come on, Gabby."

"I think she wants to see you alone," Mrs. Waring says. "I'll keep an eye on Gabby for you."

Even though I am thirty-eight years old, my heart stampedes against my ribs. What could my daughter have done? Talked back? Had a temper tantrum? Hit someone? Bitten someone? In the ten-second walk to Myrna's office, my mind races through dozens of possibilities.

I stick my head into Myrna's office.

"Come in. Take a seat, Mrs. Hirsh."

Myrna is exactly what you would expect an administrator who takes her job very seriously to look like. She's about fifty-five with short, scooped-up, butterscotch-colored hair brushed to the side, octagonal eyeglasses with clear frames, sensible shoes, and pleated skirts that fall below her knee. Every sweater she owns seems geared to some holiday. It's only the beginning of October, but already she's decked out in a black sweater with a big orange pumpkin on it. When she speaks, it sounds like her throat is stuck in her nose.

"Mrs. Hirsh, you have a remarkable little girl."

I smile. So this is what it's about, my remarkable little girl.

"She's so advanced we think she should be moved into first grade.

What a precocious little girl she is. Mrs. Hirsh, you should be very proud of the way you raised her. Perhaps at my next seminar, you could be the guest speaker? I'm sure many of the parents would love to know your secrets."

I nod my head at Myrna. She pinches her cheeks.

"I understand this is a rough time for your family."

"Well, I suppose . . ."

"Mrs. Hirsh, have you noticed any changes in your daughter, since your . . . your . . . her father moved out?"

"Well, of course, it's not easy, but she's a very resilient little girl. I think she's doing okay. Better than okay."

"Well, I'll be blunt with you, Mrs. Hirsh. We've gotten a few complaints from the parents."

My heart pounds. "Complaints? About Gabby?"

Myrna shuts her eyes and takes a deep breath. When she opens her eyes, they bore into mine.

"Yes. It seems your daughter has been using inappropriate language in the schoolyard."

"Gabby? I . . . I . . . She must have picked it up from another student. We don't speak that way at home."

Myrna gave a quick, all-knowing laugh that emanated from her nose.

"Mrs. Hirsh, I've been an educator for more than thirty years now. And every time I approach a parent whose child is exhibiting inappropriate behavior, they blame it on another student or they say the child must have heard it on television. I'm not telling you this is your fault, Mrs. Hirsh, but when a child's behavior affects other students, I must step in."

I bristle. I see red. I hate this woman.

"I don't like the way you're talking to me. I'm telling you I don't know what you're talking about."

Myrna takes another deep breath. "She called some classmates . . ." She shakes her head and leans towards me, whispering. "Well, mother and then the F-bomb. I was on the phone this morning with two very irate parents. Now maybe you don't talk this way in front of her, but, well . . ."

I take a deep breath. "It's my mother," I say, not even realizing how ridiculous that sounds.

Myrna swats her hand through the air. "Your mother?"

"My mother has Alzheimer's. She can't speak anymore. For some reason that's one of the only words she says. I have no idea why. I didn't know Gabby had heard her say these things. But I'll talk to her about it."

Myrna nods her head and squeezes out a quick smile. I can't tell if she doesn't believe me or if she's disappointed that I don't have a more nefarious explanation.

"Okay, Mrs. Hirsh, I'll try to calm these parents down, but please remedy this inappropriate behavior. I've had to mark this on her record, but if there are no more instances of this, we can put it behind us."

I want to tell her that transition is not a verb.

My five-year-old already has a record.

"Thank you," I say.

"I hope you and your husband work everything out."

Myrna gives me another quick smile. Then she buries her face in some papers on her desk. Meeting adjourned. I get up slowly and head down the hall to pick up my little delinquent.

"Gabby, do you understand that Grandma doesn't know what she's saying anymore?"

"Sure."

"Some of the things Grandma says don't make sense. So you shouldn't say them, okay?"

"Why?"

"They're naughty, naughty words."

"What do they mean?"

"It's not important what they mean. Just don't say them anymore."

"But why does Grandma say them?"

"Because she doesn't know what she's saying."

"But she must have heard them somewhere to know them."

"Yes. I guess she did."

"Where do you think she heard them?"

"I don't know."

"From you?"

"No. I don't use those kinds of words."

"But I heard you say jackass. That's a naughty word."

"Mommy shouldn't have said that. I was just angry at the driver who cut us off on the freeway."

"So maybe you were angry around Grandma and used those words."

"No. I didn't. I don't say those words and I don't want you to anymore. Do you understand?"

"Not really."

"It doesn't matter. Just don't use them again."

"I just called Cara a motherfudder. She laughed. She thought it was funny. It's a funny word. Motherfudder peanut butter."

"Just don't use it anymore."

"But why? It makes us laugh. And if it makes us laugh, how bad can it be?"

That's how it goes with Gabby, around and around. I have no idea if she'll use the word again. I'll probably spend the next month looking for a new kindergarten for Gabby and a board and care for Mom. Someone could make a small fortune figuring out how to combine them. Hilda's Board, Care, and Kindergarten. After all, there's not much difference between a five-year-old and a seventy-five-year-old.

When we get home, the woman up the street is moaning again. She's had more sex in the last few days than I've had all year. Gabby looks at me. She wants to tell me that we need to rescue this damsel, but she doesn't. Instead, Alex's Lexus turns into the driveway and she runs to it.

"Daddy!" she screams. "Daddydaddydaddy!"

I forgot he was coming to take her to a Bob the Builder–themed party. He gets out of the car and hoists Gabby into the air. She squeals.

"Who are you supposed to be?" Gabby asks him.

Lately she's been asking random people this. "Who are you supposed to be?" I think she's being unintentionally profound. After all, isn't everyone acting? Trying to be something they're really not? It seems especially fitting today. Who the hell is Alex—Xander—Hirsh supposed to be? He barely resembles the man I met in Manhattan a few years ago. His hair is too perfect, his goatee too manicured. His muscles ripple like never before. He wears a plain long-sleeved white T-shirt underneath a red short-sleeved T-shirt. And he's got on baggy faded jeans that look like they're really expensive. I check the back of them for a label and see big pockets with swirls on them that look like horseshoes. Alex? In True Religions? I want to say something, but bite my tongue instead. This is not Alex. Where is the messy hair? The flab? The wrinkled Polo shirts? The Levis? Had he been like this for a while and I'm just noticing it? Is this the result of Rose's grooming? Or is this what newfound love does to you? Makes you better than you really are? Or at least more fashionable?

Right then it hits me. Alex is not mine anymore. He's gone. He's Xander. Even if Rose is having a torrid affair with Colin Farrell, he'll move on. But he'll never be back. It's a wallop to my gut. All the air is sucked out of me. I have been living an illusion, thinking somehow this will work out, but it's over.

I will not cry. I will not cry. I will not cry.

"I'm supposed to be Daddy. I'm supposed to take you to a party, remember? Are you ready?"

"No! I have to change into a beautiful party dress."

"I'll help you," I say, my voice choking in my throat.

"No! I want to surprise you and Daddy."

"Just don't wear that Cinderella gown. It's filthy."

She rolls her eyes at me and runs into the house. I stare at Alex. He looks at me. The Moaner moans. Alex smiles and looks in the direction of the moan. He stares off for a long time.

"Are things going okay here," he finally asks.

"Sure."

"I'll get the mortgage check in the mail," he says. "You need anything else?"

"Answers. How are things with you and Rose, Xander?"

Alex shuffles his feet. The Moaner moans again and he looks off in her direction.

"You know better than anyone that you can't believe the tabloids. I really have just been keeping to myself. I just need some time, Ally. I know it sounds clichéd, but I guess I just need to find myself. Please, give me this, just for a little while."

"When will that be?" I say. I hate myself for sounding so desperate. His eyes seem to squirm in their sockets.

"I don't believe you," I scoff. "And don't make me read about it somewhere. You owe it to me. Most of all, you owe it to Gabby."

Alex/Xander opens his mouth to protest, but nothing comes out. Instead we stare at each other for a long time.

"Ohhhhohhhhh." The Moaner punctuates the tension for us.

I flash on our first date. A small Italian restaurant on Mulberry Street. We sat and talked for hours as if we'd known each other forever. Halfway through the meal, Alex kissed my hand. "I think we're going to spend the rest of our life together," he whispered. A chill sped through my whole body because I'd been thinking the same thing.

Up the street, The Moaner finally climaxes.

"Tada," Gabby says. She's dressed in a floor-length red velvet Christmas dress that Aunt Maddy sent her last year. She looks at me, expecting me to tell her to change. After all, it's eighty degrees. But I just want them to go to the party so I can be by myself.

"You look beautiful," I say.

Gabby beams, jumps into my arms, and hugs me. "I love you more than anything."

"Me, too," I say, smiling as wide as I can, knowing that in a few minutes I can collapse on my bed in tears.

7

Potty Mouth

I stare at the coffee shop photo, the one of the newborn baby in its mother's arms. When the waitress stops by, I ask her if it's for sale. I've never bought art from a coffee shop before, but I want this photograph. I look at it and can't help but feel calm.

"I think so. I'll check with the owner."

She heads to another table and takes orders. I look over and recognize the three women sitting at the table. Their children are Gabby's classmates. One of them was the one wearing the Winnie the Pooh sweatshirt the first day. She smiles and waves at me. I can't remember her name. The others look over and wave.

"Come join us, Alice," says Winnie the Pooh mom.

I have been a publicist for fifteen years. My job is to remember names, to pepper sentences with names as often as possible. Maybe that's why in real life I fight it so hard. I remember nothing. Susan? Karen? Carol? She could definitely be one of those, but she isn't. I grab my coffee and head to their table while rummaging through my brain for possible names.

I smile at the women. "Hi," I say, mustering as much friendliness as possible. "I'm Alice Hirsh. My daughter's Gabby."

"Take a seat. We're all horrible procrastinators trying to forget about all our fucking responsibilities," Winnie the Pooh says.

I didn't expect Winnie the Pooh to curse.

The other women introduce themselves to me. There's Renee, who was once a model and occasionally auditions for commercials. She's wearing a Juicy Couture sweatsuit that looks like it's never seen the inside of a gym, although she does have a perfect body. Her breasts seem more like cartoon images of breasts.

There's Amy, who works part-time as an accountant. She's perfectly coiffed in a white silk shirt, black skirt, and sling-back pumps.

And then I remember. *Nancy*. Nancy is the owner of the Winnie the Pooh sweatshirt.

They tell me their children's names. When Renee mentions her children—Sam and Cara—I cringe.

Mudderfucker.

I decide to mention it because I'm certain they've all discussed it already.

Renee swats her hand. "Oh, that's your daughter? It was really not the biggest deal in the world. I wasn't even going to say anything to Myrna but . . ." She shivers. "God, that woman just drives me nuts. She calls me in the office the other day like I'm some kid in need of discipline. Then she tells me that she strongly suggests I enroll in her seven-week parenting seminar to learn about problem ownership. Whatever that means. She says Cara's exhibiting 'inappropriate behavior.' She had a temper tantrum because she hadn't slept and now I'm the worst parent in the world. So when she told me that, I just mentioned that how come my daughter goes to school every day and the only thing she's learned so far is to say motherfucker?"

"I'm sorry. I've had a talk with Gabby about it."

"I didn't even know it was Gabby. Cara loves Gabby. She talks about her all the time. But Myrna is insane. She launched a full-on investigation. She was hoping it would be some enormous scandal. Sex and drugs."

"Well," I say. "My mom has Alzheimer's. For some reason the only words she uses are cocksucker and motherfucker. Don't ask me why, because she never said those things pre-Alzheimer's."

"God, that's horrible," Renee says.

"It is. But I guess it's kinda funny, too, in a weird way. Maybe my mom's making up for all the cocksuckers and motherfuckers she should have said when she was of sound mind."

"You're right. We probably all need to say cocksucker and motherfucker more," says Nancy. "Maybe it's a way to prevent senility. Cocksucker. Motherfucker. I feel younger already."

"Nancy," Amy whines, acting shocked.

I laugh. "You should have seen Myrna's face. She was so disappointed. She was hoping I'd tell her about some down and dirty fighting I've been having with my husband."

There, I put it on the table. I didn't care. These women know. Everybody knows. So why not? Why be secretive when some alleged friend of mine is telling the tabloids that Alex wasn't happy? That we fought all the time? That I was a shrew?

"Yeah, we heard about your situation."

"How could you not? It was just all over the tabloids."

"It must be a tough time for you."

"It is," I say. "I just feel really bad for Gabby. She's too old to lie to and too young to really know the truth."

For some reason I tell them everything. It just pours out of me. I tell them more than I've told Judy or Lauren or Claire. I even told them about the realization I had the other day when Alex/Xander picked Gabby up. Maybe it's because they don't know me or Alex. They don't know about Al Squared. Or maybe it's because these women seem like the type you can just tell anything to. I'm not sure.

"If my husband cheated on me, I'd kill him," Amy says. "I can't even imagine."

"God, that's horrible," Nancy adds. "I met your . . . your, um, husband? He was at that birthday party the other day. By the way, did anyone think that party was just a tad over the top? I mean, a Ferris wheel in the backyard? Please. It's ridiculous."

"Oh, lighten up, it was cute," Amy says. "They just went all out for their kid. What's wrong with that?"

"Cute? What's a kid gonna expect from life when at five he's already getting Ferris wheels and hoedowns and pony rides? You can tell he's already a spoiled little brat."

"Nancy, that's not nice," says Amy, rubbing her temples. "Listen, guys, I've got another migraine. I'm going to head home to take a nap. I'll call you later."

"I hope it wasn't caused by my foul mouth," Nancy says.

"No. I think I can handle your mouth, Nance."

Amy kisses everyone—including me—good-bye, throws some money on the table, and leaves.

"That woman gets more migraines than anyone I know," Renee says. "Has she had a CAT scan or anything? Maybe she has a raging tumor."

"No idea. I think life just stresses her out. Everything stresses her out. I mean, I love her, but I think I stress her out, too," Nancy says, turning to me. "So anyway, your husband shows up and people act as if he's Tom Cruise. It was crazy. These women were fawning over him."

"He dumps his wife and becomes a celebrity."

"I'm sorry, but that Rose Maris is a fucking skank as far as I'm concerned. You're much more beautiful," Nancy says. "And I'm not just saying that to make you feel good. Renee, didn't I tell you that the other day?"

"She did."

Maybe I can overlook the Winnie the Pooh sweatshirt.

I am filled with love for these women I barely knew a moment ago. I feel the way I did the other morning at Gabby's school. I don't want this moment to end. I want to order another latte, sit here all day, and forget about everything else—the filthy house, the laundry, the lawyer I need to see. I never want to leave. I want these women to like me. I want to be invited to coffees and playdates and girls' nights out.

"We should do a playdate," Nancy says, as if reading my mind. "I hate playdates, but maybe we could make it cookies and milk for the kids and vodka for the mommies."

"Sounds good to me," I say.

I turn towards the window and my heart bangs in my chest. It's Johnny, the paparazzo, exiting a black Subaru Outback with a camera dangling from his chest. I gasp.

"What is it?"

"That's this photographer who stalked me and took photos of me looking horrible."

"I'll spill my latte on my girls to distract him," Renee says, nodding to her chest. "You head out the back way, through the kitchen."

"You should let him just take your picture. You look great," Nancy says.

I smile. Then I leap out of my seat and head for the back exit.

"We'll call you," Nancy says.

I turn back and smile again. Renee. Nancy. Amy. I'll remember their names.

Dear George,

Your e-mail took me by surprise the other day. It was great hearing from you. You sound like you're doing great.

God, it's horrible. Two greats in three sentences. I can't even write an e-mail. If I wait much longer, he'll think I really labored over this. I have to respond today or it will be too late to ever respond. But what do I say?

George. Maybe he had been the one for me all along, but I was too young to know it. Should I tell him that I have a daughter named Gabrielle, too? Should I tell him that I haven't forgotten about him? That I still think about him? Think what if? What if? What if? How many what ifs can one person have? Do a certain number of what ifs constitute a failed life? How can I make sure Gabby never has a what if?

Dear George,

I am at a loss for words. Of all the people in my life, I never ever expected to hear from you again. Your e-mail completely took me by surprise. I'm sorry for a lot of things, but mostly I'm sorry for the way I treated you. I wish things could have been different, but what can I do? I was twenty-something and very stupid. Now I'm a wise old lady. I can't believe how old I am.

What should I tell you about my life? I have a daughter. She just turned five and her name is also Gabrielle. She's incredible. I am taking a hiatus from work and am just really learning how incredible she is. She calls windshield wipers rainbow makers. She thinks she's a princess. She's got it all figured out. I'm not her real mommy. There's a queen out there just waiting to tell her that she's really her daughter and a princess of some land far away from here. Sometimes, when she's particularly angry with me, she convinces herself that I stole her from her queen mother. She dresses in gowns all the time. Whenever she meets someone, she asks, who are you supposed to be? She thinks the entire world is dressed up in a costume and we're never really who we are. She's right, I suppose. At least in L.A., she's right. And maybe that's the thing. We're always right when we're five. Everyone teaches us how to be wrong until we're wrong all the time.

My mom has Alzheimer's. My dad died five years ago. Heart attack. I never told you this, but after we broke up, my father wouldn't speak to me for months. He was very angry. I think he was secretly in love with you. He actually said, "Don't introduce me to any of your boyfriends again, because I don't want to be hurt like this when you break up with them." Anyway, my parents really liked you.

My mom lives a few blocks away from me at a board and care. She's about to get kicked out of it for, of all things, bad language. Can you believe my sweet mother? That's what Alzheimer's does to you. It takes away everything. Or maybe it gives you the truth you lost when you were five. She calls people cocksuckers and motherfuckers. Maybe she's right about them.

I'm probably making no sense. It's been a tough last few weeks. But Lauren and I are thinking about going to the reunion. It could be fun. Although a different fun since the last time I was on campus, I'm sure. I really toned down the drinking.

Thanks for the e-mail. I don't think a transportation reporter sounds that horrible. At least you always followed your dreams.

All the best,

Alice

Before I have time to think it over, I hit the send button. I'm sure when I reread it, I'll regret sending it.

"Alice, you must rid yourself of the baggage from your past, not embrace it," Dr. Phil would say.

• • •

"We must maintain the integrity of North Pole Way," Sherri says when I walk into the meeting at her house. A group of ten people sit around a table, listening intently. "Last year, we seemed fractured. Maybe we've stopped trying to get to know each other and our interests. There seemed to be a lack of communication. This year, I think everyone should submit their ideas to the Holiday Board before executing their designs."

"*Holiday Board*," someone asks. "What holiday board?"

"The one I'm electing this evening," Sherri says. "We need unity on North Pole Way."

Gabby is spending the weekend at Alex's bachelor pad. I wonder how it's going. She hugged me so tight when he picked her up. Gabby has never been away from me. Sure, I've taken business trips, but this is different. She's the one who's gone. I miss her already. I want to call her right now and see if she's okay.

I wonder if anyone has seen me enter this room. I want to sneak out, call Gabby, and head to a movie. Anything is more productive than this. Sherri said the entire neighborhood would show up. There's only a handful of people.

"Has everyone met Alice . . . Hirsh? Alice lives at 4612 Monet Drive."

"Hi, Alice," they say. "Welcome to North Pole Way."

"I'm so glad—and relieved—Alice showed up," Sherri says. "Up until a week ago, she was in the dark about North Pole Way. She had no idea what living on this block entails."

"We're a regular bunch of Santa's Elves," a chubby guy in the corner says before bursting into hearty laughter. "So, Sherri, did you invite our friends on Pissarro to the meeting?

There's some more giggles. Pissarro's the street above mine, where The Moaner lives. All the streets in the area are named after impressionist painters—Monet, Sisley, Cezanne, Renoir, Pissarro. There's a sign when you enter the area that reads: WE MAKE GOOD IMPRESSIONS. Every time I pass it, I fantasize about vandalizing it.

Sherri shakes her head and pinches her cheeks. "I've had the police there four times, but they think it's funny. I swear, Bob Stone just has his girls give the cops, well, you fill in the blanks."

"That's the rumor," the chubby guy says. "Maybe I'll go up there and complain."

More giggles. Sherri catches the puzzled look on my face.

"Honey," she says to me. "Don't tell me that you don't know about Bob Stone either."

"Well, it sounds like whoever's living there is having fun."

The chubby guy looks up. "Your realtor must have been brilliant, keeping you in the dark about all the ho, ho, hos on the block."

Chubby laughs so hard his face turns purple.

Sherri rubs her neck, as if this conversation is causing her stress.

"What Tad over there is trying to tell you is that they shoot pornographic movies there," she says.

"Yeah," says Tad. "Bob Stone is the king of porn flicks. He makes a few a week, the lucky S.O.B."

Sherri clears her throat. "We've been trying to get them shut down for years now, but everyone takes it as a joke. The last cop I had here said I was just jealous that I wasn't in any of them. Can you imagine? Our property value is going straight to hell."

For a moment I feel what I can only characterize as relief. I'm glad it's not some happily married woman having great orgasms a few times a day. I don't want to know about people like that.

"Really?"

"I don't want to . . . to destroy the integrity of this meeting by talking about that horrible place. I don't want that house to participate. Besides, no one drives up there anyway. Let's forget about it. We have more important items to discuss. Who wants to head up the Holiday Board with me? Anyone? Anyone?"

Sherri's eyes dart around the room. When they land on me, I smile. Then I look down at the table.

"Okay, how about our newcomer, Alice? We could use some new blood."

"That's a great idea," Tad says.

Sherri smiles at me as if she's bestowing a precious gift.

"There's no way. I have too much going on right now . . ." I am chairwoman of the *Holiday Board.* I have to ensure the "integrity" of North Pole Way by making certain every house has a holiday theme and that no two houses have the same holiday theme. Last year there was the famous Spongebob Debacle, where three houses had Sponge-Bob displays. There were also two Simpsons Christmases and two Shrek displays. I don't know what any of these characters have to do with Christmas or Hanukah, but I decide to keep my mouth shut.

Sherri tells me she'll be putting a note in everyone's mailbox. Within the next few weeks, they must call me to get the board's approval. I'm supposed to make sure no one overlaps. I think Sherri believes she's somehow helping me feel welcome in the North Pole community. But being in charge of anything is not my forte.

Take for example my life.

When I return home I check my e-mails. There's nothing from George. Dr. Phil was right. I never should have answered his e-mail. I probably scared him. I took the mystery away.

"She's still in love with me, just as I suspected. Just like she was the day I pulled her off the hood of my car and drove off to a better life while she barfed on the curb. A life without drama. Look how stable my life is now compared to hers. The best thing I ever did was dump her ass, which, by the way, looked enormous in the Enquirer *photo."*

The house is so quiet without Gabby. I want to run into her bedroom and listen to her soft, deep breathing. I love watching her sleep. It's so peaceful and uncomplicated.

I pick up the phone to call her at Alex's. Then I put it down. No, I can't check up on them. If there were problems, they'd call me. If I call, I'm just being nosy, clingy, annoying.

I remember that Gabby hasn't pooped in five days. Ever since Gabby was three, she has been terrified of pooping. She'll hold it in for a week, each day becoming more and more unpleasant. Nothing seems to work. She's developed an almost superhuman immunity to bran, fiber, and mineral and flaxseed oils. We've bribed her with candy, ice cream, trips to Disneyland. Some experts out there have even given it a name—Anal Retention Disorder or Fecal Retention Syndrome. These experts say these children feel like they're losing a part of themselves and want to keep it inside. Or they say children with the condition want to control everything around them, including their crap.

I wonder if she's giving Alex a hard time with this.

"Alice, don't use your child as currency in your marriage," Dr. Phil would say.

The next day, Hilda stands by the front door, arms akimbo, a scowl on her Nazi face. I want to drive on without stopping, but she's waiting for me. I like to visit Mom when she's not around, but ever since Trinity left, she's become a permanent fixture. I take my time unbuckling, turning off the engine, opening the door, hoping she'll be distracted by a phone call, a dirty diaper, anything. I look up. She's still waiting.

"Good morning Hilda," I say as pleasantly as possible as I attempt to breeze by her into the house.

"Vee must discuss your mussa," she says, her eyes cutting into me.

"Is there a problem?"

"Her language is inappropriate for my board and care," she says.

Inappropriate? God, is there any word more annoying in the English language? When all else fails, call something inappropriate and you'll get instant respect even if you don't know what you're talking about. Inappropriate. Unacceptable. Offensive. Those are the catch-phrases for the mentally challenged.

"My clients do not like to be subjected to such vulgar expressions. Zey are a genteel group of people who vant to relax in comfort during zair golden years. Yesterday your mother called Dorothy a muzzahfucker. Ze woman was a singer in her church choir. I cannot tolerate zis here."

"My mother has Alzheimer's. She doesn't know what she's saying."

Hilda shakes her head as if this were the silliest thing she's ever heard. "I haff no choice," she says.

I can see her in Auschwitz, standing in the showers, about to turn the dial. *I have no choice.*

"No choice?"

"You must find another board and care. There have been too many complaints."

I look in the living room. The Laugher rocks back and forth on a couch in front of the blaring television. The Satellite does a lap through the living room.

"Complaints?" I yell, furious. "Complaints from who? These people are all vegetables."

"She must go ASAP." Hilda brushes her hands together. *Case closed.*

Blinding white dots of fury dance in front of my eyes. My body shakes. I want to punch this woman.

"You shouldn't be running a board and care. You should be shoveling people into ovens," I hiss. "Don't you know this is not my mother? This is fucking Alzheimer's!"

Her body flinches as if I've just punched her and she gasps. "Now I know vair she gets her foul mouth. I vant you and your mother out of here ziss instant," she says.

"Gladly. But let me tell you, I'll be reporting you to the Los Angeles . . . Los Angeles . . ." I scan my brain for some bureaucracy in charge of board and cares but nothing comes to mind. "Well, some Los Angeles association," I say.

I push past her into the living room. One of the new employees whose name I never learned walks my mother toward the couch. She's about to plop her down.

"*No!*" I yell as the residents and workers look at me in horror. I didn't mean to scream so loud, but if my mom sits down, it will take hours to pull her up. I clear my throat and smile at this Filipino girl who looks like she's not even twenty.

"I'm going to take my mother home."

The girl looks at me as if this is a ridiculous notion. She's thinking, "*How can this American woman who is nearly twice my age care for her own mother?*" She smiles at me without looking at me. She gently guides my mother toward me.

"Here you are, missus," she says to my mother. "Your daughter is taking you to the home." She looks up at me and nods. "I help?"

I begin to shake my head yes when I hear Hilda behind me, inhaling loudly.

"Thank you, Maria," Hilda says. "Please attend to *our* residents."

Maria nervously looks at me. Then she pries my mother's fingers off her wrist. She pulls my mother's hand into mine.

"She is such a nice lady," Maria whispers. "I will miss her."

Hilda peers out the window as I struggle to get my mother to the car. Every step seems to take an hour. She shuffles her feet a centimeter at a time. I didn't realize that my mother had forgotten how to walk. She doesn't bend her knees or lift her legs. I have to coax each leg to remember until we finally get to the car.

I am relieved when we make it to the car. My back hurts from pulling at my mother. My head pounds. When I open the passenger door, my mother won't sit.

"Sit, Mom, come on. You can do it." I lean her against the side of the car and show her. I sit and stand. Sit and stand. I push on my mother's back to get her to bend her body. Despite the Alzheimer's, she is still strong. She remains rigid and upright.

"Jesus Christ, Mom, come on, just sit," I say, straining not to yell as sweat pours down my face. Mom looks at me and her eyes fill with tears. She opens her mouth and wails. I wonder when my mother had her teeth brushed last. Since Trinity left, I'm sure no one has taken the time to brush her teeth for her, and she'd never do it on herself. The smell of her breath is like water in a vase of flowers that has been dead for weeks. It is the smell of rotting organs, muscles, flesh. It's the smell of death.

From the corner of my eye, I see Hilda at the window. She wears the same smile she had when Hal died. I wrap my arms around Mom and start crying.

"I'm sorry, Mommy. I'm sorry. I just don't know how to do this. I wish you could help me. I can't do this alone."

I have no idea what to do next. I pray for a miracle. I close my eyes and take a few deep breaths.

Someone says, "Alice?"

I look up. Nancy—Winnie the Pooh mom—sits in an idling Dodge minivan.

"Nancy!"

"I thought that was you," she says, getting out of the van and heading to us. "Can I help you guys?"

I wipe my eyes and nose. "I'm trying to get my mom to sit down, but she just won't. I don't know what to do."

"Let me see what I can do. What's your mother's name?"

"Mary."

"Come on, Mary, you can do this," Nancy says, smiling. "Let's show Alice that we can do this without her, okay? We don't need Alice's help, right?

She speaks in a soothing voice. Mom almost seems to give Nancy a mischievous grin. In a few minutes, she's sitting in the passenger seat.

"See, that wasn't so bad," Nancy says.

"You're amazing. Are you a nurse or something?"

"No, but my grandmother lived with us growing up. In her last years she had dementia, which I guess is the same thing as Alzheimer's. Your mother seems like a sweetie. They're just like kids. Sometimes it's easier for a stranger to get through to them than it is for their own flesh and blood."

I hear kids fighting in the minivan.

"What are you doing here anyway," I ask.

"We live up the street," she says. "My little boy was the one who noticed you. He said there's Gabby's mommy."

One of her children begins to scream.

"Well, I guess that's my cue. I leave them alone for a minute and they beat each other to a pulp. We're on our way to soccer practice. Just another crazy Saturday. But if you need anything, just call. I mean it, really, Alice. Please call me."

She jots a number down on a piece of paper and hands it to me.

"If I don't hear from you, I'll bug you, okay?"

"Okay."

More than anything, I want to ask her to follow me home and help my mom into the house, but I don't. I was brought up not to impose, not to ask favors, to figure out how to do it alone, to bear the burden. "Never rely on others" was my family's secret motto. I remember making pancakes with my mom in a snowstorm when we ran out of eggs. I suggested running next door to borrow some from a neighbor. Mom vehemently shook her head. "I don't want to be beholden to anyone," she told me as she tossed the batter into the garbage, and we ate cereal instead.

It isn't until I am in my driveway that I see Nancy's minivan.

She gets out and smiles at me.

"I could use a break from being a soccer mom anyway," she says as she heads to my passenger side door.

Nancy stays with me for a few hours. But the moment she leaves, I realize my mother needs a diaper change. I don't know what to do. I've never changed my mother before. I can change baby diapers, no problem. But this is beyond me. I hope one day Gabby doesn't have this dilemma: to change a diaper or let Mommy wallow in her own excrement. *Come on, Ally, you can do it.* I find a box of Depends, open it up, and grab a diaper. I cover the bed in the guest room with a sheet. Then I go back to the living room to get my mom.

Alex couldn't have planned his departure better. I wonder what he would have done if he'd been here for this. He'd probably be on the phone with every board and care in the region until he found a place with an opening. He'd be cashing in on favors. Or he'd put her in a nursing home and convince me it was for the best. He'd find a way to sue Hilda. If nothing else, Alex was effective. He knew the right people.

I stand frozen in the living room with a diaper in my hand.

"Mommy, come with me," I say, knowing she won't respond. I head towards her and grab an arm. It's a dead weight.

"Cocksucker," Mom mumbles at some unknown thought. "Motherfucker."

I wonder if Dad's looking down at us and crying. I hold my breath. "Come on, Mommy," I say. I think about calling Nancy, but can I really ask basically a stranger to help change my mother's diaper? I inventory my friends. They'd all come up with some excuse. Only Lauren, my acupuncturist college friend, would help, but she's in Rochester. I wonder how many real friends I have.

The phone rings. I race over and pick it up.

It's the second miracle of the day. Trinity.

"I am calling to tell you that I no longer am employed at Hilda's board and care. I am living with my seester in Reseda, but want to tell you what a pleasure it was working with your moother. He is a berry lovely lady. And Maria call and say he left the board and care. If you ever are in needing for someone in helping you taking care of your mother, I want to give you a phone number where you can be reached."

"How fast can you be here?"

"Please excuse me?"

"Do you want a job right now?"

"Yes. I am looking for employment."

I stare at the diaper in my hand. "Come to my house as fast as you can. You're hired."

8

Mashed Potatoes

Trinity, my mom, and I sit at the kitchen table eating chicken, broccoli, and mashed potatoes. I sigh. What a day. But not only have I persevered, I've also whipped up a three-course meal. A healthy meal for my mom, whose flesh is dangling off her bones. Trinity smiles and tells me everything's delicious. I try to eat, but I haven't been hungry in weeks. Mom doesn't eat, either.

"Mommy, you really have to eat something. Please."

"Come on, Mary," Trinity says, putting the fork into my mom's hand. Mom holds it for a second and then it falls to the floor.

I get my mother another fork.

"If you don't mind, I will feed him myself," Trinity says.

"My mother doesn't eat on her own?"

"Not really," Trinity says, keeping her eyes on the table as if she's embarrassed that I don't know this fact about my own mother.

I watch as Trinity scoops up mashed potatoes with a spoon and touches my mother's lips with it. My mother's mouth is squeezed shut, but Trinity is persistent. She taps and taps the spoon against my mother's lips. Finally, my mom's mouth opens a little bit and Trinity pries it wider with the spoon. Trinity turns the spoon over in my

mother's mouth and dumps the potatoes in. My mother rolls the potatoes around in her mouth until she finally swallows them. My
God, at this rate she'll be done eating in the morning.

"If you don't mind, you should puree everything for your
moother. The chicken, the broccoli, everything."

"Puree?"

"He doesn't really chew anymore."

"My mother? Doesn't chew? At all?"

"No. Just swallows. But he love the potato. Right, Mary? Don'
you love the potatoes?"

My mother stares straight ahead. I get the feeling that she doesn't
love potatoes or chicken or anything anymore. She's still breathing,
but there's no joy left. What's the purpose of life if you can't even enjoy mashed potatoes?

Trinity had arrived at my house about a half hour after she had
called. I helped her change my mom's diaper. (Okay, an exaggeration.
I watched her change my mother's diaper.) Then we devised a plan.
I'd convert the guest house in the back to my mom's apartment. Trinity would live there with her. It's got a bedroom and a living room.
Trinity thought that since my mother wanders the house at night, it
would be better if they stayed in the guest house—especially since
there's no oven for her to play with. I also think Trinity liked the
idea of some privacy.

The guest house already had a bed, a pull-out couch, and some
sparse furnishings. I had planned to eventually turn the place into my
home office. One day, I'd write my novel there. Instead, tomorrow I
will head to Home Depot and Pottery Barn and Crate and Barrel and
convert the space into a mini board and care. I'll get bolts for the door
so Mom can't wander at night. I'll find all the baby proofing equipment that I was saving for our next child—the covers for the switches,
the plastic locks for the cabinets—and mother-proof the guesthouse.

Trinity spoons more potatoes into my mother's mouth. It's the same routine, the slow tapping on my mother's lips. The prying of my mother's mouth. The turning of the spoon. The dumping of its contents. The sloshing around. The eventual swallowing. Repeat. I can't watch anymore. I get up to do the dishes.

A few minutes later, someone pounds at the door. Gabby! I look at my watch—seven P.M. She's been away for two days and I thought I'd enjoy the break, but I miss her more than I imagined.

"Mommymommymommy," Gabby squeals, leaping into my arms. "Mommy!"

"Baby!" I slather her pudgy cheeks with kisses. I breathe in her scent, like sugar cookies just out of the oven. Alex stands there, hands in his black Armani pants pockets. His head is bowed. After eight years, I know that look. He's guilty.

Yes, of course, he's guilty of many things. But there's fresh guilt written all over him. He shuffles his feet. He wants to leave before Gabby blabs something.

"Did you have fun, baby?"

"Yes. It was lots and lots of fun. Daddy's apartment is right on the beach. I could watch people surf from my gigantic bedroom window. I collected shells and pebbles. I have a big bucket outside for you. Then Daddy took me to a fancy restaurant and I got a big sundae for dessert that I couldn't even finish. It had like five different flavors in it. It was ne-normous. We went to the Santa Monica Pier and we rode on the Ferris wheel three times and the carousel two times. And then we—"

"Listen, guys, I should get going. There's a lot of traffic out there and I have a long drive back," Alex says, his eyes grazing my throat.

"No, Daddy, please don't go. Stay here. We can paint my shells."

"We'll paint another day."

"No! I don't want you to go. I want you to stay here with me and Mommy. Now! I don't want you to go back to that stupid apartment. This house is so much better. Why would you want to leave?"

"Gabby, I'll see you in a few days. We'll paint shells then."

Gabby scowls. "I hate you. You're mean and you don't even love me anymore."

Alex bends down to Gabby. "Of course I love you. You're my princess."

"If you loved me, you'd stay here with me and Mommy."

"Listen, me not living here has nothing to do with you, Gabby. I promise I'll see you in a few days. We'll do something real fun."

"Mommy's fun, too," Gabby says, almost pleadingly. "She's much more funner than she used to be. She even talks Barbies with me."

"I'll see you in just a few days. Okay, Gabster?"

He moves closer to the front door.

"Will that girl be with us again?"

Girl?

Girl?!

Could she be talking about Rose? Of course she's talking about Rose.

Alex's mouth flops open. His eyes bug out. His ears turn red— Alex's tell-tale sign of complete embarrassment.

Girl?

For some reason what upsets me more than anything else—than even the fact that Alex outright lied to me again, that he exposed Gabby to Rose—is that Gabby considers Rose a girl. Gabby calls my friends ladies or women. Rose, just a few years younger than I am, is considered a girl. A girl!

I struggle to remain silent. I bite my lips. I don't want to fight in front of Gabby.

"Will she, Daddy? Will she?"

"She wasn't with us that much, Gabby. She just stopped by." Alex speaks in a strange sing-songy voice.

"For like hours and hours. I liked her doggie. She was cute.

Mommy, can we get a Chihuahua? I want one that I can dress in beautiful clothes, just like that girl does. You should have seen this doggie. She was wearing a furry pink hat and a matching pink jacket. The girl let me feed her doggie biscuits. You have to remember to keep your hand flat or a dog might bite you. Can we get a Chihuahua? I want to name it Ariel Cinderella."

I don't hear a word. My rage is bigger than the rage I felt at Hilda's. It wants to explode all over the place. Instead I take a deep breath and hold it in while it rattles inside every nerve in my body. I start trembling.

"Gabby, why don't you go in the kitchen. We have a visitor." My voice is low, shaky, and drained of any emotion. I barely recognize it.

"A visitor, yay!"

As Gabby shuffles off, I stare at Alex. My face is beet red with fury.

"What the fuck, Alex?"

"Al, it isn't what you think. I never invited her over. She came back from Toronto and showed up unexpectedly. I only let her stay for a little while."

"Alex, I'm so sick of your lies."

"This isn't a lie."

"It's all lies. You told me you were using this time to find yourself. Instead, you're shacking up with that vapid actress right in front of Gabby. Don't you even care about your daughter? She's confused enough as it is. This is so not fair."

"I love Gabby more than anything in the world. I didn't do this to confuse her. I made Rose leave after a few minutes."

"You never should have let her come over. I thought you wanted to spend the weekend with your daughter. If I'd known, I never would have allowed this."

"Don't blow this out of proportion. Rose didn't know Gabby was there. I didn't let her stay very long."

"Long enough so Gabby could feed her rodent macrobiotic dog biscuits."

"Alice, don't. It was all completely innocent."

"Innocent? *Innocent?* Nothing's innocent. What's the deal, Alex or Xander or whoever you are this week? Who are you supposed to be anyway?"

"Alice, I swear. This break has nothing to do with her. It's about me."

I can't help but laugh. How clichéd, I think. It's like he's reciting bad movie dialogue again.

"Get out of here. I'm calling my lawyer tomorrow."

Alex is my lawyer.

"Ally, please, give me some time to sort through all this. I haven't seen Rose in weeks. I didn't want to see her."

"Get out of here," I hiss.

I slam the door, lean against it, and take a few deep breaths. It's quiet in the kitchen for a few seconds. Then I hear Gabby and Trinity stifle giggles.

"Oh, Mary, shame, shame. That is a very naughty word," Trinity says. "You must not say that word in front of your little granddaughter."

The phone rings. I want the machine to pick it up, but instead Gabby does.

"Who's calling please," she says. "One moment." Then she screams, "Mommy, it's some lady for you."

I pick up the phone. "Yes?"

"Hello, Alice? It's Debbie Sutton from 4819 Degas."

"Uh-huh."

"We wanted to do Spider-man this year for the holidays. The boys just love it. We're hoping no one else has dibs on it yet."

She pauses. She's waiting for me to weigh in.

"No. You're the only one," I say, not really knowing for sure.

"That's great news. Great news!" Debbie sounds almost too re-lieved, as if I've just informed her that the biopsy was benign. "Any-way, you're going to love it. We'll have Spider-man spinning a web. And guess who's caught in it? Santa and his reindeer! And then we were going to—"

"Sounds great," I say, cutting her off. "Don't ruin the surprise for me." Ho ho ho.

"Is that all you need to know?"

"Sure."

I feel like there's more I'm supposed to do, but I can't remember what. Why would anyone ever want me to be in charge of anything? I hang up.

I walk into the kitchen. Gabby is spooning potatoes into my mother's mouth.

"Look at me. It's like I'm a mommy and this is my baby."

"Grandma and Trinity are going to be living here."

"Yay!" She stands up and hugs Trinity's legs. "I'm so glad you're here. Our life's a mess."

"Gabby!" I say.

Trinity holds Gabby's face in her hands.

"It's true," Gabby says. Does she ever stop talking? The girl couldn't keep a secret if her life depended on it. "I visit Daddy at a 'partment at the beach. He's got this tiny beard now. Mommy hasn't gone to work in weeks and weeks. But we have lots of casseroles. But casseroles make Mommy sad. She says people give you casseroles when they feel sorry for you."

"Gabby!"

Trinity smiles, rubs my arm and stares into my eyes. Her coal-black pupils dart back and forth as she speaks.

"You Americans expect too much out of life for real happiness. When you come from the place I come from, where every meal is a gift, where people live in cardboard shacks on top of garbage, you don' want anything except for what is necessary. They say the American way is the best, but sometimes I not sure. So many people have everything but really nothing at all."

I stare at the floor, thinking about how to respond when Gabby exhales a world-weary sigh.

"I know what you mean," she says. "All I want is a Bratz doll, but Mommy won't let me have even one."

When I tuck Gabby in that night, I read her Cinderella for the thousandth time. She loves this story. Almost all the stories she loves have one thing in common: the mothers are dead. But that's true with nearly every fairy tale. Cinderella. Snow White. Hansel and Gretel. Beauty and the Beast. The Little Mermaid. Bambi. The Wizard of Oz. The moms are also dead in my favorite childhood books, Nancy Drew. And *Hannah Montana,* the Disney show Gabby's babysitter loves, features a dead mom who sometimes appears as a ghost. The list is endless.

"That's why we need Daddy back," Gabby says as I read a part close to the happily ever after.

"Why?"

"Because he's a boy and boys are always the rescuers."

There's so much to say about this. Fairy tales have been around as long as people could communicate. Mothers and grandmothers would tell their children stories about Cinderella or Snow White or Sleeping Beauty. But the stories were so much different than they are today. They were tales about virtues eventually overcoming adversities. The heroine was always clever, brave, strong, and good. In some early versions of the story, Cinderella performed feats of courage, much like Hercules, to test her mettle and smarts. And the fairy godmother was not just some bag singing "Bibbidi-Bobbidi-Boo," but the ghost of Cinderella's mom, protecting her from evil.

But when Charles Perrault wrote down what eventually became the most popular version of the tales, the female heroines were diluted into a one-dimensional character saved by a clever, brave, and handsome prince who whisked her away to happily ever after. I want to explain all this to Gabby, but I know she'll get that blank look on her face as her brain clicks off.

So instead I say, "Girls can be rescuers, too."

Gabby flashes a patronizing smile. "Mommy, no, they can't." She ticks off a list with her fingers. "The prince rescues Cinderella from the stepmother. The prince wakes up Sleeping Beauty with a kiss. The prince kisses Snow White alive. See, Daddy's our handsome prince. And once he comes back you can live happily ever after."

"Gabby, we don't need a handsome prince to make us happy."

"Yes, we do. Everybody needs a handsome prince."

It's hard to argue with a five-year-old who must always be right. I quickly scan my brain's fairy tale repository.

"Look at Rapunzel," I say. "She's the one who finds the blind prince and her tears make him see again. It sounds to me like she's the rescuer."

"Mommy, the only reason she got out of the tower was because of the prince. She'd still be up there, just like the lady up the street. Maybe if we rescue the lady up the street, I'll believe you."

Rescue the porn actresses? My daughter doesn't give up.

"We'll see about that," I say. Then I proceed with caution. "So . . . that lady stopped by Daddy's? Rose?"

Gabby grabs her teddy bear tighter and squirms in her bed. "I think tomorrow we should go up to that house and save that princess. She's very lonely and very, very sad. I hear her crying. Maybe her prince hasn't shown up yet and we can help her find him."

"Did you like her?"

"Mommy, I like every princess. You know that. My favorite is

Ariel. Then Belle. Then probably Cinderella. But what I don't understand, Mommy, is that if everything's supposed to change back at midnight, why doesn't the glass slipper?"

"I don't know. You're right. It doesn't make sense."

"My least favorite princess is probably Snow White because I don't understand why she eats that apple. Everyone tells her not to open the door for anybody. She's kind of stupid, if you ask me."

"Do you like that Rose woman?"

"She seems nice, I guess. Her teeth are so white." She squints at my mouth. "Your teeth are not so white. They're a little yellow."

"My teeth are yellow?"

"Well, compared to hers. But I think yellow is really pretty." She smiles at me as if trying to mask her pity. "I like yellow much more than white. Yellow is my favorite color, after pink. I think your teeth are beautiful."

"Thanks." I make a note to buy teeth whitener tomorrow.

"But I really, really like her dog. Do you think we could get a Chihuahua?"

"Let's think about it."

"I hate when you say that. It means no. Why do you say no to everything?"

She's right. I say I'll think about it when I really mean no all the time. It's my way to avoid a meltdown instead of being honest. But why can't we have a dog? I always thought we'd have another baby. I figured a baby and a dog would be too much. But now it doesn't look like that baby's coming anytime soon—despite what Faye says.

"Okay, okay, we'll get a dog. Just give me a little time. I promise."

9

Vanilla Ice Cream

Everybody is in bed, so I can finally exhale and convulse into tears. My husband is in love with someone else. My mother can no longer chew. And to top it off, my daughter thinks my teeth are yellow.

I fix myself a double vodka tonic and check my e-mails.

Dear Ally,

It was good to hear from you. Isn't the Internet great? Without it, we would have gone our entire lives without ever speaking again. And here we are—sort-of friends. I'm glad you'll be going to the reunion. I know Mike, Jack, and Riley will be there, but I don't know who else from the old gang is planning to show up. I've lost touch with a lot of people over the years.

Will you be taking Gabrielle? I'd love to meet her, but I think I'll be leaving the family behind. They've both got their final exams that week.

But I'll be sure to bore you with lots of pictures.

George

I read it a dozen times. He keeps it pretty neutral, but makes a point of mentioning he'll be going solo. Is he hoping I'll get the hint and leave Gabby at home? Or is he just casually mentioning it so I won't get the wrong idea? I'm clueless. Or maybe I'm just desperate. I need to feel that someone somewhere is thinking about me, because my husband barely knows I exist anymore.

When Alex dropped Gabby off, did he rush back to Rose? Right now, as I'm reading sex and romance into innocuous e-mails, is he having sex and romance? I guess Rose didn't fall for Colin Farrell in Toronto. Could the tabloids be right? Could she really be in love with my husband?

Is my husband in love with her? I want to believe he isn't. I want to believe it's some weird infatuation that's coming to an end. The spell's been broken and he wants his old life back. Being away from Gabby must be killing him. But do I want him back because he misses Gabby? No. He must be in love with me, too. I can't take him back for any other reason. I will not use Gabby as bait, no matter how tempting it might be.

I open wide and look at my teeth in the mirror. Gabby's right. They're yellow. Too much coffee and red wine, I suppose. When did that happen? I rummage through the bathroom cabinet and find a mouthpiece and a tube of whitener. Alex must have been bleaching his teeth for Rose months ago. I squeeze the tube and the gel squirts into the mouthpiece. Then I put it in my mouth.

I look ridiculous. I study my face. My forehead is wrinkled and my eyes look swollen. Maybe George will be shocked when he sees me.

I wonder if I should try Botox. I can't imagine injecting my face with botulism, but it seems a lot of people do it without any problems. Maybe I should try Restylane, Radiesse, Juvéderm. Perhaps I should treat myself to an endoscopic browlift. If my mother could speak, she'd tell me I'm being self-absorbed. The only time my mother even had a manicure was when I forced her to go with me the day before my wedding.

I give myself a facial. I smear green clay that's supposed to rid my face of old, dry skin and make me look younger and refreshed. I know it's bullshit, but I'll pretend to believe. Just like we must convince ourselves that we may be older, but we're smarter and better and happier.

As the mask hardens on my face, I head to the liquor cabinet and fix myself another vodka tonic. I take a few gulps, while thinking of my response to George. I know if I write to him now, I'll most likely regret it in the morning. My logical side says to put if off, but the booze-influenced side has rendered me warm and mushy. Why not tell him how much I wish I'd never let him get away? Why not ask him if he still has feelings for me?

I turn around to head to the computer when I nearly collide with Trinity.

"Wha—?" I say, my mouthpiece flying out to the floor. Trinity goes to pick it up.

"That's okay," I say as I bend down to pick it up.

"Are you okay, missus?" she says, eyeing me funny. I forgot I have a green mask on my face.

"Sure. I was just . . . well, just . . . well . . . Can I get you anything, Trinity?"

"I was going to ask you for ice cream. Every night, I put your mommy's water pills and heart medicine in vanilla ice cream for him to swallow. He love the vanilla ice cream."

"I know," I say, smiling. "My mother ate a scoop of vanilla ice cream every night when I was a kid. She was so addicted to it that she'd give it up for Lent."

I find a carton of ice cream buried in the back of the freezer. There's about a mouthful of crystallized vanilla left. It probably hasn't been touched since Alex started dieting and going to the gym—around the time Rose became a client. I hand it to Trinity. "That's all I have. Tomorrow I'll buy more."

Maybe there is some joy left. Mom remembers ice cream. She still savors the sugar, the cream, the vanilla bean, just like when I was a child. She'll roll it around in her mouth until it melts. Then she'll smile as she swallows it.

"Good night, missus."

"Good night," I say.

The liquor buzz is gone. I decide to head to bed and compose that e-mail tomorrow.

10

Wicked Stepmothers

Suzannah Oakly won't get off the phone. She lives down the street at 4819 Sisley Court right at the intersection of Monet. I don't get the impressionist artist theme that runs through the neighborhood. There's no reason for it. This area doesn't resemble the French countryside. There are no cobblestone roads or cute cottages or fields of poppies. People don't ride around on rusted old bikes with baguettes under their arms. Instead, it resembles the San Fernando Valley suburb that it is. Faux Spanish-style stucco tract houses with bright orange tiled roofs next to monolithic Persian palaces next to nondescript rambling ranch houses. There are Hummers, SUVs, and minivans parked in the driveways and on the curbs.

Anyway, Suzannah's explaining in detail her plans for a Shrek Christmas.

"I hired a company to design a Santa Claus Shrek. He says ho ho ho and then makes a farting sound. Of course that's Dennis, my son's, idea. Fiona will be Mrs. Claus. My children are so excited. Puss in Boots and Donkey will both be reindeer. I'm working on some other design elements. For instance, we're creating a North

Pole that will incorporate swamp-like themes. The elves, who'll be mini ogres, will make mud canes instead of candy canes. It's going to be very unique and special."

"Yes," I say.

"Last year we spent months planning a SpongeBob Christmas. Did you happen to see it?"

"No. I just moved in a few months ago."

"That's too bad. I feel it would really be helpful if you were better acquainted with North Pole Way. Perhaps I could come over with the DVD of all of last year's decorations? Anyway, we turned our lawn into the bottom of the sea. And you know what happened? The Mullens, just a few doors down from us, did the same thing. They copy everything we do. Everything! Did you see their cars—a yellow Hummer and a black Range Rover, just like us. The kids were devastated. That's why I'm really pleased you've volunteered to do this for us. Promise me this won't happen again, Alice."

"Don't worry," I say, wondering if everyone around here is this insane. I jot down Shrek next to Oakly on the yellow legal pad I've been using for this assignment. I'm surprisingly organized about this. After all, you can't have your neighbors hating you.

"If you want to come over to take a look at the diagrams, I'd love to show them to you. Then I can give you the DVD," she says.

"That sounds great, Suzannah."

"Well, I'm just looking at my calendar—"

"Mommmy! *Mommy*! The poo-poo's coming."

"I'll call you back," I say.

Gabby races into the house, discarding clothes. She heads towards the bathroom. Celia, her sometimes babysitter, follows behind shaking her head. When she's not babysitting, Celia, a struggling actress, goes on auditions or dresses as princesses for kiddie parties. That's how I met her. She was Ariel at a party Gabby attended before we moved. Gabby spent the whole party following her around and staring at her, so I asked her to come over and babysit when we needed a night out or when Gabby had a day off from preschool. At first Gabby was tremendously disappointed when Celia showed up without a costume and without her butt-length red wig.

"I wanted Ariel! She's not Ariel! She's *just a girl* and she doesn't have fins or beautiful red hair!"

Eventually Celia's personality won her over. Now Gabby adores her. Once a week after school she babysits. They usually go to a park. Celia likes hanging out at parks where celebrity kids go. Sometimes she'll drive Gabby twelve miles to Studio City where the celebrity quotient is higher than around here. She and Gabby work as a team. Celia will spot the celebrity kid or someone she imagines is a celebrity kid. Then she'll have Gabby go over to play with him or her. So far, according to Celia, Gabby's played with the children of Tom and Katie, Reese Witherspoon, and Denise Richards. Celia doesn't know for sure if the kids are celebrity kids, but she convinces herself she sees a resemblance to some star. Then she befriends the nannies in hopes they'll introduce her to their famous employers and she'll be discovered.

"How many days has it been?" Celia asks.

I think about it. "Five. Give or take a day."

"She was at the park squirming the whole time. I could tell she had to go because she wouldn't run or anything. She just sat on a spring horse. Her body looked like one big question mark with that tiny stomach bulging out. But, of course, she kept saying she was fine, to leave her alone. And then the minute we're halfway home, she starts screaming. She wanted me to carry her."

I sigh. "She's five years old and she's been doing this for nearly two years. She's going to hurt herself."

"Maybe he holds it in because he's afraid of losing more."

It's Trinity, standing by the doorway with a bag of Depends in her hands.

"Who?" Celia says, confused by Trinity's pronouns.

"Gabrielle," Trinity says. "He has lost the family life he has known so he is holding onto the poo-poo. It's comforting to him."

I know she means well, but Trinity has a knack for making me feel like, well, shit.

"She's been doing this for years. Before there were any problems," I say, gritting my teeth.

"Children are very sensitive. Maybe he felt the problems before you did. Gabby is a very smart little girl. Maybe he has radon for it."

So even Gabby's anal retentive disorder is my fault.

Gabby cries and moans. "Ow! Ow! *Ow!*"

I go to the bathroom. Gabby is crouched over by the toilet. Her Cinderella dress lies in a pile.

"Get out, get out," Gabby screams.

"Baby, it's okay."

"Get out and *close the door*."

I do as she says and stand outside the door. My poor baby.

"May I?" Trinity volunteers.

"Sure."

Trinity heads into the bathroom. "Shh, little one," she whispers.

I stand outside the door listening to Gabby's little grunts. Trinity quietly sings a lullaby.

A few minutes later, Trinity comes out. "Everything fine," she says. "Everything fine."

I head to the bathroom. Gabby has flushed the toilet, but it's clogged. I grab the plunger and get to work.

"You have got to stop doing this."

"It hurt."

"That's because you hold it in for so long. Why do you do that?"

"It's yucky."

"Everyone makes poo-poo. Even princesses. That's why they're so beautiful."

"No, they don't. I've never read a fairy tale about a princess making poo-poo." She looks hard at me.

"What is it?"

"Is that girl a princess?"

"What girl?"

"The girl with the Chihuahua."

"No."

"Her hair is so shiny, just like Rapunzel's."

"Not really."

"And her teeth are really white and sparkling, like a princess's," she says, studying me.

"You think so?" I say, frowning.

Gabby gives me a fake Hollywood smile. "Yellow's still my favorite color for teeth."

I think about all the hours spent with whitening trays and strips the last few weeks. I open my mouth wide. "My teeth aren't yellow anymore. Are they?"

She squints at them. "Well, sort of yellowish. Maybe like yellow-white." She smiles at me as if this is some kind of compliment. "Your teeth remind me of buttercups."

"Thanks."

"So, is Daddy going to marry her?"

I gulp. "What?"

"Is Daddy going to marry that girl?"

I don't know what to say because I have no idea. My heart pounds. Gabby stares at me. "I don't know."

I shut my eyes tight for a second, bracing myself for Gabby's tears. When I open them, she's got a smile on her face. She nods to herself.

"What is it?"

"Well, if Daddy marries Rose, does that mean I'll become a princess?"

My four-foot Benedict Arnold.

"No," I snap. "That means she'll be a stepmother. You know, they're nice now, but once they marry daddies, they become wicked."

Gabby's eyes widen in horror.

I am a horrible person.

11

The Rescue

Gabby is outside playing princess. I watch her through the window. She chats incessantly to herself as she twirls around the lawn. She's at a ball, I imagine. A prince is falling in love with her. She dances and leaps and spins. She is so happy and innocent at this moment. I wish I could bottle it and keep it forever.

Yesterday, when she cartwheeled across the lawn, a bunch of stones fell out of her pocket.

"Gabby, why do you have rocks in your pocket?"

"Leave me alone," she said as she started collecting them and shoving them into her pocket.

"Gabby, they're too heavy. Besides, when you cartwheel, one could smack you in the head and that would really hurt."

"I don't care. Leave me alone. *Leave me alone!*" She screamed and screamed until she started bawling. Then she threw herself on the ground, clawed at the grass while her legs kicked and kicked.

"Calm down, honey, calm down."

"Go away!"

"Gabby, honey, I just don't want you to hurt yourself."

I rubbed her back as she lay on the grass, her little body convulsing with sobs. Finally, she calmed down and raised her tear-stained face.

"I don't want him to send me to the woods."

"What? Who?"

"Daddy."

"What are you talking about?"

"If Daddy marries Rose and she becomes my stepmother, she might have Daddy send me to the woods just like Hansel and Gretel. I want to be able to find my way home."

I hugged her tight. "Sweetie, no one would ever send you to the woods. Daddy loves you so much. He'd never hurt you."

"It doesn't matter. They all love their children, but they do it anyway."

"Those are fairy tales. It's not real."

"Yes, it is. You even told me."

"Mommy was being silly. I'm sorry. Trust me. Mommy would never let anything bad happen to you. Neither would Daddy."

She looked hard at me, like she wanted to ask me something very important. I prepared myself for what I imagined would be a heart-to-heart. Then she looked past me at a painted lady flittering through the cosmos. She grabbed her yellow butterfly net and began chasing it. She raced across the lawn. Her butterfly net swooped up and down while the butterfly darted around her. It seemed to be taunting her, as if aware of her intentions.

I turn on my computer to check e-mails. There's an e-mail from George.

Dear Ally,

What's new? Haven't heard from you in a while and thought I'd check in. The kids and wife went away for a few days to visit the in-laws in Florida. I have the house to myself for the first time in what seems like forever and I have no idea what to do with myself. I thought it would be easy. I spent years living by myself, but I seem to have forgotten how to function without lots of noise. So, I thought I'd see how you were doing . . .

Gabby comes in for a snack. I quickly shut my computer and head to the kitchen. As I'm spreading some peanut butter on apples, the phone rings. Lately, the only people who call are neighbors announcing their holiday plans. This time, it's my boss. He tries to be friendly with about ten seconds of small talk, but I can hear his aggravation.

"So, Alice, when will we be blessed with your presence?"

I wish I'd screened. I usually screen precisely because of calls like this. I like to be prepared. Now I'm on the spot.

"Well, would it be possible to have a few more weeks off? Without pay, of course."

There is a pause and a sigh.

"Quite frankly, I'm surprised we haven't heard from you, Alice. I thought you'd be checking in with some of your accounts, but you haven't. I know you're going through a lot, but well, to be quite frank, I feel you've really dropped the ball. You don't seem to be committed. Your clients are concerned. They don't like being passed along."

"Claire and Judy are great. They know all my accounts very well."

"It's not the same thing, Alice, and you know it."

"Just a few more weeks, okay?"

"How about a week from Monday?"

I gulp. A week from Monday? At the very least, I wanted until after the holidays.

"Can I get back to you later? I just need to check on a few things."

"Later, when?" I can practically hear him gritting his teeth.

"By the end of the week?"

He sighs. "How about end of day tomorrow?"

While publicity is not my true calling, I am damned good at it. I have a knack for getting my clients press, even when it appears utterly futile to everyone else—my boss, my colleagues, even my client. I'll dig and dig until I discover some angle, some spin, and voilà—press. For years and years, I was addicted to this challenge. I'd work day and night searching for the story behind the person, the product, the event, the restaurant or store. When I was pregnant with Gabby, my clients begged me to come back. I promised them I would. I even cut my maternity leave from four to three months. I felt invaluable.

When I hang up the phone, Gabby's in my face.

"I know who that was and I don't want you to ever go back to that place. I want you here with me."

"Gabby, you're in school most of the day."

"I'll never ever see you."

"Of course you'll see me. You get out of school at three. I'll be home about two hours later."

"It's not just two hours. It's hours and hours and hours and hours."

"Gabby, I'll be home in time to make dinner."

Gabby snorts.

"What does that mean?"

"You say that now, but then you'll work later and later and later. You did that all the time at that horrible, stupid, ugly place. I hate it."

"It won't happen. I promise."

Gabby rolls her eyes.

"Gabby, please. This time it will be different."

I know that sounds idiotic. Such an empty promise. The phone rings again. I'm certain it's going to be Judy, who has probably over-heard the entire conversation with my boss. She's been calling me every day. I pick it up quickly before Gabby hears who it is on the answering machine.

"Is this Mrs. Hirsh?"

I don't recognize this voice. I assume it's going to be someone about to tell me what kind of cartoon character will be adorning their home for the holidays.

"I'm sorry to bother you. My name is Elise Manning. I just wanted you to know that you're not alone."

"What? Who are you?"

"My husband left me for Rose Maris. And there are a bunch of women just like us. I wanted you to know that we're here for you. We meet for drinks sometimes. And we all have the same story, basically. The gestures of friendship . . . Did she send gifts home with your husband? Did you go out to lunch with her?"

"No, dinner," I say, suddenly feeling dizzy.

"She probably told you how sorry she was to be taking so much of your husband's time. She's *sooooo* thoughtful, isn't she? Did she sit next to you and talk your ear off and make you feel like you were becoming best friends?"

I'm silent.

Elise hiccups out an angry laugh. "She's a head case. My husband was the architect for one of her homes. He left me two years ago for her, but he came back. They always come back. We're still working through a lot of things. I don't know if it will ever be one hundred percent right for us. Rose Maris messed me up for life. But I'm not alone. Neither are you."

"Well, I guess that's good to know." I don't want to be on the phone with this nut case, especially with Gabby nearby. How did she get my number anyway? We're unlisted.

"Mark my words, she'll leave him. She always does. This is all a big game for her. She's bored with her life so she steals other people's lives."

"Uh-huh." I don't know what to say to her. I don't know why she's calling. I look out the front window. Gabby is outside, chasing butterflies.

"There's a group of us. And we're not a bunch of losers crying over the past. We're all well-educated, attractive women with careers and families. I just wanted you to know that we're here for you. If you give me your e-mail, I'll give you more information on the group."

I give Elise my e-mail address, but I have no intention of being part of a Rose Hater's Group. Sure, I hate Rose. But I feel like she'd absolutely love the idea of a bunch of jilted, angry women getting together to obsess over her.

I check up on Gabby as soon as I hang up. I open the front door, expecting to see her galloping around chasing butterflies, but her net is on the lawn and there's no sign of her.

"Gabby? Gabby?"

I run to the guest house. Trinity is combing Mom's hair.

"Have you seen Gabby?"

"No. He not here. He came in here before and said he was look-ing for the princess in the tower. I said that was very nice. He has such an imagination."

I head back outside and survey the lawn.

"*Gabby!*"

The front gate's ajar and a magic wand is tossed on the grass next to it. Rage and fear race through me. Gabby knows she's never sup-posed to leave the property. I run toward the road.

"*Gabby!*"

"*Ohhhhhhhh! Ohhhhhh! Ohhhhh!*"

I suddenly know exactly where my daughter is.

I run into the house for my car keys. As I empty out my hand-bags, I try to figure out how long this Rose Hater had chewed my ear off. Rose had monopolized my life again, and in the meantime, my daughter was out exploring the world of porn. I head to the bed-room and scan my dresser for my car keys.

I think of all the minutes of my life that I've lost searching for keys. I've probably wasted years because my head's such a disorga-nized mess. Alex never lost his keys. He had a place for everything.

"Why don't you always put them in the same place when you come in the house and you'll never have to think about it," he'd say. Of course it made sense, but I never did it anyway. My keys would follow me into the bathroom, into the kitchen, into the living room. They'd turn up in the pantry, on top of the washing machine, on the toilet, in the cupboards. Sometimes I'd wonder if they were possessed by some demon that would play hide and seek with me until I lose my mind. Come to think of it, maybe this is the beginning stages of Alzheimer's.

Ah hah! The keys. Right next to the blow dryer in the bathroom. I pick them up as the doorbell rings.

Gabby stands in front of me, beaming. She's holding hands with a buff woman in her late thirties with long flowing corn-husk blond hair and big boobs. She's wearing tight, dark blue True Religions and a tight Ed Hardy T-shirt with a peace sign dangling over a cross. Mascara runs down her face and her eyes are bloodshot.

I am so furious I can't even speak. I stand there with my mouth hanging open as I think of ways to punish Gabby. No television ever. No ice cream. No candy. I'll burn every one of her princess dresses. I'll throw away her magic wands and butterfly nets. I'll never take her to Disneyland.

"Mommy, see I told you, fairy tales are real. This is Rapunzel."

Rapunzel nods and smiles sheepishly. Gabby turns towards Rapunzel. "My mommy thinks fairy tales are stupid, but I knew one day I'd rescue you. I told her."

I take a deep breath and exhale. My heart skitters. I open my mouth and my voice comes out like a restrained growl.

"Gabby, how many times have I told you not to leave the yard? How many times? You never listen, though. Do you have any idea how worried I was?"

Gabby still smiles. Nothing fazes this girl. She turns to Rapunzel. "See, I told you my mom would say that."

Rapunzel smiles nervously at me. Her eyes are bloodshot. I wonder if she's on some kind of drug. I also wonder if she's the one I
heard moaning a few minutes ago.

"I'm sorry about all this," she says.

"Okay," I huff out. I turn to Gabby. "Go to your room. *Now.*"

Gabby is shocked. She was expecting parades and fanfare. Her
mouth hangs open. "But . . . but . . ." She turns from me to Rapunzel,
and back again. She glares at me. "No. I will not go to my room."

"Gabby!"

"You never understand anything. She's a princess who needed to
be rescued. I rescued her. You're the one who said that boys don't always need to be the rescuers, so I did it. I rescued someone and now
you're being so mean. You are the meanest mommy in the world."

Do you ever look at yourself and wonder how you got there? I'm
being screamed at by a five-year-old while a porn star looks on. Next
to me are neighbors obsessed with Shrek and SpongeBob and
Rugrats. I've got a porn house above me and cartoon-obsessed
people on all sides of me.

We make a good impression.

Mr. Rogers never imagined a neighborhood like this. I never
imagined a neighborhood like this. I don't even know who I am.

"Well, I better go now," Rapunzel says. "Nice to meet you, Gabby."

Gabby turns to me; her face is red.

"You can't let her go. She was all the way at the top of the hill and
the evil king was screaming at her, so I helped her escape. I know
you never believe me, but it's true." She looks at Rapunzel. "You
have to stay with us until the handsome prince finds you."

The porn actress smiles. "Well, you're a very smart little girl,
Gabby. I hope you always believe fairy tales." She smiles sadly at me.
"You have a wonderful, beautiful girl. I'm sorry she scared you like
that."

"You have no idea," I snarl. I just want this to end. I want this woman out of here and back up the hill snorting her coke and having her gang bangs and moaning at the top of her lungs. I want to get out of here forever. The minute she leaves, I'll put this house on the market. With any luck I'll be out of here before the holidays so I will not have to put up one ornament.

"Yes, I do have an idea," she says softly, her eyes locked with mine. "I have a boy who's five, too."

Gabby's in her room. And I'm sipping tea with Ruth. A regular Swiss Mocha moment with the former porn star, better known as Jill Chris Monroe.

When I tell her that name sounds vaguely familiar, she smiles and says, "Charlie's Angels."

I give her a strange look.

"Farrah Fawcett was Jill Monroe, and Cheryl Ladd, who replaced her, was Chris Monroe. As a kid, they were my favorites. I wanted to be them when I grew up." She forces out a smile. "I guess dreams can come true."

Ruth is no longer in the business. She gave it up when she got pregnant with Connor, her five-year-old son. She has nothing to do with her son's dad, but she's married to a doctor who's helping in her quest to erase her past. That's why she was at the top of the hill this morning. She's single-handedly trying to buy all the tapes and DVDs of every movie she's ever made. She put ads in trades and offers rewards for anyone who sends the tapes to her P.O. box.

"I don't want Connor to ever know about my past. But I don't know if it's possible, not with that man," she says, nodding to the house above me. "I went up there to get the master copies of movies. He had promised me. But today he just laughed. He's making too much money off of it."

She sips her tea and looks out the window. "I know you think you have problems," she says to me. "And I'm not saying you don't, but at least you don't have my past. When I became a porn actress I wasn't thinking about children. I wasn't thinking about anything, actually." She lets out a bitter laugh, indicating to me that it's a long, sad story, but she doesn't want to go there. "So now, every time I see one of my movies, I buy it or steal it and then I burn it. Whatever it takes to rid the world of my oeuvre."

I didn't expect a porn actress to use the word oeuvre.

"Gabby is a real sweetie. She saw me yelling at Bob the slob, and came over to help. She grabbed my hand and the next thing I knew, I was running down the hill with her. I couldn't help myself. I wanted to be a part of her little adventure. In a way, she really did save me."

The doorbell rings. It's Nancy. I invite her in, wondering what a woman who wears a Winnie the Pooh sweatshirt would think if she ever discovered the woman at my table is a former porn star. But I doubt she's ever seen a porn flick in her life.

"Oh my God, you're Jill Chris Monroe, aren't you?" she says, putting out her hand. "I'm Nancy."

I look shocked. Nancy laughs. "Ally, I've been married for ten years. We've got to find some way to keep it exciting."

"Well, if you wouldn't mind throwing them all away, I'd really appreciate it. I'm trying to rid the world of movies like *Head in the Class* and *Three's Humpin' Me*."

Nancy promises to discard all her copies of Ruth's movies. Then she invites Ruth, who has no mommy friends, to our next playdate. She informs me that I'll be hosting it.

"It'll be good for you. There's nothing like a playdate at your home to make you forget about all your problems."

I guess I give her a confused look.

Nancy laughs. "You'll see."

The next day when I go to school to pick up Gabby and have another chat with Myrna, Alex is waiting out front.

"Alex?"

"Didn't you get my e-mail?"

"E-mail?"

"I figured that was the best way to get in touch with you since you check it a million times a day," Alex says, as if this is something that's annoyed him for years. "I know you've been screening calls."

Yesterday I forgot to check my e-mails.

"I'm meeting with Myrna. She sent a note to me about Gabby's language."

I had received the same note, but I had no idea that bitch had sent one to Alex, too.

Dear Mrs. Hirsh,

It has *again* been brought to my attention that your daughter, Gabrielle, has been using inappropriate language in the classroom and on the schoolyard. Please meet with me at 2 P.M. tomorrow to discuss this very serious matter. I hope we can work together to resolve this problem before we must take it to the next level. I have fielded several complaints from anxious parents. As our handbook outlines, we are a zero tolerance school.

Thank you in advance for your prompt attention to this most delicate matter.

Last night I asked Gabby what had happened.

"Didn't I talk to you about not using those bad words?"

"Mommy, I couldn't help it. When Cindy told Joey I had a crush on him it made me so angry. I wanted to kick her and punch her, but I stopped myself. I thought you'd be proud of me. You always say I should use my words."

"Not those words. What did you say anyway?"

"I called her a mudderfutter."

"Aha. Is that it?"

"And a codshucker."

The school bell shrieks. Gabby runs out of the classroom. She sees both of us and beams.

"Daddy! Daddy!" Gabby leaps into his arms.

"Daddydaddydaddydaddy." She slathers him with kisses.

Alex hoists Gabby in the air and she's got her legs wrapped around him. My insides are exploding. And I imagine this is how malignant tumors begin. You reign in your anger and the imploding fury forms cancer cells. Why didn't Myrna address the letter to both of us, so I'd have some advance warning? How can Alex stand here as if nothing is wrong? And why doesn't Gabby love me as much as she does Alex? I know she's only a child, but I can't help feeling so very hurt.

Alex jiggles Gabby in his arms and kisses her neck. "I hope you didn't say anything too horrible," he says to her.

She laughs and rubs her nose against his. "Daddy, I love you."

"I love you too, Gabbybabbysabby."

Myrna calls us in to her cramped office. She asks Gabby to wait outside. Her face is expressionless and I wonder if Gabby's about to be expelled.

"Good afternoon, Mr. and Mrs. Hirsh." She gives us a tight little smile. "Thank you *both* for coming here today." She pauses for a moment as if waiting for one of us to say something. "Even in times of crisis, it's imperative to your child that you form a united front. I commend you both."

Again, the tight smile and a pause. Her eyes skitter from me to Alex and back, as if waiting for one of us to confess something. Anything.

I return the little smile and nod. I refuse to look at Alex.

Myrna sighs and stares at some notes on her desk. She clears her throat.

"As Mrs. Hirsh is well aware, there have been some complaints from parents regarding their children's language. Our staff did some investigating and it led to your daughter." She stares at me. Another tight smile.

"I know Mrs. Hirsh attempted to remedy the situation, but it seems your efforts at this point have been unsuccessful. I thought we could brainstorm and come up with a solution before more serious measures must be taken."

Alex nearly jumps out of his seat. "Serious measures? What the hel—heck is Gabby saying? From the way you're speaking you'd think she was saying really horrible things. My daughter would never—"

"Mr. Hirsh, we consider Gabby's language to be highly inappropriate."

Alex's ears turn bright red. His eyes pop out of their sockets. "With all due respect, I think you're blowing this out of proportion. I'm sure it's my fault. I occasionally use damn and ass. You know how it is on the freeway, when you're stuck in traffic."

He gives one of those chuckles that he's hoping is contagious. But Myrna clears her throat and pinches her mouth. "Gabrielle's words are far worse than those, Mr. Hirsh. But even so, as I outline in the student handbook, we are a zero tolerance school."

She clears her throat again. "As Mrs. Hirsh is aware, your daughter has been using some horrible profanities. I hate saying them aloud myself, so please excuse me."

She bites her lower lip as if this is too much to bear, but I know she enjoys spitting them out. I swear I see a flush of excitement flash on her face. She stretches her neck out towards us and lowers her voice. "She's been saying mother F-er and well, C-S-er."

Alex's eye bulge. "*What?*" He looks from Myrna to me and back again. "This is a misunderstanding. We don't use those words." He turns towards me as if waiting for an explanation. "Ally?"

I shake my head and smile. *No big deal.* "She's not really saying it like that. She's saying mutterfudder and codshucker."

Myrna burps out a tiny laugh. "Mrs. Hirsh, the parents here aren't making that kind of distinction. They send their children here to learn and grow as human beings, not to come home with filthy mouths."

"I don't understand this at all," Alex says.

"Well, Mrs. Hirsh mentioned her mother has been using these words and—"

Alex guffaws. "Your mother? Your *mother*?" Still laughing, he turns towards Myrna. "Her mother wouldn't even know what those words meant."

"Maybe this is something you two need to discuss as co-parents. All I know is what I've been told. I was hoping we could come up with a solution. I think the first thing you must determine is why is Gabby using inappropriate language. Ask her, 'Why did you say that?' Is she seeking attention? Expressing anger? You must determine if she's having problems with language or emotions. Perhaps I could recommend a child psychologist."

Alex stands up. "Thank you for your time, Mrs. Schafly. I can assure you that Gabby is fine—emotionally and linguistically. This was just a fluke. I will talk to her. This won't be happening again."

Myrna is perturbed. From the looks of the pile of papers on her desk, she had a whole lecture planned.

"I hope you can work this out for Gabby's sake. She is an extraordinary child."

I stand up. She extends her hand and I shake it. It's so weak it's like holding a leaf. I can tell she doesn't buy any of this. She doesn't believe Alex can get Gabby to stop cursing. She also doesn't believe Gabby picked this up from my mother. In her mind, Alex and I run around, throwing things at each other while screaming cocksucker and motherfucker.

"I hope this is the last we'll see of each other—on this matter," she says.

We head out the door. Gabby's no longer in the lobby. I spot her outside on the swings. A teacher's aide is pushing her. I wave at her and head outside. Alex follows.

"So where did she really pick up these words," Alex says, his voice a contained fury. "Is this what you and your friends have been calling me?"

Anger pulsates through my body. To disguise it, I give a fake laugh. "Don't flatter yourself, Alex. It's the truth. I read it's not completely uncommon for Alzheimer's patients."

"Maybe you should limit Gabby's exposure to your mother."

"Exposure?" I turn towards him and speak in a flat, even tone as if I'm not on the cusp of losing it. "You're talking about my mother as if she's nuclear fallout or some kind of virus. Exposure?"

Alex coughs. "Maybe she shouldn't be living at your house. I have some contacts who could put you in touch with a good nursing home. I don't think this is healthy for Gabby."

I don't think this is healthy for Gabby? A bomb has been detonated inside me.

"Alex, please don't tell me what's healthy for Gabby." My voice is louder than I want it to be. "After all you put her through. This is *my* mother. She's not going to be hidden away just because she has Alzheimer's."

Alex closes his eyes and breathes deep. "Alice, I'm sorry. I didn't mean it the way it sounded. Alzheimer's is a horrible disease. Your mom needs professional care at a place that can handle people like her. That's all I mean. It's too much for you or Gabby."

"Well, we're doing just fine," I growl. "You left *us*, so stop telling *us* what's best for *us*."

Xander. They say every seven years people change. Every cell in their body is different. Their metabolism is different. Why can't their brains be different, too?

I stare at him and hate him so much right now. Then something distracts me. A tiny cough.

I turn toward the swings. Gabby stares at me, tears running down her face. The teacher's aide has her arms tightly wrapped around Gabby as she shoots us a pleading look that says, *"For the sake of your child, stop acting like monsters."*

"Oh, Gabby," I whisper.

I head towards her. I want to wrap my arms around her and tell her I'm sorry. But she runs past me and jumps into Alex's outstretched arms.

That night, I dream about Alex. He has a brain tumor and that's why he's been acting horribly, he tells me. He says he is going to die. I am happy. "Oh, at least that explains everything," I say.

In my dream I suddenly remember I was supposed to call my boss at the end of the day. This jolts me awake. I look at my clock. 11:55.

Alex is not going to die. He just doesn't love me. I feel sick.

I think about my Gabby. I can't abandon her now.

I leave a message for my boss. I make a joke about it literally being the end of the day. Then I ask for just a little more time. A few more weeks. I'm not sure if he'll agree or fire me. And I don't really care.

12

Home Invasion

my shows up at the house a half hour before the playdate is supposed to begin.

"I hope this isn't an inconvenience, but would it be okay if I dropped Amanda off and left?" She clutches her head and squeezes her eyes shut. "I have a killer headache. All I want to do is go home and go to sleep."

"Sure," I say. I wonder if this woman has had a CAT scan or an MRI. Renee's convinced Amy's dying of a brain tumor. Nancy thinks it's some weird food allergies.

I can't believe a bunch of kids and their moms are on their way over any minute. I am not in the mood for this. I have not been in the mood for anything lately. Gabby's beyond excited, though. We haven't entertained in ages. I haven't been much fun for Gabby at all.

The last few weeks, a fierce depression has taken up residence. I can't shake it. During the day, I'm exhausted, slogging around, having difficulty doing the slightest chore. Even something as simple as making the bed has become overwhelming.

Thank God Trinity's here. She's taken over and become a mother for a thirty-eight-year-old child. She makes beds and cleans. She miraculously removes stains from Gabby's princess dress. She gives my boss excuses for me when he calls to see when I'm coming back to work. For me, the question is no longer when I'm coming back to work, but will I? I can't imagine being back there. But then again, I can't imagine being anywhere except curled up in my bed.

Here I am, though, about to host a playdate. I look at Amy. I should feel grateful, I suppose. At least I don't have a tumor buried inside my brain.

"Gabby's in her room playing," I tell Amanda. "Why don't you tell her to take you outside and play."

I have put everything outside—food, drinks, toys. The thought of a bunch of kids trampling around the house makes me nervous. I know so many moms think nothing of it. They surrender their home to the kids and their friends, barely wincing when they hear a crash or shattering of glass. They'll blow bubbles, feed the kids spaghetti, let them rampage through the house with squirt guns. They must be on Zoloft. Other than Gabby, I can barely tolerate children.

"Gabby," I yell, again in my weird sing-songy voice. "Go outside with Amanda."

"Is Nancy coming over," Amy asks.

"She better," I say. "This whole thing was her idea."

"Well, could you ask her to take Amanda home for me? Tell her to call my cell about a half hour before she leaves. I don't like Mandy to see me lying in bed in the middle of the day. I'll try to make myself all perky for her."

"Sure thing. I'll tell her."

She winces and clutches her head. She takes a deep breath.

"Poor Nancy. She's pretty stressed lately. The bar she and her husband run isn't doing very well. They might have to close it. Thank God my Glenn has a stable job. Accounting might not be glamorous, but it pays the bills. Plus, Glenn's so motivated and so devoted to his family."

"That's great," I say, although I don't know why she's flaunting her great husband to me. It's like she's thinking out loud or convincing herself of something.

She presses her index fingers to her temples. Then she grabs onto the sides of the door to steady herself. "Well, I guess I'll go."

"Amy, are you sure you're okay to drive?"

"Yeah, I'll manage."

But the thing is, the moment she steadied herself in the doorway was the moment she lost me. I don't believe her. She overacted. There are no tumors or allergies or headaches. This is about something else. But what?

What the hell is wrong with you, Alice? You are too cynical for words. The poor woman has a splitting headache and you're doubting her? How guilty will you feel when she dies of a brain tumor?

I don't know. Something doesn't feel right. But what could be the reason a person would fake a migraine? Could she hate playdates that much? Then again, people do get desperate when they don't want to do something—especially when it involves lots of children. A few months ago, a nanny in Encino told police that a man was roaming the local playground attempting to buy babies. She sent Encino moms into panic mode. Turns out, she concocted the story because she hated going to the playground.

I walk Amy to her white Range Rover.

"Feel better," I say.

She nods her head, grimaces, and turns the ignition. As she drives away, I read the frame around her license plate: "Love my life as mommy and wife!"

In a half hour the place is teeming with kids, most of them holed up in Gabby's room, trying on dresses and playing with Barbies. It's another beautiful Los Angeles day, but, as usual, most residents don't seem to notice the weather. If you're from a place like New York, you treat each sunny day as a gift. As much as I've tried, everyone's migrated inside. Nancy's in the kitchen, whipping up a batch of Mojitos.

When Ruth walked in a few minutes ago, the women stopped what they were doing and stared. I guess I'm the only Valley resident who wasn't familiar with Ruth's oeuvre.

Now Ruth holds court with a bunch of moms in the kitchen. They keep asking for sex tips. I cringe. Ruth came here today to escape her past and just be a mom. That's what Nancy and I promised when we invited her.

But Ruth just laughs. "I think the best sex is a mental thing anyway."

I leave the kitchen for a few minutes to survey the damage so far and throw away juice boxes, half-eaten cookies, and Goldfish crumbs.

When I return, a bunch of women are listening intently to Ruth as she discusses something.

Nancy plops down next to Ruth. She sips a Mojito. I inhale the mint and the rum.

"I'll take any advice I can get. My husband is totally going through a midlife crisis," Nancy says. "If I didn't know any better, I'd swear he was having an affair. He doesn't seem interested in me at all."

"Well then, make yourself interesting," Ruth says. "Spruce it up. Buy a costume. Buy a sex toy. Learn to pole dance. Surprise the hell out of him. I promise he'll be interested. They're all interested. You just have to be different."

Ruth has been married to Connor's pediatrician for three years. They met a few hours after Connor was born. She thought he was cute in a nerdy way, but definitely wasn't thinking romance. "Who thinks about that stuff after you give birth? It's the last thing on your mind. He was the perfect catch. A Jewish doctor. He was in his late forties and, best of all, never married. No baggage.

"For the first year of Connor's life, I didn't know what I was doing. I had never imagined being a mother. As you probably guessed, my mom wasn't much of a role model. Even as a little girl, I never, ever played with dolls. And I had no friends with babies to call for advice. So I called Melvin up all the time about every little thing. I figured he thought I was crazy, but I was so petrified I'd do something wrong to this little baby."

She wipes away tears. "I love Connor more than anything in the world, but I felt I didn't deserve him. Every day, I lived in fear that God would realize his mistake, punish me for my life, and take Connor away from me. In my mind, every cough was tuberculosis. Every fever was going to reach one hundred ten degrees. Every bad night of sleep was a sign of some evil invading his tiny body. I could barely function."

Ruth blows her nose and Nancy puts her arm around her. "I wish we'd known you then, Ruth. I would have told you that we all feel the same way to some extent. Babies are a miracle and no one feels worthy. No one."

"Maybe it's a good thing that I didn't know any of you, because that's how I got to know Melvin. He was always there for me. I didn't think anything of it. I just assumed doctors would speak to you for hours any time of the day if you needed them. One day, he blurted out that he usually didn't spend this much time with a patient. But since this patient's mother was so special, he couldn't resist."

We listen to her, completely riveted. Who would have thought a porn star could have a great love story? Faye was right. I am too quick to judge.

"He stared so hard at me with these steely eyes and, well, the rest is history. He didn't even know about my past. And when I told him, he didn't care. He said, 'You are a beautiful person. I love you for

who you are. Not what you've done. I can't imagine my life without
you.' "

"*Wow!*" we all say again.

An hour later, Nancy, Renee, and a few other moms are slightly tipsy.
Nancy's mixing another batch of Mojitos and I watch as she pours
in nearly a whole bottle of white rum. I take a few sips of one and
my throat burns. It's much too strong for the lightweight I've become. Someone clicks off the endless loop of Disney princess music
and locates KBIG's Noontime Disco Workout. "YMCA" blares.

I take inventory of my living room. It seems big, stark, and cold.
More like a warehouse than a home. The white walls are bare except
for the entertainment center with the steroid TV. There are no photographs or artwork to give the room a cozy feel. I had so many
plans for this place when we moved in. But right now it has the look
and feel of one of those model homes up for sale with the hotel fur-
niture and the vases filled with artificial flowers. Mind you, I don't
have fake flowers, but they would fit in perfectly with my style
choices, or lack thereof.

Trinity and Mom come into the kitchen from the guest house.
The moms say hi and Mom actually smiles and says hi back. Renee
starts having a conversation with Mom about how pretty her hair
looks and Mom smiles and nods her head. I wonder if Renee has any
idea that my mom isn't really there. She keeps going on and on about
how thin her hair is and how lucky my mother is to be able to wear
it in a bun. Mom keeps smiling and nodding.

And then Mom's expression changes. She suddenly hears the
music. It's the BeeGee's "Stayin' Alive." Mom's head starts bobbing
and she shuts her eyes.

I wonder if somewhere she remembers that *Saturday Night Fever*
was the first album I ever bought. She drove me to Musicland on the
Post Road where I purchased it from some cashier wearing a Led

Zeppelin T-shirt who told me that disco sucked. When I got home, I blasted the music. Mom and I tried to imitate John Travolta's moves.

Mommy, Mommy, look at me. Remember? Remember? Remember? Just make some eye contact and I'll know somewhere you are still there. Please.

Mom stares off into the distance with a smile on her face. Her head continues to keep the beat with the music.

"Oh, Mary, you like disco," Renee says, still completely clueless.

Arms swaying, hips slightly gyrating from side to side, Mom moves into the living room near the stereo with Trinity in tow. She slowly spins around and then puts her arms around Trinity's shoulder and clumsily waltzes around the room. Trinity holds herself rigid, but when Nancy and I start clapping, she loosens up a bit. Some of the other mothers circle around them, dancing.

I stand back, watching and grinning. This is one of those rare moments when I actually forget about everything. Mom seems like Mom again—carefree, lost in this dance. After the music stops, I can almost imagine her saying, "Well, I better get back to the kitchen and fix dinner. Your father will be home soon." For a second, I have forgotten about Rose and Alex and Alzheimer's. I am a daughter watching her mother waltz around a room. I am a mother surrounded by other mothers whose children are playing with dolls and princess dresses and teddy bears, whose husbands are at work, but who will return to us in a few hours. We'll greet them and smile and be happy and safe and cozy in our lives.

Ruth puts her arm around me and squeezes me.

"Ruthie," I say. "My mom can move."

She smiles at me strangely. "Honey," she says while rubbing my back. "You have a . . . um . . . a visitor."

"Huh?" My heart pounds. Alex? Ruth's concerned look confirms this. It's got to be Alex.

"Alex?" I ask her, my throat closing up on me. Isn't this how it always works? When you suddenly forget, that's when they show up, begging you back, telling you it was all a big mistake.

Ally, I love you. I'm so sorry. I'll do whatever it takes to get you back. I know I don't deserve you, after all I put you through. But these last months made me realize how much I adore you. How I can't live without you. How you're the only woman for me.

Ruth shakes her head. "No," she says, her voice slightly shaky.

I squint at her as if trying to decipher something.

"Ruth?"

"It's . . ."

"Yes?"

"Her."

13

We're in the Money

There's an enormous limo idling outside my gate. An Armani-clad chauffeur stands next to it. I feel rage bubbling within me. If she's going to come to my house, can't she at least be discreet? Why the hell is she here anyway?

"Oh, Ally, I'm so sorry. I forced Alex into this whole thing, but he's in love with you. You're all he talks about. I just wanted you to know this. He wants to come back so bad, but he's afraid you'll never forgive him. Well, forgive him, Ally. The man really loves you."

"Hello, Ms. Hirsh, Rose would like a word with you," the chauffeur says. "Would you mind stepping into the limo?"

"She can't get out and talk to me?"

"Well, Ms. Hirsh, she would, but ..." He smiles condescendingly, then tips his head across the street to a cluster of paparazzi gathered there. In my fury, I hadn't noticed them. They snap away at me. I refuse to look in their direction, although I do wonder if Johnny's one of them.

"Rose, come out. Give us something. A quick smile. Anything."

The driver opens the door and I quickly jump into the limo. I practically sit on Rose's lap.

"Sorry," I mumble. Sorry? *Sorry?* What the hell am I saying? She steals my husband and I tell her I'm sorry for sitting on her lap? What am I doing in here anyway?

Rose slides over on the seat.

"What are you doing here? What do you want?" I shake my head and tug at the door handle. "What am I doing here? I've got to go."

Rose grabs my wrist.

"No, Ally, wait, please."

"What? What could you possibly say to me right now?"

She stares at the floor as she speaks. "I'm sorry about all of this. I mean it, Ally. You're such an incredible person. Xands and I never meant for any of this to happen."

My hand reaches for the door.

"No, please. I know there's no reason you should talk to me. If I were you, I'd probably have killed me by now, but just hear me out for a second." She rummages through her pink leather Prada handbag and pulls out an envelope. She holds it out for me.

"I don't need your apology letter."

With perfectly manicured peach-colored nails, Rose adjusts her oversized Fendi sunglasses. "It's not an apology," she says. "Go on, open it." She suddenly sounds excited.

I shoot her a confused look.

"Please, Ally, I think you're going to like this, a lot."

My heart palpitates. Maybe it's from Alex. Begging me back. Rose vigorously nods her head. "Open it."

I shouldn't open it. I should just leave. Instead, believing that this envelope contains the keys to my eventual forgiveness of Alex, I tear it open.

Then I stare at its contents in complete disbelief.

Pay to the order of Alice C. Hirsch. $1,000,000.

I can't speak or move.

"Ally, it's the very least I could do." Rose smiles as if everything's going to be just *Great!*

"*What*? You think I want or need your money? You think you can buy my . . . my forgiveness?"

Rose takes off her sunglasses and gives me a look—a mix of pity and contempt. "Oh, Ally, I wasn't trying to buy your forgiveness. I want to buy Xander a quick divorce."

I'm paralyzed. I want my hand to squeeze the door handle, but my body betrays me.

Rose smiles as if she's going to bestow some great news. I can't help but think that Gabby is right. Rose's teeth are whiter than a fresh piece of chalk. They're neon white.

"It's over, Ally, face it. He's not coming back. So why not get something out of it? Be smart. Help me and I'll help you."

My mouth hangs open. This woman is beyond insane. She's not even human. I will my hand to the door handle, but it's limp against my leg. I can't escape.

"Believe it or not, I love him. This is not some boy toy of mine, if that's any comfort to you. I'm in this for the long haul. He's a man among men, Ally. I'm sure you know that. I want to make it official." She giggles like she's telling her best friend the good news. "I can't believe I'm saying it, but I want to get married. I want to have a baby. Xander wants a baby very badly, too."

I think about the baby again. Maybe it will come back, just like Faye said. Maybe it will return to Alex but not me. Maybe Rose will have the baby that was supposed to be mine. I feel dizzy. My stomach turns. I am going to throw up all over this limo.

"Alex already has a baby," I choke out.

"I know. I know. And I love the Gabster."

The Gabster?

"She's not yours to love," I sneer. "And she never will be."

The door opens. Ruth grabs me and pulls me out.

"Get the fuck out of here and never come back, you piece of shit asshole," Ruth snarls.

The paparazzi click away as the limo screeches down the block.

"Party's over, boys," Ruth yells.

Ruth puts her arm around me and leads me back into the house.

Inside it's quiet. Everyone has left. Trinity straightens up while Connor and Gabby lie on their backs watching *Beauty and the Beast*.

I slump down on a chair, shut my eyes, and breathe deep.

Ruth sits next to me, rubbing my hand. We don't say anything for a long time. From the TV, Mrs. Potts sings about a tale as old as time.

"You know, I know her," Ruth finally says. "Not well. We were both starting out in the business at the same time. We were up against each other for some roles."

"Roles? You mean Rose was a . . . ?"

Ruth shakes her head and laughs. "No. I didn't come out here planning to be a porn actress. I came out here hoping to be, well, what Rose Maris is now. We got here at the same time. We'd always be at the same auditions for the same cheesy horror movies and sitcom pilots, it seemed. Believe it or not, we both were typecast as the wholesome girl next door. As you probably guessed, she wound up getting the roles."

She shakes her head and laughs. "Stupid me. You wanna hear something funny and a little catty?"

I nod.

"What I did in front of the camera, she did behind the camera. She's a star. I'm a washed-up porn actress desperately trying to forget my past."

I begin to cry. Not because of Alex or Rose or what just happened in front of my house. It suddenly dawns on me that this woman I barely know has done something remarkable for me. By coming outside to rescue me from Rose, Ruth put her past back in the news for all to see—Melvin's colleagues, Connor's teachers, other parents. She's spent the last few years trying to escape it. Tomorrow, her photo and her former profession will most likely be glaring from a newspaper because of me.

I cry harder, remembering my first impression of her. How I wanted to get her out of my house, away from Gabby, away from me. In just a few weeks, she's become a true friend. I understand why Melvin was drawn to her, despite her past. I think again of Faye and how she said I've missed many opportunities because I judge too fast and too hard.

I stare at Ruth and I can't get the words out to say thanks, but she smiles at me.

"It's going to be okay. I promise. I know you don't believe it now, but it really will be one day."

14

A Thousand Things

Before school, Gabby asks me to read her *Cinderella* for what has to be at least the thousandth time. After I finish, Gabby tells me the secret to all fairy tales. She says they're divided into three parts. There's the really bad stuff at the beginning. Then there's the stuff in the middle that's still pretty bad, but at least there's a little hope. And last, there's the happily ever after. The prince kisses the princess and she's alive again. Or awake after a deep sleep. Or the shoe fits. Or the girl in the tower cries and the prince has his vision restored. Gabby believes life is the same way. She says one day, no matter what, everyone gets their happily ever after.

I nod and smile, but I don't tell her the truth. "Okay, honey," I say. It's the best I can do.

The phone rings. Monica Brent who lives on Cezanne Court explains that she wants to create a holiday in New York City motif. "We'll have skyscrapers, scaled down, of course, Rockefeller Center with skaters and a big tree, holiday shoppers on Fifth Avenue. It will be quite spectacular. I'm assuming no one's come up with anything nearly as original."

No wonder Sherri laughed when I said I'd string up some lights. These people are all fanatics. Who has time for this?

As she talks, I rummage through the drawers for my pad with the list of all the Christmas displays I've collected so far. It's vanished.

"We need to celebrate our individuality as a neighborhood. We have to change the mindset of people who assume everything is about Christmas. There are a lot of other holidays going on besides Christmas. I plan to incorporate them all in my New York holiday vignette."

I finally hang up with Monica and rummage through more drawers for my legal pad. "Have you seen the big yellow notebook that was in this drawer," I ask Gabby.

"Yes," she says.

"Well, where is it?"

"It's not there," she says matter-of-factly.

"I can see that, but where did it go?"

"It's in my room."

I'm relieved. Silly as it sounds, that pad is the only part of my life that's been organized lately. I've collected ideas from about fifty houses now—everything from Santa on the roof, elves in the toy factory, dancing candy canes, to SpongeBob, the Rugrats, Shrek, Dora the Explorer. If I lose that list, I don't know what I'll do. I bet the neighborhood would hold a public lynching. They'd hang me and then string me with lights. The perfect holiday display.

"Could you get it for me?"

"Sure."

Gabby runs down the hall. When she returns, she proudly holds up the legal pad.

"Isn't it beautiful?"

I grab the pad from her. Every page has been painted over. Big, broad strokes of colors. Blacks and reds and blues and greens and oranges. My notes are devoured by paint.

"Gabby!" I snarl. "This was Mommy's. You have paper every-where."

"No, I don't. I ran out about three hundred and seventy-nine days ago. You never buy me anything. Connor and I wanted to paint, but you were outside and so was his mommy, so I found this. Isn't it beautiful?"

"Go to your room."

I think about what to do. I could call Sherri and get a list of all the phone numbers to every house in the area. Then I could call and pretend I'm confirming decorations. But that sounds like a full week's work. Something for tomorrow, or the next day. Right now I have to get Gabby to school.

I drop Gabby off at kindergarten. Then I go to the coffee shop down the street and order a latte. I sit in my usual spot. I look up but the photo I love is gone. In its place is a painting that resembles a Thomas Kinkade. A country cottage with too much light, too many flowers, and too much cobblestone. I take all of this as a bad omen.

Ruth shows up a few minutes later and says I look depressed.

I tell her something I haven't told anyone yet—I called Alex after Rose's visit.

She shakes her head. "Ugh."

"I'm so sick of these games. He was my husband for a long, long time, and now he's this stranger. I want answers. I was furious at him for letting Rose come over. He said he had no idea."

Ruth laughs. "That sounds hard to believe."

"I know, but I believed him. He said that's what Rose is like. She takes things into her own hands. He said she shouldn't have done that, but it's her style."

"To be a psycho?"

"That's what I said. Then I asked him if that's what he wants, a divorce."

"And he said?"

"He got silent and said no, but I knew he was lying. He must have told Rose that he wanted a divorce and she just got sick of him waiting to grow balls, so she took it into her own hands, right?"

I want Ruth to disagree with my assessment. But she seems to be contemplating something. After a minute, she says, "What are you holding on to?"

I feel my throat choking up as my eyes tear. I shake my head. "I don't know . . . everything? My life as I know it? My life as I thought it would always be? And I guess I'm afraid of being alone."

"You're doing great," Ruth says. She reaches out and squeezes my hand. Then she sips her latte and thinks about something. "So what would you do if tonight Alex or Xander, or whoever he is, comes by, tells you how sorry he is, and begs you to take him back?"

"I wouldn't take him back. How could I? After all this?"

Ruth stares at me and smiles like she knows I'm lying. She's got to be the smartest porn actress ever.

"Here's a game I used to play with my friends when we got our hearts broken," she says. "You've got to forget about the good times and think of all his flaws. Even Melvin, who I think is the greatest man in the whole world, has flaws. When we are in love, we have to bury the flaws or we'd drive ourselves crazy. But you should look at all the stuff you've buried and dig it up again and then put it all in the past."

I nod. "My mom. Every weekend I'd go with Gabby to visit her, but Alex hardly ever came. I accepted his silly excuses even though I knew I shouldn't. I pretended I understood. But he should have been there for me. He said my mom didn't know the difference, but I did."

"That's what I'm talking about," Ruth says. "That's enough reason to kick his sorry ass out for good."

"And he always, always, always gave in to Gabby. If I told her no about something, like say she wanted ice cream and I said no. She'd throw a fit and Alex would give in. He'd say, 'Come on, Al, let her have a little ice cream.' He'd always undermine me and she'd get her way. It got to a point where she stopped asking me for anything and went directly to him. And I let this happen. Now I'm trying to undo the damage, and let me tell you, it's very hard."

Ruth smiles at me. "See, if you stayed with Alex you would have created a brat. You saved Gabby and that's a good enough reason in itself." She takes a long sip of her latte. "Do you still have that check?"

I giggle and nod. "Yup."

"Well, you should divorce his sorry ass and cash that check."

"I dunno. It seems, well, sort of degrading."

Ruth laughs. "I know degrading, trust me. And that's far from it. Besides, you could do something spectacular with that money. Imagine all the fun you could have."

It's true. A million dollars is a lot of money for me. It would take me over eight years of really hard work to make that kind of money. But I don't think I can do it. It's letting Rose win. Giving her the last word. Telling her I can be bought.

The waitress comes over to ask if we want something else.

"You haven't been here in a long time," she says. "I just remembered that I have something for you."

She returns a few minutes later with a package wrapped in brown paper. She puts it in front of me.

"For me? Are you sure?"

"Sure I'm sure. I've been holding this for a while now. Open it."

I do.

It's the photo. "Baby, Five Minutes Old." I smile hard for the first time all day.

"Wow! This is great," I say, staring at it. "How much do I owe?"

"Nothing," the waitress says, smiling. "J.D. wanted you to have it." She pulls a pamphlet from her dress pocket. "He's having an exhibit in Studio City in a few weeks. Here's the information. He said he hoped you'd stop by, with some friends."

Ruth looks at me quizzically. "You know him?"

I shake my head. Then I look at the pamphlet—Photographs by J.D. Wolfe. "I've never met the guy in my life."

Ruth laughs. "It sounds like you have an admirer."

I snort. "He probably has me confused with someone else. Besides, I'm a real catch. An almost forty-year-old woman with a five-year-old."

"You're almost forty?" Ruth says. "I thought I was the only oldie in the group. Geez, Ally, you look like you're barely thirty."

Ruth grabs the pamphlet from my hand. "I still think we should go to his exhibit. You never know."

Jingle Bell Rock

It is Christmas Eve and I am struggling to feed my mother a puree of beef, broccoli, and potatoes. Since yesterday, Gabby has been at Alex's Marina del Rey condo with all the other divorced dads and children. There will be a holiday parade complete with Santa, presents, toasted marshmallows, and fireworks.

Trinity is with her sister, having a quiet dinner.

Feeding Mom has gotten easier. It's become like meditation. But whereas in traditional mediation, you concentrate on your breathing—in and out, in and out, ham sa, ham sa—in this form, I focus on the simple motions it takes to get the food from the plate into my mother's stomach. Unwavering patience is my religion. I must not think of anything except the movement of the spoon. Scoop up the puree. Pry open Mom's mouth. Push in the spoon. Turn the spoon over. Dump out its contents. Watch as my mother sloshes the food around in her mouth. Catch the food that drips down her chin with the spoon, shovel in that food. Watch again as Mom sloshes it around until slowly, ever, ever so slowly, she swallows it. Begin again.

I forget about all the chores I need to get done and all the problems in my life. Instead, I become one with the rhythm of these motions until I am numb. Until there is nothing else I can think about.

I'm not complaining. It feels good not to think about anything but the spoon.

When I am done feeding Mom, I wipe her face with a wet cloth and remove her bib. Half the food I fed her has fallen out of her mouth and onto her lap and the floor. I wonder how many calories my mother actually gets in her body. She is so thin. When I dressed her this morning, I was shocked by how skeletal her body looked. Her bones jut out of her transparent skin as if death is not waiting for an official notice, it's already taken up residence.

I slowly hoist Mom out of her chair and guide her to the couch. I plop her down to face the Christmas tree. I bring the hot chocolate I made in an attempt to be festive and sit next to her. With the fire blazing, the tree glowing, and the hot chocolate to imbibe, we could almost be a Thomas Kinkade painting. Although I'm sure none of Tommy's figures look as cadaverous as Mom or as sad as I feel.

About two weeks ago, Sherri Gold from 2804 Delacroix came to the house. She wasn't bubbly this time.

"I thought you were on top of things, Alice, but today I've been fielding complaints from many of the neighbors. There's two Spidermans. Three Simpsons. Four—did you hear me—*four* SpongeBobs. I thought last year was a disaster, but this is worse. Much worse. This is the worst year ever. And we had a committee! How could this have happened?"

I used the standard response I've been giving the bill collectors, the water company, the gas company, Gabby's teachers, my boss. "I'm going through a divorce, Sherri, okay? I haven't been able to get it together."

Sherri closed her eyes and massaged her temples. "I understand, Alice. I really do. I've been there. A lot of us have been there. But I

wish you had just come to me and told me this was too much for
you. I mean, you did volunteer."

"I did? As I recall, you volunteered me."

"You could have turned it down if you wanted to," she says. "Re-
gardless, you should have come to me if it wasn't your thing."

"I know. I know. I should have. It was on my list of things to
do, but well, I never got to anything on that list," I said. It's true.
For weeks I had "Call Sherri" on the top of my to do list. But it just
seemed too strenuous. Every day, I told myself I'd do it tomorrow.
Until tomorrow was the moment when Sherri was at my house
screaming at me.

Then I forced out a smile. "But did you see my decorations?"

Sherri didn't say anything. She just gave me a look of pity.

I don't know why I added that. My decorations aren't something
to be proud of, and I know it, even Gabby knows it. But I figured
maybe quantity could replace quality in Sherri's eyes. After all, the
woman is bedazzled up to her neck in rhinestones and faux dia-
monds and just about anything that sparkles.

"I had to talk the neighbors out of coming over here with pins to
pop everything," Sherri said.

A week earlier, I had gone to Target and bought all of their inflatable Christmas decorations. There's an enormous Santa, Mrs. Claus,
elf, Grinch, reindeer, candy cane, Christmas tree, and a snow globe.
Trinity and I had spent a day positioning them on the lawn while Mom
supervised from a chaise lounge.

I thought it looked festive enough. Well, I knew it was pretty
lame, but I thought it would look wonderful to Gabby.

But as I drove back to the house after picking Gabby up from
kindergarten, I realized how horribly cheesy it looked. It was
haphazard—the Grinch looming over a candy cane while Santa stood
next to the snow globe. It was a mishmash and bizarre and almost
menacing. Gabby sniffled when she saw it.

"What's wrong," I said, trying to sound as enthusiastic as possible.

"It's not beautiful," Gabby said. "It's not magical. It's ridicleus. I wanted a fairy tale. This isn't a fairy tale."

"Did you see the snow globe? Snow falls while the snowmen sing 'Jingle Bell Rock.' "

"I hate that song. It's like someone took a song that doesn't sound like Christmas and forced the words jingle bells into it. It's stupid."

I hate that song, too, but I didn't know why until Gabby just explained it.

"Well, I think our house looks very festive."

"I think our house looks like the Christmas aisle at Target," Gabby sniffed.

So now the neighborhood hates me. Gabby is disappointed in me. She had begged me to create a princess wonderland. She'd even drawn pictures of her "vision" of snow blowing and fairies dancing and princesses milling about. Every day I promised Gabby that we'd get to it soon, but the days rolled along while I remained stagnant. Another undone thing on my to do list.

"I knew it," Gabby had said. "I just knew it. You promised and it didn't happen. Just like the dog. You said we'd get a dog, but where is it?"

I sip the hot chocolate as I sit next to Mom. It's cold and the chocolate is clumpy.

Christmas in Larchmont: As soon as Thanksgiving was over, Mom would turn the house into a fantasy of lights, colors, and smells—a glorious confection of pine from the spruce and spices from her nonstop baking. Every day, it seemed, I'd come home from school and embark on another holiday task, whether it was decorating cookies, stringing popcorn or cranberries, arranging the Hummels in the crèche, making a wreath, caroling with friends, or wrapping gifts for neighbors.

Now the neighbors hate me. I have blow-up Santas on my front lawn. My daughter is with my soon-to-be ex-husband. I am sitting on a couch staring at a Christmas tree that I had nothing to do with.

I tried hard to get in the spirit—I really did. I bought a Christmas tree. I hung up a few balls, but I lacked energy. And Trinity seemed to be having so much fun with Gabby that I felt like I didn't belong. It felt like I was dead and watching from beyond the grave while my daughter and her surrogate mom happily continued without me. They sang and laughed as they pulled out the decorations that have been in my family for half a century. I felt like a downer, slogging through the motions. I could sense that Gabby knew I was acting. So when the phone rang, it seemed like a perfect escape.

It was my boss. I had told him I'd be back right after the New Year. He was calling to make sure I wasn't going to flake out on him again.

"Sure," I said. "I'll see you January second." After all, Gabby will be fine. It's probably the best for both of us. Gabby will be at school most of the day. I'll start fresh. Get my life in order. Be invaluable again. Plus, work will help me take my mind off my life. Isn't that the point of work anyway?

I hadn't even shopped for Christmas presents for Gabby until a few days ago. The shelves at Target and Toys "R" Us had been picked clean. Gabby really wanted a lifesize Barbie, but they had none left. Instead, there was a generic-looking doll that was three feet tall. It was made with that really stiff plastic and its face was expressionless with wide eyes and a puckered mouth. The fingers were too long and narrow and attached to each other like a fin. The clothes were sewn on and couldn't be removed. I also found a trunk filled with princess clothes, which I figured she'd love. I filled my cart with as many dolls and toys as possible. I tried to convince myself that Gabby would love most of these gifts. Quantity over quality again.

Gabby was still in school when I got home, so I spread the toys on the living room floor and took inventory before I wrapped them.

Every year I tried to get a gift that would thrill her, but this year nothing seemed outstanding. The doll I'd gotten her was as horrible as my inflatable decorations. I went online, hoping there would be a lifesize Barbie doll available somewhere. Anywhere.

"Missus!"

I flinched. Trinity had snuck up on me. She was holding giant Barbie—the one Gabby had wanted.

"I found this the other day. I knew he wanted it badly, so I bought it just in case." She paused. "I know you been berry, berry beesy."

"Trinity!" I stood up and hugged her. "I don't know how to thank you. How much do I owe you?"

"Nothing. I want to give him something. But put it under the tree and tell Gabby Santa brought it."

"Thank you so much. I don't know what I'd do without you," I said.

She smirked at me and then pulled out a box. "For you, missus. A little gift."

"Trinity! You should be saving your money."

"Take it, please," she said.

I opened it. It was a sterling silver bracelet with a small heart locket. I unclasped the locket. Inside was a picture of Gabby, in her Cinderella gown, holding her butterfly net.

"Thank you, Trinity, but I can't take it." She must have used a lot of her savings for this. The poor woman sent most of her money back to Manila. She probably had nothing for herself.

"No. You must. I would be very hurt if you did not. I wanted to cheer you up. So it is a gift for me, too—your happiness."

"Well, thank you. It's beautiful. Very beautiful."

I look at my watch. Gabby still isn't home and it's getting late. Alex was supposed to have her back sometime tonight so she can wake up in her own bed on Christmas morning, just like she always does.

I imagine she's begging Alex to let her stay at the condo with marsh-mallow roasts and caroling and Santa on the beach and fireworks and too, too many gifts. It's Mom's bedtime, so I hoist her off the couch. She quietly moans—every joint in her body aches. Then we shuffle toward the guest house. She stares at me, smiling, as if I'm the mother and she's trying to make me happy. I lay her on the bed and change her wet diaper. Then I tuck her in. I don't attempt to brush her teeth. She just bites on the bristles until I let go. She only allows Trinity access to her mouth.

Since Gabby isn't home yet, I read Mom *The Night Before Christmas*, just like she used to do for me. I read it slowly, trying to remember the spots where she'd add suspense, pause, whisper, shout. Before I get to the part where Santa commands the reindeer to dash away, Mom is asleep. I watch her for a few moments, her mouth wide open, her breathing labored. Then I kiss her cold, moist forehead, switch on the baby monitor, and head back to the house.

A few minutes later, Gabby is home. Alex drops her off along with boxes and boxes of presents.

I can tell Gabby is in a bad mood.

"She's got to be really tired. She had a really, really busy day," Alex says proudly.

"Yeah," Gabby says. "I saw Santa and toasted marshmallows and opened lots of presents and played with my best friend, Charlotte. I wished Charlotte lived near me. I miss her so much."

"Gabs, you just met her yesterday," Alex says. Then he adds all too merrily, "Well, give me a kiss, okay, baby?"

I brace myself.

"*What*? Daddy, you can't go! It's Christmas Eve. I want you to see me open my presents. I want you to stay. That's what I asked Santa today. For you to stay here with me and Mommy. For you to love Mommy again. Why don't you love Mommy anymore?"

Alex bends down and stares into Gabby's eyes. Their noses practically touch. "I still love you and I love Mommy."

He gives me a smile. I wonder if he's saying this to console Gabby or if he and Rose have finally and inevitably broken up.

"Then stay! *Stay! Stay!*"

She clings to Alex's neck.

"Come on, Gabby. I've gotta go."

She lets go of Alex and balls her fists.

"This is going to be the worst Christmas ever," she screams, running down the hall into her bedroom. The door slams.

We stare at each other for a long time.

"What do I do?" Alex says. For the first time since I've married him, he looks helpless. I'm convinced he has been dumped and he's waiting for an invitation to stay. Do I ask him? Do I really want him here? What's best for Gabby?

"If you want, you can come back in the morning to watch Gabby open presents."

Alex looks at the floor and shuffles his feet. And I know he has plans with Rose.

"Well," he starts. Then he coughs into his hand.

"No," I interrupt. "It's probably for the best if you leave. You go. I'll deal with Gabby."

That's become my mantra. He gets the Santas and marshmallow roasts and the laughs. Then he leaves. I get the tears and the tantrums and the I hate yous.

Gabby's sobbing into her Sleeping Beauty pillow. I sit on her bed and put my hand on her back. She stiffens.

"Leave me alone," she screams. "I hate you."

I stroke the side of her tear-streaked face. "Shh, Gabby. Shhh."

Her whole body hiccups from sobs, so I keep rubbing her back until she begins to calm down.

"I'm so sorry, honey. I'm so sorry."

She turns to face me. "No, you're not," she says angrily. Her eyes narrow. Her mouth is taut.

"Why are you so mad at me, Gabby? Why?"

"Because," she says, again hiccupping. "Because . . . because you're supposed to make everything right. You're supposed to be magic."

I smile and grab her face. I feel tears slide down my cheeks.

"I'm not magic, sweetie."

"Yes, you are. And you're not using your powers. I want you to fix everything. I want to have the fairy tale back. I want Daddy back. I miss my daddy. I miss my daddy." She buries her face in her pillow and sobs again.

"I know, honey. I know you had a lot of fun with Daddy, but I promise tomorrow—"

Gabby sobs even harder. She turns towards me. Her face is red and hot. Her eyes are tiny slits bubbling with tears. She wants to say something, but every time she opens her mouth, she cries even harder.

"Shh," I say. "Shh, you don't have to talk anymore."

"I . . . did . . . not . . . have . . . fun . . . at . . . Daddy's." She hiccups out each word. "It was horrible. Santa Claus was not the real Santa Claus. He laughed too hard and too much. And everyone sang Christmas carols, but no one really knew the words, so it was stupid and boring. But everyone laughed too hard like it was the funnest thing in the world. It wasn't fun because you weren't there. I missed you so much, Mommy. I miss you and Daddy together. I don't like this."

I am crying, too. I lie down next to Gabby and we look into each other's face as tears stream out of our eyes. We wrap our arms around each other.

"I'm so sorry. I'm so sorry." I keep saying this over and over again because I don't know what else to say. We lay there for a long time, just staring at each other, until Gabby's eyes get heavier and heavier. She struggles to keep them open, but fatigue gives in. I watch her body relax as she begins to breathe softly. I pull up the covers, cuddle her, and stare into her precious little face until my eyes get heavy, too.

Before I fall asleep, I tell myself that I can't go back to that job. I'll leave a message for my boss tomorrow and tell him I quit. Who am I kidding anyway? I'm not invaluable to my clients. My Gabby needs me more than ever. I will be here for her every day. I will make things as good as possible for her. I think about the present I will give myself—I will file for divorce.

Soon I can't think anymore. Exhaustion has settled into every bone of my body. I feel that I have never been this tired in my entire life.

I drift off, holding onto my daughter, and we sleep deeply, both of us silently hoping to hear Santa's reindeer on the roof.

Part Two

Still Bad But a Little Hopeful

I

A Child's Song

We are over the Grand Canyon," the pilot informs us in a nasal and staticky voice.

He's been doing this every few minutes for the entire flight. He tells us where we are. Then tells us we're socked in, so it's impossible to see any of these places.

"On a clear day, you would be looking right into the mouth of the canyon. A breathtaking sight," he says.

I am on my way to Rochester, New York. From there, I'll meet up with my friend Lauren and head to a small town on the Finger Lakes where my college is located. Most people go to reunions to flaunt their success and their good-looking spouses. I wonder what I'll say.

"Hey, everyone, it's me. Alice. I'm unemployed. My husband left me for another woman. I have a daughter who's five and who hates me a lot of the time."

They'll look at me funny and laugh, unsure if I'm making a joke or not. Then they'll tell me that I look great.

"Well, my daughter tells me my teeth have yellowed and I have lines underneath my eyes. But thanks for lying to me anyway."

But at least I'm thin. All this sadness has melted my love handles and gut. Divorce becomes me.

Why am I going?

When it comes down to it, there's only one reason: George.

We've been exchanging e-mails for months now. A little innuendo here. A little flirtation there. It has been half a year of foreplay and I'm going slightly crazy.

"You should be creating a future for you and Gabby, not retreating into the past," Dr. Phil would say.

But I deserve it, don't I? It's the beginning of June. The last few months have been exceptionally draining on me. I filed for divorce. I officially quit my job. I ripped up Rose's check. (I know. I know. It was a lot of money—but could I have lived with myself?) I put the house on the market and then took it off, decided to put it on again and then took it off. (Sherri Gold, the realtor, hates me more than ever.)

Before I left for this trip, I visited Faye again. As a matter of fact, she's one of the reasons I'm here, on this flight. She promised me the plane wouldn't crash.

"Your life is undergoing great change," Faye said, her gray eyes darting back and forth, inhaling my soul. "There's someone from the past who will be entering your life again. Someone you were very antagonistic with. But you helped change his life and he will soon return the favor. He is handsome, with striking eyes. If you let him in, he will become important to you. I think you are shutting him out, though."

"Who? Who?" I said.

"I don't see a name, just these beautiful eyes. It is someone you have met."

"George," I said. "It's got to be George."

Faye shook her head. "I'm not certain. Maybe."

"Oh, Faye." I roll my eyes and snort. "Anyway, should I go to my reunion?"

"Absolutely."

"Why?"

Faye pinches my cheeks as if I'm a tot.

"It's a chance to get crazy. Also, it's an opportunity of a lifetime. You get to see all the fat, bald, middle-aged men who used to be the hunks on campus. You still look like you're in your twenties, so flaunt it and have fun."

"Uh-huh. So this isn't your psychic opinion."

"No, Ally. This is just a sixty-year-old's observation. The exceptional men from our youth usually disappoint in middle age. But go. Enjoy. Be merry. Don't think so much. Stop worrying so much."

Then she stared at me and a trouble look crossed her face. "And please, Ally, please really, really listen to the safety instructions at the beginning of the flight."

My eyes bugged out.

Faye laughed. "You're too easy to get."

On the drive home from Faye's that day, Ruth called.

"I'm taking you shopping," she said. "Meet me at King's Fish House at the Commons for lunch."

We sat outside the faux New Orleans facade, picking at salads. Out of the corner of my eye, I watched a man devour Ruth. She's changed her look during the last few months. Her hair is shorter and more of a honey blonde color. Her clothes are a little more conservative—so she'll fit in with the PTA moms, I suppose. She's even getting laser treatments on her back to remove a tattoo of an angel.

However, hard-core Jill Chris aficionados still recognize her.

This guy kept stealing glances. And I could feel him waiting for a lull in our conversation. I kept talking about anything to prevent him from coming over.

It didn't matter. He finally summoned the courage. He awkwardly stood by our table, waiting for one of us to look up. I refused to. He coughed while nervously playing with coins in his pants pockets.

"Excuse me, you're Jill Chris, right," he asked. "I just want you to know I'm a really big fan. I think you're amazing. My name's Todd Mott."

"Thanks," Ruth said, barely looking up. She stabbed at some lettuce.

He stood there, his mouth hanging opened. "You've given me a lot of pleasure over the years. *A lot.*"

I felt like this guy was going to start pleasuring himself in front of us.

Ruth turned toward him and spoke gruffly. "Well then, Todd Mott. Can I ask you a big favor?"

Todd looked like he was going to explode. "Sure. Anything."

"Do you have my DVDs at home?"

"All of them. Hidden, of course. My wife—"

"Would you send them to me?"

"Huh?"

"If I give you my P.O. box, will you send me every DVD that you have? Everything."

"Um . . ."

"If you send me every single copy, I'll send you one hundred dollars for each. Tell all your friends, too."

Todd looked confused. "Okay."

"Promise?" Ruth pulled out a business card with her name and a P.O. box number on it.

"Anything you say, J.C. You have no idea what you mean to me."

She held out her hand. Todd shook it and didn't let go until Ruth finally pried it away. Beaming, he walked away from the table.

Ruth watched him as she wiped her hand with a napkin. "Gross, was he sweaty," she said.

"You think he'll send the DVDs?"

"I'm always surprised by how many do. At first I told Mel that this would never work, but he said, 'You have no idea of the almighty power of the buck. It'll beat sex any day'. So far, I've gotten stacks and stacks of DVDs back. I know I won't wipe it out, but I want to make it harder for Connor to stumble on it. If only I could get Stone to burn the originals." She thought about this for a moment. "Well, I guess one day I'll probably have to tell Connie, but I hope it's a long, long way off. And I hope he's old enough to sort of understand why Mom did the things she did." She laughed sadly and stared at her plate. "First, I guess, I'll have to figure it out, too."

After lunch, we headed to Nasty Kitty, a lingerie and sex toy shop on Ventura in Tarzana.

"We've gotta find you something sexy," Ruth said.

"I don't know why I'm here. George is probably still married. I'm reading into things."

"Be prepared. You'd hate to have everything going well and then remember you have on big ol' gray underwear with a big ol' hole in the crotch."

The saleswoman was a short, big-breasted woman with peroxide blonde hair and a squeaky little voice. Her eyes followed Ruth around as Ruth plucked up various nighties.

"Look at this one," Ruth said, laughing as she held up a skimpy little police uniform. "The badge says Officer Nasty."

"Maybe I'll wear that during my next parent conference with Myrna."

The squeaky-voiced saleswoman was right behind us. "That would look great on you," she cooed to Ruth. "It looks like it's your size. A two? Why don't you try it on? Please."

"I'm not in the market today. I'm shopping for Ally, my friend. Do you have any recommendations?"

Squeaky could barely hide her disappointment as she surveyed my body.

"How about a Rabbit? You look like you could use one," she decided.

"A Rabbit?" At first I thought she was talking about a furry costume with ears and a fluffy tail. Then I realized she meant a vibrator.

"That's our top of the line," Squeaky said, holding up a vibrator with rabbit ears. "Every woman should own one of these. Do you?" She studied me. "You don't, do you? Honey, do you even know where your G-spot is?"

I instinctively stepped back, half expecting this woman to stick her hand down my pants. Instead, she pulled one of the Rabbits off the shelf and fondled it.

"This is the Rabbit Habit. It's a good choice for a first-timer." She turned it on. The bunny ears spun. She rolled her eyes skyward, as if just watching this thing was getting her all hot and bothered. "I use the Habit a few times a day. I haven't had a man in years."

She beamed at me as if this was some kind of wonderful accomplishment. I felt like she was waiting for some kind of acknowledgment. "Good for you," I said.

"Trust me. This thing is better than anything a man can give you."

It didn't happen. I grew up in a strict Roman Catholic household and was shuttled to Catholic schools until I broke free of it in college. I associate a rabbit with Easter and Easter with Christ on the crucifix. How could those ears ever bring pleasure? I'd be thinking of Jesus dying for my sins, including the one I would be committing at that moment. Besides, cute bunny ears? Did some inventor see a little rabbit hopping through the fields, munching on a carrot and think, *Wow! I'm so aroused!* But then again, what do I know—I'm so repressed.

Instead, I wound up at Victoria's Secret, where I bought a black lace bra and matching undies. Just in case.

George. George. George. What am I thinking? Maybe he is happily married. Maybe his wife decided to come along. I was placing way too much stock in a few silly e-mails. I haven't figured out the art of interpreting e-mails. It's too easy to jot out a few thoughts and hit send. Writing e-mails doesn't mean as much as sitting down at a desk, putting your thoughts on a piece of notepaper, crumpling it up, and beginning again and again until it's perfect. With e-mails, you might say more, but the words have less meaning.

"It's a little bumpy up here. We'll be experiencing some turbulence for about the next twenty minutes or so, so please, buckle up and remain in your seats."

Gabby is spending the weekend at Alex's condo. I packed her suitcase and left it by her bed. Later, when I lifted it, I was shocked by how heavy it was. I assumed Gabby had added her hardcover collection of fairy tales. I unzipped it and discovered dozens of glinting white rocks and pebbles. She must have painted the stones in our backyard white.

"You weren't supposed to open that," Gabby whispered when she caught me.

"I thought we discussed this already," I said. "No one is going to take you into the middle of the woods, honey. You know your daddy loves you."

"The Daddies always love their kids, but that doesn't stop them from doing horrible things to them. Especially if their wives tell them to."

"Daddy isn't married to Rose."

"But I think he's going to be, don't you?"

I sucked in a deep breath. How to answer such a question? According to the magazines and my Hollywood friends, they should have been broken up by now. But they're not. And maybe they never will be. Maybe this is the real thing for both of them.

"I don't know," I finally said.

"You say that a lot lately."

"I know. I'm sorry."

"You say that a lot lately, too."

The pilot broke into my thoughts. "We're beginning our descent into Rochester International Airport."

A few hours later, Lauren and I check into a Ramada right off campus. I stare out the window at the lake while Lauren unpacks.

"It's strange being here," she says. "I feel like in some ways it was just yesterday, and in other ways it was a million lifetimes ago."

"I just still can't believe how old we are," I say. "How did all this time go by between then and now? God, life was so easy and we made it so complicated. I thought it was so important to get straight As. And what did it matter? No one has ever asked to see my report card."

"That's why I was so much smarter," Lauren says. "I never tried to get straight As. I just drank too much."

They start arriving. Sarah, the quiet, bookish one; Beth, the boisterous, athletic one; Dawn, the effortlessly smart, party girl one; and Liz, the sexy, slightly slutty one. We tell each other how great we look. We say we look the same, but we're lying. At the very best, we are tired versions of our younger selves. Our eyes are puffy and lined. The whites have a pinkish cast now. Our hair isn't as shiny as it was. Our waists are thicker—except for Liz, who is as thin as she was in college and is flaunting the hell out of it, strutting around in a skin-tight racerback and mini shorts.

We planned it so our rooms are all right next to each other's. We are in and out, checking out wardrobes, applying makeup, chatting.

"I have a rule I'd like to announce," Beth growls. She's the lesbian of the group. Despite the fact that she had declared her love for

Matty Reynolds all through college, we all secretly knew the truth, although she officially came out tonight when she showed photos of her partner, Jeannine, and their adopted Cambodian baby.

"Once we leave this room, we can't talk about spouses or children. Whoever does will have to drink a shot."

I smile so wide it hurts my cheeks. Kids? Who has kids? I feel like I'm twenty again where every night held a surprise. We'd spend the night at a bar, scanning the crowd and watching the door. Would tonight be the night when I'd fall in love? Make out with a stranger? Flirt with a crush? The possibilities were endless back then. And it doesn't seem much different right now.

Someone has burned a CD filled with late eighties hits. Milli Vanilli segues into Madonna who segues into Phil Collins. I sip my margarita slowly—I want to be slightly tipsy but not drunk and slurring when I see George. I don't want him to think I'm the same old Ally. No, I'm older and better and soberer!

That night, no George. We attend every party the reunion committee holds. I even drag my friends to the crew party, because George rowed in college. But he's a no-show. I casually ask his friends about his whereabouts, but no one's seen him. No one even seems to know for sure if he is definitely coming. Maybe he got stuck on a deadline. Maybe he chickened out.

It isn't until the next night, at a party on the quad, that I see him. I am filling my Styrofoam cup with beer, when he walks out on the quad. I'd been secretly searching for him for the last twenty-four hours, and had begun to think he had a last-minute change of heart. I watch as he hugs some people and my heart throttles my ribs. I didn't expect this nervousness to overwhelm me. My Styrofoam cup is vibrating, my hands are shaking so hard.

Get a grip on yourself, Alice, I tell myself. I gulp at my beer.

It's always been my problem. As cool as I try to be, my body betrays me. My voice cracks. My hands shake. My face turns purple.

My ears go magenta. My emotions are always written in bold all over my face: Nervous. Scared. Confused.

The yeasty smell wafting from the beer keg next to me makes my mouth parch. I fill my cup up again. *Gauge yourself, Alice. You don't want to be slurring, dancing naked, and making an ass of yourself.* I am a middle-aged woman who has gone through childbirth and divorce. I change my mother's diapers. Why shouldn't I be able to talk to an old boyfriend without being blitzed out of my skull?

He looks better than I remember. Maturity has been a kind accomplice. It has chiseled away the boyish awkwardness from his features. His face seems more angular. His hair has grayed, but in a sexy, Richard Gere kind of way. He looks calmer, wiser, self-actualized.

I want to secretly watch him for a few minutes, but then someone approaches. I don't remember his name, I just recall that he was annoying then and is most likely annoying now. A person's look might undergo a major metamorphosis, but it seems the personality he was born with remains pretty much intact, or accentuated.

"Hello," I say, overly friendly to compensate for the fact that I have no idea what this guy's name is.

"Hello, Alice," he says, a weird smirk plastered on his face. "So, what's it like being a celebrity?" His beer and cigar breath bangs into my face.

"Huh?"

"I was at the dentist a few months back. *People* magazine was the only thing they had. I never look at those types of magazines, but I was bored and there was nothing else there. So I flipped through it. And there you were. I was so completely freaking out. I told everyone in the waiting room that I knew you. I was like, I went to school with her and now her husband's banging Rose Maris! That's so fuckin' cool."

This loser will go back to whatever cheesy upstate New York town he lives in and tell the locals how he spent the weekend with a celebrity. I thought it was an L.A. thing—people qualifying their lives by their close proximity to the famous. A few days before I came here, Gabby went for a checkup. Out of the blue, the pediatrician boasted how he had just removed a splinter from Dakota Fanning's sister's hand. Every dry cleaner's, hardware store, and Chinese take-out joint has 8x10s of "stars" who allegedly patronize their businesses. My gyno practically has a shrine to Heather Locklear where his diplomas should be. I suppose that brings many women comfort. "*Oh, he examined the vagina of the former star of* Melrose Place*! He must be good!*"

"Great," I say as I walk away.

I scan the quad for George. I spot him immediately again. He's wearing khaki shorts and a light blue T-shirt. I wonder if he remembered that I told him blue was his best color. I suddenly feel ridiculous in this snug-fitting sundress. I wonder if I have love handles that I couldn't see in the hotel mirror. I wonder if I need a fresh coat of makeup. It's been hours since I've applied it. I rummage through my bag for my lip gloss and quickly rub on a fresh coat.

The minute I saw him, I was in love again. It's as if the all those years have evaporated. I can barely remember Alex.

As I watch George talking with some professor, I imagine our future. We'll rekindle what we once had. Then we'll get married and have a blended family. We'd have to come up with cute nicknames for the Gabbies. We'd tell everyone about our romance. How we never got over each other. How we were always meant to be together. We'd live in a place where there were no tabloids. No *People* magazine.

"He was asking about you," Lauren says.

"Who," I ask, but I can't help smirking.

Lauren chortles. "Yeah, right. I'm not playing that game. We're too old."

"Is his wife here?"

"Not only is she not here, he doesn't have a wedding ring on."

"Really? Well, maybe he's one of those guys who never wears it."

"Oh, please. He's here for you. Why don't you go over and talk? He's over there, talking to someone who's really drunk. Go over and rescue him with something witty."

"Let him come here."

"What are you, still in college?"

"When in Rome . . ."

"By the way, did you see Nick? He looks horrible. All bald and fat. I can't believe I obsessed about him for four years."

"You girls are so catty."

I recognize the voice immediately—a slight twang of that upstate "A" that seems to emanate from the top of the nose. My heart palpitates again. George has snuck up on us. It's funny. I spent all weekend searching for him and suddenly he appears at my side. I don't know what to do. I turn slowly and feign confusion, like I have to place his face. This is ridiculous, but I can't remember the last time I've been caught off guard like this.

"George," I say, standing there, my arms glued to my sides.

His eyes bore into me. "Hey there, Ally."

We look at each other and freeze. Then he swoops in to peck me on the cheek. I move my head in the wrong direction and our lips meet air. So he moves his lips to the other side. I turn my head again and we miss. I laugh a little too hard. Then I remain still while George kisses me on the cheek.

"No wonder you guys broke up. You can't even get a simple kiss right," Lauren says. "Oh, look, there's Professor Blackwell. Think I'll ask him why he didn't give me an A on my Shakespeare paper." She giggles and heads down the quad.

"So is that why we broke up," he asks.

I scrunch my face in mock concentration. "Hmmm, I think it might have had something to do with you throwing me off your car on the Upper West Side."

"I would never do something like that, unless provoked," he says, staring hard. "You look great."

"So do you."

A few hours later, we are by the lake, sitting on the dock. I'm wearing his college sweatshirt and my heart's still pounding, even faster than it does in Pilates class. What am I doing here? We had stood on the quad talking until we were the last ones there. Everyone had headed on to bars or bed. It was awkward. We didn't know where to go next. I knew we didn't want to go on to the loud bars where everyone would be wildly drunk by now. But we couldn't say, "Let's go back to the hotel." And I certainly wasn't ready to call it a night. So George casually asked me if I'd like to take a walk to the dock where he used to crew. It had been a small, splintered raft back then, but now it was glinting metal island with a bunch of canoes, kayaks, and sailboats stacked on it.

We stood on the dock as it gently rocked, staring out at the blackness. Then George sat and I followed.

"I forgot how beautiful it was out here. Actually, I don't think I knew it then."

"Me either."

"So, do you like L.A.?"

"Yeah, well," I start like I always do, about to heap L.A. with fulsome praise, but then I stop. I don't need to lie to George. "Not really. I live in the Valley, which is just a collection of strip malls and tract houses. It's pretty ugly. I miss the East a lot."

George stretches and leans back on his elbow. "I can't believe I haven't seen you in fifteen years," he says. "I suddenly feel like we're seniors waiting for graduation and life to begin. You look exactly the same, Ally."

I snort out a laugh.

"You do."

"People have been saying that to me all weekend. But they're ly-ing. You know how I know?"

"How?"

"Because I've been saying the same thing to them—and I'm lying."

George chuckles. "You're too cynical. You were the most beauti-ful girl in college and you still are. Or maybe it's because you live in L.A. and have more Botox than the rest of us."

"I'm probably the only person in L.A. over thirty who hasn't in-jected botulism into her forehead," I say. "You know what? Sud-denly I'm the oldest person no matter where I go. People call me ma'am. No one cards me anymore. I don't know when this happened. One day it seemed to just hit me that I'm old. There's nothing subtle about it. You're busy with kids and work and whatever. Then you catch your breath and it's gone."

Why am I babbling on like this?

"What's gone?"

"That thing you had that made the world stop and stare. Now someone else has it and they're flaunting the hell out of it. And part of you wants to scream, hey, I had it once, too! Doesn't that count for anything?"

"There are people who always have it no matter what. Like you, Ally."

He is so close to me. I can feel his warm breath hitting my face, the soap on his skin. I could kiss him right now. Instead, I whisper, "Thank you."

A few hours ago, I took a shower and put on my new black lace bra and panties. Then I stared at myself in the hotel room's floor-to-ceiling mirror. I studied the silver stretch marks at the tops of my hips and the pouch of skin that hangs on my stomach and won't dis-appear no matter how many crunches I do at the gym. I turned around and examined the cellulite on my butt and the tops of my legs. And my breasts—back then they were so perfect and perky. Now, if I take off my bra, I'm afraid they'll drop to my knees. How could I ever get naked for another man again? It's too traumatic. I remember reading *A Streetcar Named Desire* in high school and not understanding Blanche's need for darkness. Now I do. If I'm naked, I want to be shrouded in black. I can't imagine ever being as uninhibited as I was fifteen years ago, when I just assumed my body was flawless.

But part of me doesn't care. It's been nearly a year since I've had sex. What's to stop me tonight? A crazy, fun fling with a man I loved, who I may still love and may even have some kind of future with. I can feel the charge between us. Pent-up desire. Nostalgia. Horniness. Call it what you will.

"Don't you see, Alice? What you're doing to his wife is no different than what Rose did to you. He's a married man. You have enough baggage. Don't pick up more," Dr. Phil would say.

What's the deal with George anyway? We've talked about our kids, but he has yet to mention his wife. He's acting like a guy who isn't married. What's he doing by the lake with me anyway? He's never come out and said he's divorced or separated. And I'm too afraid to ask. I could just assume he's divorced and then continue on with a guilt-free fling. Then, if he is married, I could feign shock or surprise, but I wouldn't have committed adultery. At this moment, ignorance would be blissful. Unfortunately, I've never been an ignorance-is-bliss type of person.

My heart pounds. "So, George, what's your wife like?"

George gulps hard. For the last few hours, he's been back in college with his girlfriend, sitting on the dock where he starred as the best strokeman on the team. It's like I threw a cold bucket of water on him.

"My wife?" he says as if he's forgotten he has one.

"Ah, yeah."

"Well, we're getting divorced, Ally. The truth is, I never stopped loving you. She knows it and I know it. I came here this weekend to win you back. To start over where we left off. Will you give us another chance?"

"She's great," he says matter-of-factly.

I nod.

"She's a really good mother. She takes great care of the kids. When I checked in on them earlier, they were all doing some big papier-mâché craft thing. She really knows how to keep them occupied. And she's probably the most organized person I've ever met."

I realize I would hate her. I also realize that's hardly a ringing endorsement for a spouse. She's organized. She's good with crafts. I can't help but smile.

"What?"

"It's just a weird way to describe your wife. That's sort of how one would rave about a nanny."

"I've never stopped loving you, Ally."

"It's just that . . . well, I've never stopped loving you."

What?

When does your fantasy ever match your reality? I don't know what to do or say. I'm paralyzed. I wonder if I'm dreaming this. Maybe I drank too many beers back on the quad. Maybe I'm passed out somewhere. Nothing ever goes exactly the way I play it out in my mind, in case you haven't noticed.

What would have happened if we'd stayed together? George would never have cheated on me. He's not the cheating type.

Wait, what am I saying?

George stares at me, waiting for me to say something.

"I don't think it's working out," he says.

"What do you mean?"

"We never talk like this. I wish she'd get me. Sometimes I feel she doesn't know who I am. I wish she could look at me and know what I was thinking."

"Most people can't do that. That's why we have voices."

"That's what bothers me the most. When I tell her something and she says, 'What do you mean?' She'll give me this quizzical look, and I'll pray to myself, don't let her say it. And then it comes out. *'What do you mean?'* And I feel my heart breaking a little bit. She just doesn't get me and I don't get her."

"Oh." I don't know what else to say. Is this the lament of everyone who's been in a marriage for a long time? Is this the kind of stuff Alex complained about me with Rose?

"We were so young. I didn't know what I had with you was as perfect as it was."

Is he drunk? Why is he telling me this?

"George, it was so not perfect. Do you remember how insane I was?"

He chuckles. "Yeah, still. It was damned good. I was young and didn't know how rare it was. I thought I could find it again easily. But, well, you're pretty rare, Ally. The rarest."

It's so dark I can barely see George. But I can feel him so close to me, our arms not quite touching. If I moved just a fraction, I'd feel his skin graze my arm. We sit, not saying a word. I listen to the gentle slapping of the water against the dock. My heart seems to be pounding in my throat. We sit like this for a few minutes. Then George clears his throat.

"You know, I wish I'd stopped, turned around, and picked you up off the street you were barfing on, and helped you, and worked it out."

"Oh, you did see that. I always wondered if . . ."

He takes a deep breath and wipes his eyes quickly. Was he crying? I can just see the outline of his head, but I can feel him looking at me, waiting for me to say something, but I can't. Anything I say right now will be fraught with too much meaning and it petrifies me. So after a few minutes of quiet, except for the sound of crickets and the water sloshing around the dock, he moves a little closer. Our arms graze. It's too much. I can't sit still anymore. I turn my head toward him and we kiss.

It is a perfect kiss. Nice, soft, and slow. We kiss like this for a long time until we can't stand it anymore and we go at it, our mouths opening wider, our kisses harder and more furious, our breathing heavy. Our hands everywhere. I don't want to stop. It's magic here. The stars above. The water gently lapping below.

"Let's go back to my room," George whispers in a raspy voice.

"Okay."

We kiss for a while longer. Then we stand up and walk towards his hotel, holding hands and leaning into each other. I'm lightheaded and wobbly. My body is numb. I feel the thrill of expectation. I can't believe this is really happening. I can't remember the last time I felt this excited or made out like that for so long. My cheeks are stubble-burned, my lips are swollen. That hasn't happened in years and years and years. The cold lake air blows through my body. I can't remember when I felt this awake.

I don't care about stretch marks or cellulite or falling boobs. George adores me. He's thought about me all these years. He'll still love my thirty-eight-year-old body.

The hotel is right ahead of us, just a block away. Every step closer toward it feels full of expectation. As if even the steps we are taking are somehow part of our foreplay. We don't speak at all. George massages my hand. I feel like I may pass out.

We are in front of the hotel. George holds open the door. *This is it*, I think. *This is the moment when your life changes forever*. Once I walk through this door, nothing will ever be quite the same.

And then his cell phone rings.

It doesn't have to be a big deal. I can ignore it. He can move into the lobby and take the call, and I can pretend it is a buddy from college wondering if George wants to meet up for some drinks at Chauncey's or Holidays or somewhere.

He is holding the door, so he can't answer it immediately. His phone keeps ringing.

But the thing is, it isn't a ring at all. It isn't the Nokia Tune or the Cingular Tune or the nostalgia ring or a Stones or Beatles song, or any tune or song or ditty or melody whatsoever.

Instead, it is a child's voice. *"Pick up, Daddy. Pick up, Daddy. Pick up, Daddy."*

He fumbles in his shirt pocket as the recording of *his* Gabby's voice chimes. Finally, he locates the phone, moves into the lobby, and gives me a sheepish look. "Just a second," he mouths to me.

He whispers into his phone. It could be anybody. A friend. A neighbor. His office. His wife. It doesn't matter who it is. Despite what he feels or what he's saying or what he isn't really certain of, George is married. He has children. He has a little girl who records a message for his phone so that he'll always be reminded of her, no matter where he is—at work, out with friends, at a reunion. A little girl who is innocent in her love and in her belief that the sound of her voice could only bring joy—never guilt, never pain. Only pure happiness.

And I know—even though it's been a lifetime, because we do know each other so well, and I know he feels it, too—I don't have to wait for the phone call to end to say good-bye to him. He can't do this. He understands I can't either.

That tinny child's voice broke the spell.

I don't say a thing. He knows when he turns around, I'll be gone. So I begin my three-block walk to my hotel. We never had to explain anything to each other then, and even now, we don't have to say good-bye. Because it is good-bye. I know I will never see him again. We won't e-mail. We won't talk. We probably will never go to another reunion.

Maybe the truth is that he is just bored with his life, and I was the person from his past who could make him forget for a little while that he is a grown-up whose dreams didn't quite come true. But maybe we all get bored without saying it, and we deal with it or end it or find a way to reinvent our spouses, our lives, our marriages. Maybe George and I would have been bored with each other, too. Maybe he would have cheated on me. Maybe he would have thought about cheating on me. Maybe after years of marriage, he'd tell someone he barely knew that I didn't get him anymore. Or maybe we would have had our happily ever after. But it is too late for us now. How silly of me to think otherwise. Maybe Gabby's fairy tales are affecting me, too.

As I walk back in the pitch blackness, part of me wishes he'd run after me. But I know he won't. If he'd tried to protest, it would just sound pathetic. This is for the best.

But God, it would have been fun.

I haven't felt this horny in years. And for some reason, this makes me laugh. I didn't think I could ever feel this way again, so I thank George for that. Although I have no idea how I'll ever sleep tonight.

I guess I should have taken Squeaky's advice and bought the Rabbit Habit.

2

As Giddy as a Drunken Man

The flight on Jet Blue back to Burbank is less than half full. I have the whole row to myself. So I stretch out and read my college's alumni magazine. I drift off into a shallow sleep and dream about the weekend.

I'm still half asleep when I glance up at the tiny TV on the back of the seat in front of me. Something familiar has flashed on the screen. I blink as my brain tries to process this image.

No, it couldn't be.

I look again.

Yes, it is.

Gabby! Gabby stares at me, laughing and skipping. I grab my headset and frantically turn the dial up for sound.

Has she been abducted? Killed? Lost forever? Why else would my daughter be on television? It's my fault. God punished me for kissing a married man!

Gabby disappears and is replaced by the smarmy Billy Bush, as he gleefully announces what's up next on *Access Hollywood*.

"First up, Rose Maris and her new, exciting role—playing mommy to boyfriend Xander's daughter, Gabrielle. It looks like a match in heaven for Xander, Rose, and this five-year-old cutie-pie who may have a career in movies, too."

Oh. My. God.

There's Gabby again in a white lace gown I don't recognize. She's dancing along the red carpet in between Rose and Alex. They're at the premiere for *Dugglebub,* an animated feature about a seagull who gets lost in Death Valley. Rose is the voice for Dugglebub's love inter-est, Gaggleloo, a turkey vulture. Talk about typecasting.

I take a deep breath and think. The premiere was yesterday. There's a three-hour time difference between here and there. So while I was making out with George on the dock, Gabby was holding hands with Rose on the red carpet. I should have had sex at least!

Get a grip, Ally. This was bound to happen sooner or later. It's been months and months now. You filed for divorce. Isn't it better that she likes Rose? Isn't it better that she isn't terrified that Rose will send her out into the woods? You want your child to be well adjusted and happy. Don't you? Don't you?

Do I?

I don't know. The rational part of me says, yes, of course. I want my daughter to feel safe and secure, especially when I'm not with her. The insecure part of me says, but wait! She's going to like this woman better than me. Rose is famous and beautiful. Gabby gets to go to formal events and wear pretty dresses and have her picture taken and be on television. What more could a five-year-old want? I'm the most boring person on the planet next to this woman. First my husband. Now my daughter. Maybe even my mother in her Alzheimer's fog would like Rose better.

"I'm a pebble star," Gabby announces in the camera.

The reporter, a blond-haired woman with an enormous smile and fluorescent white teeth, asks Gabby, "And, what is a pebble star, sweetie?"

"It's a really cool kid who's not big enough to be a rock star."

They all guffaw. Alex, Rose, the reporter. Then the reporter gives a sly smirk and nudges Rose. "So, Rose, you think there are children of your own in the future?"

Rose smiles coyly, beams at Gabby and says, "Well, the only thing in my future right now is Disneyland. I promised Gabby we'd go there tomorrow."

What? I promised Gabby *I'd* take her.

I look at my watch. Twelve o'clock New York time. Nine o'clock in Los Angeles. That means they're probably in the car or limo or private helicopter or jet heading towards Disneyland. This trip must be stopped, but I'm trapped here. I can't do anything about it. With each exhale, they're getting closer and closer to princesses and teacup rides and pirate ships and carousels. This was supposed to be my trip! Mine. Rose is stealing Gabby from me.

My heart throbs and my chest tightens. I can't breathe. Could I be having a heart attack? I search the aisles. Is there a doctor in the midst of these people? I'm going to die on this plane while my daughter trills along to "It's a Small World."

Disneyland with Rose Maris. They will never have to wait on lines. They'll march right to the front of everything. Crowds will part for them. Mickey and Minnie and Ariel and Cinderella will have private meetings with Gabby. She's getting the trip to Disneyland I could never give her. We would have waited an hour for the pirate ride. A half hour for the Haunted Mansion. Minnie would have given us the standard gratuitous wave. Ariel and Cinderella would have posed for the perfunctory picture. Belle and Jasmine would have quickly ushered us on to make room for the next starry-eyed girl.

Still, it would have been our trip. And we would have had fun. Only I would have noticed how creepy it was that Pluto's eyes peered out from the mouth of his costume. Only I would have been annoyed that Mickey didn't really give us the time of day. Only I would have gotten a throbbing headache after listening to that godawful, repetitive "It's a Small World."

"You've been making empty promises to Gabby for months now. Were you ever going to really take her to Disneyland? Were you ever going to really buy her that dog?" Doctor Phil taunts me.

I had imagined that I'd spend most of the flight daydreaming about George. But I've forgotten all about him. George who? Alex who? I think about Disneyland for the rest of the trip. I try to watch TV, to read my magazines, but all I can do is picture what Gabby is doing at that moment.

I decide that she arrived at about 10 A.M. They are whisked inside by security. Then she heads directly to the Haunted Mansion. She clings to Rose when the ghost hitches a ride in their cart. Then it's the Mad Hatter ride. The teacup ride. Mr. Toad's Wild Ride. By now, Gabby's probably hungry. She'll want lunch. I'm certain it's a VIP lunch. I bet all the princesses are dining with them in some private cordoned-off area that even Roy Disney doesn't know about. Gabby's probably wearing a princess gown and a real diamond-studded tiara that Rose just purchased for her in the gift shop. All the princesses are taking pictures of themselves with Gabby and Rose. Gabby eats a burger with Mickey-Mouse-ear fries. After, Rose will order her a special sundae with extra cherries and plenty of whipped cream that will look just like Cinderella's castle.

I am driving myself insane. I can't take it. I breathe in and out. I pick up a magazine. I fumble through it. As I try to read an article, my mind wanders again. It says, as I try to read this article, *"Gabby is swinging in between Alex and Rose as they head to Toon Town."*

I pray for a miracle. I pray for rain. I silently beg the pilot to get on the intercom and tell us visibility is horrible because there's a hurricane in Los Angeles. I pray for turbulence because there's a thunderstorm in the Anaheim area. Did you hear the news? Lightning hit Disneyland and it's engulfed in flames! Disneyland is at the epicenter of an earthquake.

Nothing. Another perfect June day in Los Angeles. With no chance of precipitation. Ever. If you look out the window, you can see everything.

In the car ride home, I dial Alex's number, but hang up before it rings. What am I going to say without sounding like the jealous, jilted ex-wife. I will be a shrew. Besides, there's nothing I can do. It's 3:30 in Los Angeles. They've had most of their fun. Just a few more rides. Soon it will be dinner. Then it will be time for the character parade. Rose has probably arranged VIP seating somewhere away from the masses. What am I saying? Rose and Xander and Gabby will probably be *in* the character parade!

There is so much traffic that it takes me over two hours to get home. When I do, my head is whirring. I can't concentrate on anything. It's nearly six. Almost time for the parade. They're probably putting the finishing touches on Gabby's float.

I grab my suitcase and head to the front door of my house. "Disneyland. Disneyland," I mumble over and over like a crazy person while angrily shaking my head. I'm looking down, lost in my own world, when my body bangs into someone.

I look up, expecting to see Trinity. I gasp. It's a man. I recognize the face, but I can't place it for a moment. It's a handsome face, but it makes my stomach turn. Then I remember. Johnny. The paparazzo. He's waiting here. I'm sure he's hoping to get a picture of Gabby when she returns from her Disneyland adventure. Maybe he'll hit the jackpot and Rose will be with her. We can all pose together. The happy blended family. It's a small world after all!

Well, Johnny the paparazzo picked a really bad day to stop by.

"Get out of here." My voice is hoarse and furious.

"Alice, wait. Can I talk to you?"

"No. I never want to talk to you. Leave me alone."

"Alice, please, hear me out."

I push him out of the way. I race up to the door. "Asshole," I say loudly before I slam the door.

"Mommy, that's a naughty word."

"Sometimes mommies can use naughty words," I say, exhaling. Then it dawns on me. "*Gabby*!"

"*Mommy*!"

I hug her tight and slather her with kisses. "What are you doing here?"

"I live here, duh."

I laugh. "Oh, Gabby. I missed you. But you didn't spend much time at Disneyland. I thought you'd at least stay for the character parade."

"What? Disneyland? Oh. I didn't go."

"What?"

Gabby shrugs her shoulders. Now I'm furious she didn't go. Rose is a typical Hollywood actress. She makes false promises for the camera and breaks my daughter's heart.

Gabby wraps her arms around me. "I said to Daddy that I didn't feel like it. So Daddy and I went to the zoo instead. But it was horrible. All the animals looked dead. They barely moved. I saw a baby gorilla, though. He was drinking from his mommy's booby. Did I do that, too?"

"Yes," I say, hugging her close and breathing in her freshly baked bread scent. "But I don't understand, Gabby, you love Disneyland."

She shrugs her shoulders again. "I didn't feel like it."

I instinctively touch her forehead. "Do you feel okay?"

"Yes," she says. "It's just that . . ."

"What?"

"Well, it's a Mommy-Gabby thing."

I squeeze her so tight I'm afraid I'll crush her. I feel just like

Ebenezer Scrooge did at the end of *A Christmas Carol* when he learns he didn't miss Christmas at all. He's been given a chance to make everything right. He says he feels as light as a feather, as happy as an angel, as merry as a schoolboy, as giddy as a drunken man.

I will honor Disneyland in my heart, and try to keep it all year.

Gabby proudly tells me that she and Trinity have picked out her clothes for school the next day. The smile on my face hurts my cheeks as I tell her she won't be going to kindergarten. She'll be playing hooky tomorrow.

"Hooky, what's that?"

"That's when you take a day off from school to have some Mommy-Gabby time."

"Yay!" Gabby claps her hands and dances.

I haven't even told her we're going to Disneyland. Maybe she senses it. But I don't think so. She's just happy to be with me. Gabby grabs my hand and we spin around and around and around, until we're dizzy and laughing like we haven't laughed in a long, long time.

I feel so wonderful. So blessed to have a daughter who understands that Disneyland is more than teacups and carousels and character parades. It is a Mommy-Gabby thing.

God bless us, every one.

3

A Dicer, A Slicer, A Peeler

I've never been one of those moms who believes in throwing over-the-top birthday parties for their children. I've always felt that kids enjoy simple pleasures more than elaborate excess. My secret credo has been (well, at least for the last six years) that a child's age should determine the number of birthday guests. If a kid turns one, one friend. Five, five friends. You get the picture.

Then why have I contradicted myself this year? I've invited the entire kindergarten class. I've hired Celia, Gabby's babysitter, to play Cinderella. She'll sing, blow bubbles, sculpt balloons, and paint faces.

I'm embarrassed to admit this, but I even rented a bouncy castle.

This has been such a rough year for Gabby, so why not? In just two months, my baby will be in first grade. So screw my credos and my mottos. I have a bouncy castle in my backyard and I'm proud!

Well, it's actually the tackiest thing I've ever seen, but it will keep the kids occupied for the two hours I've invited them.

A few weeks ago, Nancy clued me in on birthday party etiquette.

"When you send out the invites, make sure you put a time limit," she said. "You know, write from, say, noon to four or whatever."

"Noon to four! You've got to be kidding me," I said. "Four

hours of little kids running around? I can't even occupy my one child that long without the rugrats eventually taking over. No way. Two hours is the maximum."

Nancy laughed. "Okay. But two hours is nothing. They'll have lunch, open presents, eat cake, and it will be time to go."

"Exactly."

I don't know why I keep visiting Faye, but I do. I think it's just because I enjoy her company. She's funny, warm, and smart. I don't think she's at all psychic. Nothing she's told me has happened. For instance, she had mentioned that George would play a big part in my life. And now I know I'll never see him again.

"I never said that," she informed me when I visited her the other day.

"Don't backpedal on me, Faye. You did."

"Don't rework my words, Alice," Faye said, admonishingly. "I said *someone*. I never named a name."

"Well, you said it was someone I had been antagonistic with. Toward the end, George and I had an antagonistic relationship. It was him and you know it. Besides, I can't think of anyone else who would fit the bill."

Faye laughed and swatted her hand through the air. "Oh Ally, you're just not thinking hard enough."

I laughed back. "Faye, if I thought any harder, my brain would short out and explode."

"Maybe you should stop thinking. I believe that's your whole problem in life. You think too much and live too little."

Hence, the bouncy castle.

Before I left, Faye gave me a solemn expression. She clasped my hands in hers.

I chuckled. "You've got to get new material, Faye. This is getting stale."

"No jokes, Ally," Faye said, her gray eyes darting back and forth. "I just want to tell you something. You are going to go through a bit of an ordeal soon, but you will get through it. Keep telling yourself over and over that it will all work out. I promise it will."

"What? I've been going through an ordeal for the last year. What else could there be?"

"I don't know. I feel it, but I don't see it. Sorry."

It's like I'm trapped in those Ginsu knife infomercials from the seventies. Just when you think you've been shown the whole sales pitch—a set of knives that can cut through aluminum cans and radiator hoses for just eighty cents each—the booming salesman's voice tells you, "But wait, there's more! A dicer, a slicer, a peeler—at no additional cost!"

Just when I think I've survived the worst of it, I hear that voice—but wait, there's more. An affair? A separation? But wait, there's more! A divorce? An angry daughter? But wait, there's more! A mother with Alzheimer's. But wait, there's more! We'll throw in a motherfucker and a cocksucker at no additional cost! But wait, there's more. A new, unknown ordeal . . .

Every day since Faye—the psychic I don't really believe in—predicted it, I ask myself if this ordeal will come today.

Perhaps the ordeal is beginning right now, I think when I open the door for Celia. It is Gabby's birthday party, but Celia isn't dressed in her Cinderella costume. Instead, she's a mess. Her eyes are bloodshot and ringed with smeared mascara. Her hair is disheveled.

"What's wrong?" I ask.

"Bryce broke up with me. For good. He said he's bored. I'm not enough of a challenge, intellectually." She breaks down and begins sobbing. Her whole body shudders with sorrow.

I hug her. "Bryce sounds like a jerk. You deserve better. A lot better."

Celia breathes in. Her nose rattles with mucus. She wipes it with the back of a hand. "Maybe he's right. Maybe I'll take some classes in archeology or something at UCLA. I've always been fascinated with the solar system. What do you think?"

What I am really thinking is that it's only a half hour before the party starts. Celia's not in her Cinderella costume. I'm not even sure if she remembered to bring it. Plus, she looks horrible. There's about a pound of mascara on her eyelashes and it's tumbling down her face like a mudslide. Her hair is matted to her head. Her breath stinks of nicotine. She'll scare the kids away.

"Well, if that's something you're interested in, you should do it—but for you. Not for him."

She gasps and shudders.

"But . . . but . . . I love him. He's the only one for me."

I sneak a peek at my watch. Then I take a deep breath.

"If it's meant to be it will work out," I say, giving her my best Hollywood smile. "But I think the most important thing you could do for yourself right now is to forget about Bryce. Think about the joy you will be bringing Gabby and her friends. How many people can do that for others? You have a gift. Does Bryce get that that is the true definition of an intellectual? Someone who can relate to children as brilliantly as you do?"

This shit is just spewing out of my mouth. It's almost like, well, dare I say it? It's almost like Dr. Phil has invaded my brain. I have become what I mock. I brace myself, wondering if Celia will fall under Dr. Phil's spell.

Celia smiles at me and wipes away tears. I can practically hear the applause from the studio audience.

"You're right, Ally. Thanks for putting this in perspective for me."

Oh my God. The man is a genius. I will never mock him again.

"Ally, that's a slippery slope. Don't make promises you can't keep," Dr. Phil warns me.

An hour later, the party is in full swing. And I am actually relaxed as I survey the lawn. Kids munch on pizza and jump in the bouncy castle. Celia wanders the property in full Cinderella regalia, blowing bubbles. The parents sit on teak chairs, sipping wine and eating the Chinese chicken salad I ordered. I feel proud of myself for pulling this off. I search for Gabby. She's laughing as she chases after a few kids. She wears a sparkly tiara and the brand-new Ariel gown I gave her this morning.

I am supermom!

I head into the house. Trinity pushes a wheelchair out the door with my mom in it.

"I am taking him shopping for pants, if that's okay," she tells me. "All this noise is very scary to him. And his pants are all too big now."

"Sure, Trinity," I say, smiling. "But take my car. It's too far of a walk to the mall."

I help get my mother into the car. Then they leave. I'm practically whistling as I head back outside with a tray of turkey, tuna, and chicken wraps.

Little Amanda nearly knocks me over. She's crying hysterically. "I saw Cinderella smoking a cigarette in the bushes and then she said a naughty word to me."

I bend down and touch the side of her face. "Shh, it's okay, Mandy," I say. "But are you sure? I can't believe Cinderella would do such a thing."

"She did. I saw and heard her with my own two eyes." She wipes her tears with the back of her hand.

I scan the lawn for Celia. Where the hell is she?

"She was smoking. Cinderella would never ever smoke. She's not a real princess. I said no handsome prince could ever, ever love her." Mandy sniffles some more. I grab a napkin from the tray and hand it to her. She blows her nose.

"And then . . . and then," she says, gasping. "She said fuck. I know that's a bad word. I hear Mommy say it to Daddy when she's very, very mad. Cinderella would never say that, right?"

"Right," I say, shaking my head. I'm ready to kill Celia. "It must be an evil imposter."

"Where's the real Cinderella? I better tell my mommy."

Of course, this is the one time Amy decides not to have a migraine. Although I saw her clutching the sides of her head a little while ago.

"Mommy! Mommy!"

I put the wraps on a table and scour the yard for Celia. I find her huddled behind a bush by the guest house, smoking a cigarette and yelling into her cell phone. She's got raccoon eyes. Mascara stains her cheeks again.

"You know what, you're wrong, Bryce. I am smart. You're just too stupid to know it, so fuck you," she screams. "You're a fuckin' asshole."

I grab the phone from her and shut it. "Celia, what the hell are you doing? You're scaring the kids."

She bursts into tears again.

"I'm sorry, Alice. I can't do this. I can't pretend to be Cinderella when my life is so far from a fairy tale."

I sigh. "Ceel, you're an actor, so act for the afternoon. Please." I strain to sound cheerful. This makes her cry even harder.

"The truth is I'm not an actress. This is the best I can do. This is the best I'll ever do—dress up as fucking Cinderella for a bunch of bratty kids. This sucks, but it's my life. Maybe if I get really good at it, they'll promote me to Goofy at Disneyland or I could wander around Graumann's in a Darth Vadar costume or I could wear a chicken costume and twirl a sign by El Pollo Loco. I'll never be a real actress. It's hopeless."

"You don't know that yet."

"Yes, I do. I haven't gotten a callback in months. When I audition,

I can see it in their eyes. They bite their cheeks to try not to laugh. I'm a joke. Even Bryce knows it. Stupid Celia. She thinks she can act. Hahaha."

"Oh, Ceel, that's not true. You're being way too hard on yourself."

"Look at my life, Ally, please. I'm sneaking cigarettes at a kiddie party in a fucking Cinderella costume. If I weren't me, I'd make fun of me."

I laugh and put my arm around her. "Ceel, one day when you're an old lady like me, you'll look back on this time and say, I wish I had those problems. It's nothing, trust me. You're only twenty-two. You have everything in front of you. You're beautiful and fun and great with kids, when you're not cursing at them. Anyway, you've got tons of boyfriends in front of you and tons of adventures. Trust me. Don't be so hard on yourself."

"That's easy for you to say. You have everything so figured out."

I burst into laughter. "You have no idea."

"Ohhhhhhhh, ohhhhh, *ohhhhhhhhhhhhh*."

"Not today," I say.

I watch parents' heads turn skyward, their ears pricked, their mouths hanging. Celia rubs an index finger around her eyes and takes a deep breath. "What the hell is that?"

"Porn house," I tell her, pointing at the manse directly above mine. "They shoot them right in the backyard. They haven't made one in a few weeks. I was hoping they'd moved."

"Ohhh, ohhh, *ohhhhhhhhhhh*! Fuck me harder!"

I hear a collective parental gasp.

"Apparently they haven't," I say. "I can't believe this is happening today."

I watch as some parents collect their kids. It's only been an hour. We haven't even sung happy birthday to Gabby yet.

Ruth rushes over to me. "This is horrible," she says. "But don't worry. We can fix it."

"Harder! Harder! *Harder!*"

More gasps from the parents. The kids don't seem to notice. They're in their own world of bouncy castles and pizza.

"How," I say.

"Let's drown them out. If we're loud enough, we'll ruin their audio and they'll have to redo the whole thing. Let's just hope we mess up the money shot." She surveys the lawn and takes a deep breath. "We'll set your speakers up outside and blast your stereo."

I give Ruth a panicked look. "I don't have a stereo. It broke," I confess, embarrassed. In happier days, we had a cheap, old stereo that worked intermittently. Alex and I had planned to buy a new, improved sound system, but he became obsessed with finding The Best. He researched systems for months. But we never got around to purchasing anything. Then he left and music just didn't seem important to me. And after the holidays, the stereo just died.

"All I have is a boom box and it's not very loud," I say.

"Ohhhhhhh, ohhhhhh, ohhhhhhhh!"

There is going to be a mass exodus. Parents shake their heads and cover their kids' ears. A few start getting out of their seats.

"What's that sound, Mommy?" I hear a child ask.

"That's another princess stuck in a tower," Gabby informs everyone. "It happens all the time."

"I know!" Celia says. She tosses her butt, stomps on it, and bolts across the lawn. I have a feeling she's going to try to distract the group with bubbles or balloons. I don't think it will work.

"*Ohhhhhhhhhhhhhhhhhhhh.*"

Dana, a mom I just met, smiles nervously at me as she clutches her daughter Sadie's hand. "Thanks so much, Alice, but we have to get going," she says, smiling so hard it looks like she's screaming inside.

"But . . . the cake . . . Gabby," I stumble out.

"Ohhhhhhhhhhhhhhhhhh!"

"Bye-bye," she says as she gallops toward the driveway.

Gabby runs to me. Her eyes are wide. "Why are people leaving my party? Don't they like me?"

Suddenly, the loud, piercing sound of feedback fills the yard, drowning out the neighbors. Celia has set up my boom box, and attached her speakers and a microphone to it.

"Testing, testing," she says. There's more feedback, so she adjusts dials.

"Turn that thing off!" a voice from above yells.

Celia smiles. She speaks in a sing-songy voice.

"Come here, boys and girls, it's time for a Cinderella sing-along."

The mass exodus halts. Kids squirm away from their moms' tight grips and race towards Cinderella. Some mothers protest. Others shrug and smile. Some—like my new friends, Nancy, Renee, even Amy—never thought of leaving. They're still sitting and eating Chinese chicken salad. It's like they know it will all work out.

Nearly two dozen kids are huddled around Celia, who has somehow cleaned herself up a bit, although she still has traces of mascara on her cheeks and her eyes are puffy, red little slits. But she manages to smile big as she stands in front of a microphone.

"Hello, boys and girls. As you all know, I'm Cinderella and—"
"Ohhhhhhhhhhhhhhhhhhhh."

Celia looks around nervously and talks faster and louder. "Well, let me start by singing the song my fairy godmother once sang to me when I needed some help. I'm sure you all know it. If you do, sing along. If you don't, fake it."

Celia closes her eyes and inhales. Then she sings at the top of her lungs.

Salagadoola mechicka boola bibbidi-bobbidi-boo.
Put 'em together and what have you got?
Bibbidi-bobbidi-boo . . .

While she sings, Celia holds the microphone out towards the crowd and the kids scream the lyrics. Then the parents join in, shouting, clapping, and stomping their feet.

When the song ends, there's wild applause, followed by silence as the moms listen for sex sounds. Celia looks over at me. I smile at her and give her a thumbs up. She shoots me an enormous grin.

Ruth rushes over and whispers in my ear, "It worked. I took a little walk up the hill and heard them cursing at us. Then they gave up and started packing their equipment. Maybe you'll get them to move. What could kill the mood more than a bunch of kiddie voices?"

I am reminded of my night with George: "Pick up, daddy. Pick up, daddy."

Celia pulls Gabby out of the crowd.

"Here's the birthday girl. How about you tell Cinderella what your favorite song of all time is."

"Well," Gabby says, thinking. "Are you going to be angry if it's not a Cinderella song?"

Celia laughs. I laugh.

"No, of course not. Just don't let my little mice friends know. They might get mad."

"Okay," Gabby says. " 'Wish Upon A Star.' "

"Great, that's my favorite, too. Let's sing it together."

They turn to each other and Celia motions for Gabby to begin. Gabby scrunches her face and stands there, her eyes wide. I don't think she's going to go through with it. She looked panicked and paralyzed.

I'm reminded of a conversation we had this morning.

"Mommy, I really want to be an actress. Can I?"

"Sure, honey."

"No. I mean like now. I want to be in the TV set. I want to sing in front of people, too. Daddy said to ask you. I said you'd say no."

"Can I think about it?"

Gabby stomped her foot. "Thinking about it always means no."

Gabby stands there and I think, *See, Gabby, I was right, you're not ready. You're still a baby. I don't want to be some crazy stage mother anyway. Sure, it looks easy, but it isn't. It's hard to be in front of a group of people and perform. I couldn't have done it, especially at your age.*

She looks so scared and so tiny as she stands there, frozen in front of the microphone. And I wonder if I should go up and grab her and tell everyone it's time for cake. But I don't. I watch her, my heart pounding away. I try to send her my thoughts.

You can do it, Gabby. Don't be scared. Mommy's always holding your hand, even if she's not right next to you. And if you can't do it, that's okay, too.

She closes her eyes and exhales into the microphone. Her breath is so loud it sounds like a hurricane. The crowd titters. Celia gives her a nod of encouragement. Gabby smiles and opens her mouth.

" 'When you wish upon a star,' " she trills.

It's a beautiful voice. Until this moment, I'd never *really* listened to it. Sure, she sings all the time. In the car, in the yard, in her bedroom, at the table, on the toilet. But I'd never really heard her. I'd smile and tell her that her voice was beautiful, but I wasn't really, truly paying attention. I was thinking about Alex or Mom or my divorce or my career or the list of what I needed to do that day.

Gabby's voice is so pure and clear. It reminds me of the brisk air of a chilly autumn day back East, when the leaves are piling in drifts under trees and the sky is tinged with silver.

Gabby is lost in the words and the music. Celia watches, transfixed, and doesn't join in. This is Gabby's moment. Her face registers bliss. The crowd watches in awe as she makes notes dance and twirl through the cloudless sky.

My daughter is right. She is a pebble star.

The song ends. The crowd bursts into applause. I look at Gabby and she's all blurry. That's when I realize I'm crying.

"Unbelievable," Ruth whispers to me, squeezing my arm. "Should I get the cake?"

My voice chokes, so I nod my head.

My daughter takes a long, deep bow and then motions for Celia to bow, too. They laugh and keep bowing. *This is perfect,* I think.

Until I hear the sirens. They seem to be coming right here.

And I hear the voice: *But wait, there's more!*

4

Lipstick, Blush, Mascara

As I head to the front door, I assume this will have something to do with the party being too loud. I figure I'll politely explain to the officer about the porn house above and we'll all have a big laugh.

He'll say, "Well, you did what you had to do. I have a little girl myself, so I completely understand." I'll invite him to stay for a piece of birthday cake. He'll stay for a few minutes, have a piece. Then he'll leave. "I'm sorry to have bothered you, Mrs. Hirsh."

But Officer Jay Tibbits stands at the front door and doesn't mention anything about disturbing the peace. He doesn't say a word. He just glares with his arms akimbo. I feel like he's waiting for some kind of confession. So I bring up the noise.

"I'm sorry. Were we too loud?"

He squints his eyes at me, confused. Then he looks past me at the bunch of women behind me, eavesdropping. He runs his fingers over his gray-flecked moustache.

"Are you Alice Hirsh?"

I nod, smiling. He frowns and slightly shakes his head. I decide that porn maker Bob Stone must give a big donation to the Police Benevolent League.

"It's my daughter's birthday," I gulp out. "We're just having a little party here. I'm sorry if we were loud."

His face doesn't change expression. "Would you mind stepping outside? I'd like to have a word with you"—he looks past me at the women clustered behind me—"in private."

He sounds too serious. What have I done? My heart races as I quickly inventory my brain for some crime I could have committed. Nothing comes to mind. I am pretty much a law-abiding citizen. Sure, I make illegal U-turns and I still don't really understand the difference between solid and dotted yellow lines. But nothing that would warrant a cop coming to my door.

He marches towards his squad car and I follow. The red siren light is still whirring. L.A. cops are the least subtle human beings on the planet.

"Do you know a Mary Fitzgerald and a Trinity Mendoza?" He frowns as he speaks.

I feel like I'm going to faint. "What? Are they okay? Did something happen to them?"

He flashes a patronizing grin. "So you are acquainted with these individuals?"

"That's . . . that's my mother. Trinity takes care of her. What happened to them?"

My heart palpitates. *They were in a car accident and died,* I think. It's my fault for so readily handing over my keys to Trinity. She's run errands alone in my car before, but I've never actually seen her drive. Maybe she doesn't have a license. I was busy obsessing over jumpy castles, face painting, and turkey wraps. I allowed my mother to be driven by an unlicensed terror behind the wheel.

The ordeal! This is the ordeal.

Officer Jay manages to curl his lips into a snarl. "Nothing happened to them." He speaks evenly, his mouth barely opens.

"Oh my God, thank God," I say, closing my eyes and sighing. My body relaxes. "I thought they were in some horrible car accident or something. Was it just a fender bender?"

Officer Jay shuffles his feet and coughs. He's getting bored and annoyed with me.

"No, Mrs. Hirsh. It wasn't a fender bender," he says, slowly and deliberately. He pauses. Then he removes his aviator sunglasses and narrows his eyes at me. He pauses and licks his lips. "Your mother and her friend were apprehended for shoplifting."

"What?"

He studies me. I feel as if he's trying to determine whether or not I'm an accomplice.

Officer Jay's eyes dart back and forth as he explains to me that Trinity and my mother were spotted by a store manager hiding jewelry and clothing in the back of my mother's wheelchair. According to Officer Jay, my mother would pick something off a counter and put it in her wheelchair or in a pocket, and Trinity would readjust my mother's wheelchair while stuffing merchandise underneath my mother's butt or legs.

"Are you sure of this," I say. "I can't imagine Trinity doing something like this."

He gives a weird smirk and an obnoxious chuckle. "So, Mrs. Hirsh, does that mean you can imagine your mother doing this?"

I huff. "Officer, my mother has Alzheimer's. She doesn't know what she's doing. But I can't imagine Trinity would . . ."

"Mrs. Hirsh, I checked your mother's wheelchair. It was filled with merchandise. Lipstick, blush, mascara, and a pair of stockings."

All the things my mother used to buy for herself when she could, I think. I remember as a child, she was always buying the latest lipstick shade and new blush for a night out with Dad.

Officer Jay continues to study me. "My question to you is, has Ms. Mendoza ever done this before?"

"Never."

Someone is tugging at my leg. It's Gabby. She nods her head at me. I shoot her a "be quiet" glare.

"Are you certain? Has she ever come home with expensive gifts for you? For your family?"

"Never," I say quickly and with certainty, although as soon as the words leave my mouth, I flash on the sterling silver bracelet Trinity gave me for Christmas. It dangles from my wrist right now.

"Mommy, what about—"Gabby says.

"Shh, honey. Not now," I scold.

"But I was just going to tell you—"

"Gabby!"

Officer Jay bends down, smiles, and looks Gabby in the eye. "So, is this the birthday girl? What are you, sweet sixteen today?" He winks. She giggles. God, is she easy.

"No. I'm only six."

"Six. No! That can't be. You have to be at least seven."

She giggles some more. "No. Six. I swear."

"Wow! I thought you were much, much older. You're such a big girl! Well, birthday girl, what did you want to tell us about Trinity?"

"My mommy might get mad at me. I don't think she wants me to talk."

Officer Jay pats her head. "Of course she won't get mad at you, right, Mommy?" He looks up at me with a big grin on his face. "Your mommy looks like someone who always wants you to tell the truth."

"Sometimes she does and sometimes she doesn't," my little traitor replies.

Officer Jay nods encouragingly.

"Well . . . There's this Claire lady who's friends with my mom. She gave me a Snow White gown for my birthday and I don't like

Snow White because she eats the apple when everyone tells her not to—du-uh. Mommy said to tell her I like the dress. So I did. But I will never ever wear it!"

Officer Jay smiles. "Well, that makes sense. You don't want to hurt this Claire lady's feelings. I think you made the right decision there." He smiles hard at her as if she's the cutest thing he's ever seen. "So what about your friend, Trinity?"

"Well, sometimes she brings home these presents for me when she's out shopping. Like once she brought me clothes for my Barbies and a magic wand and a crown and lots and lots of candy. Is that okay? Did I do something wrong?" She looks at Officer Jay like she's going to cry. "Am I going to jail?"

He pats her head and smiles at her. "No, of course not, sweetie."

Then he stands up and looks at me. "You're sure Ms. Mendoza hasn't exhibited this behavior before today?" He bites his cheek, like he already doesn't believe me.

Hilda. I remember Hilda telling me she fired Trinity for shoplifting, but I didn't really listen. After all, Hilda kicked out my senile mom for cursing.

"No," I say. But I wonder if this cop will track down Hilda and she'll seek revenge by saying she warned me. I'll probably be sent to jail for perjury or something.

Trinity and my mom are sitting in the back of the squad car as if they're criminals. Only in Los Angeles, where Paris Hilton does time yet O. J. Simpson gets away with murder! I want to scream at Officer Jay for this, but I know if I do, my mother will somehow be locked in the county jail getting a full-body cavity search. So I just shake my head, bite my tongue, and try not to cry.

Officer Jay tells me he's just giving them a warning, but next time the store owners will press charges. He says he's seen this before—caregivers taking advantage of their wards. "It's an old con game with these foreigners," he stage-whispers. "I assume you'll be firing her." I nod my head. I feel like it's what I'm supposed to say. Trinity watches me. She looks so hurt and betrayed. She puts her head down.

Trinity and I hoist my mother out of the backseat while Officer Jay watches, shaking his head. "That's why I make sure I take my vitamins every day," he says.

I smile warmly as if he's a dear friend. "Take all the vitamins you want. It's not going to keep Alzheimer's away."

Inside the house, Trinity keeps her head down.

"Trinity, what were you thinking?"

"I am so sorry, missus," she says, shaking her head. "I am so, so sorry."

She shuffles off, still staring at the floor. I run to my bedroom and rummage through my jewelry box. Nothing seems to be missing.

I'd forgotten about the party. Ruth, Nancy, Renee, and Amy are cleaning up while their kids play in the backyard with Celia. I realize that Judy never showed. She had told me she wouldn't miss Gabby's party for the world. But lately she hasn't been keeping her promises, or returning my calls and e-mails, for that matter. I made excuses for a while, but I know what it is. Ever since I've quit, she's distanced herself. I had miscategorized Judy. She wasn't a friend. She was just an office friend. She doesn't need me anymore.

When I first met Judy we had instantly clicked. She was hip and urbane with a wicked sense of humor—the perfect friend, I thought. Now I look at this group with its porn star past, fake boobs, frumpy Disney clothes, migraines—not the friends I'd have ever picked, yet they chose me and they're perfect. I watch them, cleaning up my mess, chatting and laughing.

"You guys didn't have to stay. Thanks so much," I say.

"Don't thank us," Nancy says, smiling. "We're still waiting on the cake."

Nancy and I light the cake and head outside, singing happy birthday to Gabby. She makes a wish and blows out the candles. I ask what she wished for, but she won't tell me.

As we eat the vanilla cake with chocolate frosting, I see Trinity exit the guest house with her suitcase.

"It's probably for the best," Amy says.

"But she's such a sweetie," Ruth says.

"Ruth, you've got to be kidding me, the woman's a criminal."

"She's great with my mom," I say. "How many people do you know who can change a grown woman's diaper?

"She gets me really cool presents," Gabby adds.

"Oh, I bet," Amy says, turning to me. "Alice, how do you know she hasn't been stealing from you?"

I shrug. "I don't."

"You could so easily find someone else. People like her are all over the place. They're a dime a dozen," Amy says. "They'll work for next to nothing. I could have my housekeeper call some of her friends."

I think of the night months ago when Trinity rushed over and changed my mother's diaper and comforted me. I felt like she was a miracle.

I run after Trinity.

"Trinity, what are you doing?"

She keeps walking.

"I cannot stay here after what I did to you and your family. I am so ashamed."

I grab her wrist. "Wait, Trinity. Don't go yet."

"I am so ashamed."

Trinity and I sit alone in the kitchen. I pour the Filipino Winona Ryder some chamomile tea.

"People like your mother when they have that disease of the brain, they put things in their hands. They cannot help it," she says, her eyes watery. "They are always grabbing. Most of the time, I don't even see it until I am home. They have jewelry in their pockets or next to them in wheelchair. Most of it is junk. Things a store would never miss. And no one notices. No one looks at old people. Most people are afraid of them. No one says anything, because they don't want to see them. They don't see me either. I am just a Filipino lady pushing around old people."

She smiles and shakes her head, but she still won't look at me.

"Then, I see your mommy doing it at store and I get so scared. Instead of putting it back, I hid it in wheelchair. I didn't want any trouble. I don't want to go back to Manila. But I don't take things. I never steal in my life. I just don't put things back."

If this were Gabby, I'd tell her it was still stealing. I think about the sterling silver bracelet dangling from the chain. I run my fingers over it. Is Trinity lying to me? Did she steal this bracelet? The presents for Gabby?

"Trinity, if you needed money or things, you could have asked."

"I swear, missus, I never take anything for me. I just don't put back because it scares me to make attention for your mommy. Because I have to bend over and go through pockets and sometimes he screams when I take things away. And then, suddenly, everybody notices an old person. But I leave all the things at the church for the poor—to make sure God doesn't punish me. Store owners don't notice, but God does. God sees everything. The good and the bad."

I sigh. "Well, these shop owners noticed. They treated my mom like a criminal."

"I'm so sorry, missus. You are like family to me. Your mommy is my mommy, too. I love him like I love my own mother in Manila."

What do I do? Is she telling me the truth? If I keep her, can I ever really trust her? And what kind of message am I giving Gabby? That it's okay to steal?

But if I let her go, will I ever find someone else to change Mom's diaper? To have the patience to feed her for hours and hours just to get a few calories down her throat? Will Mom even let someone else brush her teeth? Caregivers may be a dime a dozen, but there's no one like Trinity. She loves my mom.

Unconsciously, I run my fingers along the bracelet again.

"I buy that for you with my own money," she says. "I promise, missus. I wanted to make you happy. You so sad at Christmas. It was the money for a present for my mommy, but you seemed to need something more. I knew my mommy would understand."

I stare at her. And crazy as it may sound, I believe her. She sees that I believe her and she smiles.

"Oh, Alice, you are like a daughter to me," she says. I don't think she's ever called me by my name before.

I laugh. "Trinity, we are practically the same age."

She shakes her head. "Age doesn't matter." She reaches out her hand to me and holds my face. "You are like a daughter."

I can barely speak. "Thank you."

5

Someday My Prince Will Come

Gabby and I sit at the coffee shop. We order ice cream sundaes with extra mounds of whipped cream. We are celebrating her first commercial, although the celebration has lost its luster after Alex/Xander dropped her off.

When Gabby arrived home, she was giddy and bubbly. But Alex/Xander's face registered pure fury. He smiled hard at Gabby. With fulsome cheerfulness he said, "You go play. Let me and Mommy talk for a minute."

I imagined that he'd finally been dumped by Rose and was extra cranky.

I cleared my throat and spoke carefully. "How'd it go?"

"Oh, you know how it went." He practically spit the words out.

This Xander guy was completely insane. Maybe Alex had always been crazy, but I was too close to notice.

I coughed out a laugh. "Alex, how would I know how a commercial shoot went when I wasn't even there?" I spoke as if he was a small child I was trying to amuse.

"It was an embarrassment," he barked out.

I nervously scanned the room to make sure Gabby wasn't eavesdropping. I couldn't believe he was saying this about his daughter.

"Well, maybe it just isn't her thing," I said.

Alex guffawed like a crazy man. "You made sure of that, didn't you? The poor kid begged and begged for this. Rose pulled some strings with the director. And then, you. You go and sabotage the whole thing."

I opened my mouth and gagged. Then I said, "What the hell are you talking about, Alex?"

"Don't act all innocent with me," he said. "You know exactly what you did. And you may think you're hurting me, but you're just hurting Gabby."

I stared at him in complete disbelief. "What?"

Alex's eyes bulged. They looked like they'd pop out of their sockets and rip through me like bullets.

"It's called fiber, Ally. Give her some. She hasn't gone to the bathroom in at least a week. And she told me she had rice with dinner last night. What were you thinking?"

Because Gabby refuses to poop, we've always tried to steer her clear from binding foods like bananas, pasta, rice, cheese, bread. But last night, Nancy and I took the kids out for Chinese food. We had been engrossed in a conversation about how to make Nancy's bar more profitable. I had come up with a plan, including a mom's night out to bring in new business for them. I also created a publicity campaign. I was so wrapped up in my ideas that I hadn't noticed Gabby wolfing down mounds and mounds of rice.

"It's not like I let her eat rice on purpose," I said.

Alex cackled. "Nothing with you is ever an accident, Ally, you know that? You never take responsibility for anything. Well, let that poor girl's broken heart be on your conscience, not mine."

"She looked pretty happy to me."

Alex angrily shook his head. "You know what happened? She was totally unfocused. Then instead of saying her lines, she said, 'The poo-poo's coming, the poo-poo's coming.' She ran off the set. It was a disaster."

Oh God, I think. *Poor Gabby. My poor baby.*

"The director knows, well, me, so he tried to be a good sport about it. But do you have any idea how pissed he must be? He wasted the entire day. And I can't even begin to imagine how much money was spent."

"Alex, this is not my fault."

He glared at me. "This is something she wanted that you were totally opposed to. And guess who won, as usual?"

My heart pounded and my head throbbed. "What the hell are you talking about? I know this is what she wanted. If I was totally opposed to it, I wouldn't have let her do it at all."

"Well, you let her do it, didn't you? You just made sure she screwed up so you'd win in the end. This is Ally's typical passive-aggressiveness. Isn't it?"

Gabby skipped into the room, dressed as Cinderella. She was still beaming. She was as oblivious to our anger as she was to the disaster of the shoot.

"Are you still talking about me? Did Daddy tell you how funny I was? I made everyone laugh really, really hard."

Alex coughed as if trying to regurgitate his anger. "Well, give Daddy a big hug. I've gotta get going, okay?"

Alex's voice shifted from pure fury to pure love. How does he do that? Gabby jumped into his arms and squeezed him. She turned to me. I braced myself, figuring she was about to plead for him to stay.

"Remember, Mommy. You said you'd take me out for ice cream to celebrate."

So we are here, although my head is still back at the house, reliving the scene with Alex. Ever since Gabby stopped pooping years and

years ago, Alex has always silently blamed me. He believes I did something egregious during potty training. And he believed I never gave
her enough fiber. He never said this aloud until today, but I know.

Debbie, our usual waitress, comes over, smiling.

"How about Gabby comes in the kitchen and helps make her own
sundae today? That way she can make sure she gets enough cherries."

Gabby nearly leaps out of her seat. "Can I?"

"Sure."

It feels good to be alone—I don't have to fake merriment for a
few minutes. I take a deep breath and survey the walls for the latest
artwork, but the walls are barren. I wonder why. I close my eyes and
try not to think about Alex.

Gabby returns holding a tray with two sundaes. She beams.

"Guess which one I made?"

I look at them. One is a small sundae with the requisite cherry
and a scoop of whipped cream. The other looks like it will topple
over at any moment. There's a mountain of whipped cream that's
weighed down by at least a dozen cherries. Chocolate syrup bubbles
out of the sides of the bowl.

"Wow!" I say. "That looks delicious."

She sits down and we dig in. "And guess what else, Mommy?"

"What," I say. I can't remember the last time I had ice cream. It's
more delicious than I remember. I savor each spoonful, holding it
on my tongue until it gets warm and melts.

Gabby shovels in a few spoonfuls before she speaks. "The handsome prince is here."

"That's nice," I say, smiling. "Is it Prince Phillip or Prince Charming?"

She gulps another spoonful. Chocolate syrup drips down her face
and onto her dress.

She shakes her head. "No, Mommy. Really. It's the prince who
rescued us."

"Oh, that's nice. What kind of spell were we rescued from?"

Gabby rolls her eyes at me. "You don't believe me. But it's true. It's a real prince. The prince who rescued me and you. I'm going to go get him."

Gabby stands. Her entire dress is dripping with ice cream and chocolate syrup. I make a mental note to douse it with Shout! when we get home.

"Gabby, sit down. Your sundae will melt."

She ignores me. "I'll be right back."

She disappears into the kitchen. I wonder if I should stop her. Maybe she's being a nuisance back there. But I have no energy, so I lap up the rest of my sundae. When I'm done, I sneak a spoonful of Gabby's.

"Tsk, tsk," a male voice says as I scramble to wipe the ice cream off my face. "What will you give me to keep this infraction from your daughter?"

I turn my head towards the voice. Deep-set blue eyes with crinkles in the corners. Light brown hair.

It's him again. Johnny, the paparazzo. The man who pretended not to sell the pictures of me to all the tabloids. What does he want this time?

I open my mouth.

"Before you yell at me, remember, I have ammunition. I saw you steal food from your own daughter. She doesn't look like someone you wanna mess with."

He smiles. He's one of those good-looking guys who believes he can charm you no matter what he's done. I've never fallen for those types. Actually, I can't stand those types.

"So how much did my photos go for," I ask as my chest tightens.

He smiles and shakes his head. "Millions. I'm living in a mansion in Malibu now, thanks to you."

"Well, I'm glad my tragedy could bring you so much happiness."

He stares hard at me. I smile back, glad to have put him in his place. He shakes his head.

"First of all, I didn't sell any of those photos to any tabloids. I told you I wouldn't and I kept my word. And second of all, that was hardly a tragedy. It was an unfortunate event. It was a sad event. But a tragedy?" He stares at me and smirks. "As long as everyone's still alive and kicking, it ain't a tragedy."

I roll my eyes. "A photographer and a philosopher."

He flashes me another fluorescent, white-toothed grin. "I'm sorry you didn't make it to my opening."

I squint in confusion. "Opening?"

"My gallery opening."

I study him. I have no idea what he's talking about. He leans in closer. I can smell the breath mint he's sucking on.

"I'm glad you liked my photograph, though. It was one of my favorites." He slaps a manila envelop on the table. "I thought you might like this one, too. It's my way of saying, thanks."

It hits me. Johnny is J.D. Johnny is the creator of "Baby, Five Minutes Old" and all those other photos that I love.

My face must have changed expressions from hostile to friendly because the next moment, Johnny is sliding into the booth on the other side of the table. He takes a napkin and wipes up some of Gabby's mess.

I am too shocked to open the envelope. I just stare at him trying to figure out who he is. Good or evil? Sleazy or decent? What I am thinking? I know already—evil and sleazy!

"Open it up," he says.

Slowly I pull the photograph out of the envelope. I stare at my daughter in black and white. She is dressed in her Cinderella gown. A red feathery boa is wrapped around her neck. A magic wand is in her right hand. Her mouth is wide open in song. It's from that day.

The worst day of my life. But this evil, sleazy paparazzo has some-how managed to capture beauty.

I can't speak. I can't even catch my breath. Johnny stares at me with his soul-piercing blue eyes. He's waiting for me to say some-thing, but I don't know what to say. I'm completely flustered.

"What do you want," I whisper, my voice cracking.

He squints his eyes as if he doesn't understand.

"The story's so old now. No one cares about it anymore," I say.

Johnny smiles and flexes his thick eyebrows, like he's trying to tell me something. Could he be interested in me *that way*? He's got to be kidding me, right? He's seen me at my worst, what could he possibly want from me?

"I'm almost forty. I'm divorced. I have a child. Alzheimer's runs in my family. Aren't I a great catch?" I realize I'm saying this aloud. I hadn't meant to. I am completely embarrassed. I have assumed he's interested in me. That's the way it worked in the old days. If a guy paid attention to me, it was because he wanted to do me. But maybe that's not the case anymore. After all, I'm old. I'm divorced. I have a child. Alzheimer's runs in my family. My face burns and I can tell it's turning crimson. This makes me even more embarrassed because I know he knows I'm embarrassed.

"Aren't you full of yourself?" Johnny grins wide. "I just wanted to thank you."

"For what? That house in Malibu?"

"Something like that—for helping me reinvent myself."

Reinvent? Alex to Xander. Johnny to J.D.

"Everyone is reinventing themselves these days, it seems," I say.

"I hated what I did for a long, long time. But that day I shot pic-tures of you, and you confronted me, I knew I had enough of it all. I knew if I stayed in the game for another minute . . . Well, it was never for me."

"Glad I could help you," I say.

He winces at the sarcasm in my voice. I didn't mean it, but I guess it's just a natural defense mechanism. I flash on Faye telling me that I judge people too quickly. But come on, Faye, this is different.

"My sundae's all gone. Who ate my sundae?" Gabby suddenly is back, arms akimbo. She barks at me.

"It's not gone. It's just melted," I say cheerfully, thankful for the interruption. "That's what happens when you leave ice cream alone for a long time. But how about you ask Debbie for another scoop?"

Gabby looks at me like she's not quite sure if I'm joking or not.

"Who are you supposed to be," she asks. "Where's my mother?"

I laugh. Johnny laughs.

"I'm still your mother."

"No. My mother would never let me have more ice cream. My mother's mean about stuff like that." She eyes Johnny. "Maybe the prince is making you nicer. See, Mommy. Maybe you were under an evil spell."

My face reddens again. I giggle. I can't remember the last time I've giggled. Does that mean I like Johnny? Or J.D.? No, I'm not going to fall for someone who's reinventing himself.

He gets out of the booth holding Gabby's ice cream sundae.

"I'll get you that scoop before your mom changes her mind," he whispers conspiratorially to Gabby. He winks and turns towards the kitchen.

I laugh at the chocolate syrup stain on his butt.

Why am I even looking at his butt?

6

Little Angels

Trinity tells me that Mom won't eat.

The last few weeks have been a battle for Trinity and me to get food into my mother. Her brain has forgotten how to swallow. This is the final stage of that long good-bye, I know. But still, I struggle with the spoon. I jam food into my mother's mouth until she practically gags. Sweat drips down my face and I shake with frustration. My heart beats wildly.

Please don't die yet, Mommy, I silently beg. Even though she hasn't really been here in years, I'm not ready to let her go. I want Mom to be there for me. I want to hear her voice, whispering in my ear, calling me her little angel one last time.

"There, there, my little angel, everything will be all right."

"Come on, Trinity, you can do it. I know you can. You're magic when it comes to feeding Mom."

She shakes her head sadly. "I've seen this many, many times before, missus. He is trying to go. Maybe you should tell him it is okay."

I nod my head, but I'm thinking, *No, it's not okay to go.*

I called Mom's doctor to tell him that my mother has stopped eating. He listed the options. There weren't many. I could either hospitalize her so he could insert a feeding tube into her stomach, or I could leave her here and do nothing.

I thought and thought and thought. Neither option sounds humane to me. So I create a third choice. I keep her home and try to force-feed her. I can't imagine subjecting her to the pain of a feeding tube. But I can't just let her go without doing anything. Part of me believes if I try hard enough, I can get her to eat. If I try hard enough, I can cure her of Alzheimer's.

I saw Faye again today. Why? I'm not sure. She's become more of a therapist than a psychic. Still, I hold out hope that one day she'll predict something wonderful that I won't really believe anyway.

I didn't ask her about my mother. Instead, I focused on the more frivolous aspects of my life.

"Is it the paparazzi guy?" I asked her, realizing that was why I was there. Johnny had become my distraction from Alzheimer's, even though I've had nothing to do with him since the night at the coffee shop. I wanted to find out from Faye if he was the one she was telling me about, the one I had mistaken for George. The one I shouldn't shut out of my life, despite the antagonism.

"What are you talking about?" Faye cocked her head and grinned. I wondered if she knew more than she ever let on. But I imagine that is what she wants you to believe.

"Oh, never mind."

Faye laughed. "Oh, I forgot. You think I'll take what you say and throw it back at you as if it's some sort of revelation."

"Yeah, how did you . . . ?"

Faye laughed again and threw her arms in the air. "I'm psychic, remember? But you don't really believe anyway, although you keep coming back for some bizarre reason." She crinkled her eyes at me. "Why is it that you keep coming back, Ally?"

"You've given me really good advice. You were right when you said I judged people too fast and don't give them a chance. Anyway, I've become friends with people I wouldn't have in the past."

"The woman who wears Winnie the Pooh shirts. How evolved of you," Faye said, oozing sarcasm.

"For your information, I've also become good friends with a former porn star. How's that? When I met her, I heard your voice in my head, telling me to give her a chance. And now that I know her, I really respect her," I said. Then I struggled to casually add, "And then there's this photographer guy. I hated him, but I'm wondering if I should give him a chance, too. Not that he's asking for a chance. I'm not sure if he's asking for anything. Maybe he's just a guy who felt sorry for me. He's completely baffled me. I mean, why the hell hasn't he called?"

I realized that I was thinking out loud.

"I've never heard you so talkative, Ally."

"Maybe because I've stopped judging you. I don't think of you as a psychic anymore."

"You never thought I was a psychic," Faye said.

"Well, anyway, I think of you as a friend," I said. I felt myself blush.

Faye smiled. "Don't do that. I won't be able to charge you anymore."

I told her about my idea for Nancy's bar. I'm organizing a weekly moms' night out to drum up new business for the place. I've written up press releases and gotten some mentions about it in the local papers. There will be a $10 cover charge. For an additional fee, women can get private consultations with Ruth for love or sex advice. There also will be a manicurist and a chick flick in the back room—although any movies starring Rose Maris are banned. I asked Faye if she'd like to work as a psychic there.

"Of course, you'd take a cut of the profits," I added.

"I have a better idea," she said, smiling. "How about I do my stand-up routine?"

"Deal." I wondered if she was funny on stage.

"Now, what is all this sadness I see around your porn star friend?"

I smirked and swatted my hand in the air, thinking Faye must have assumed I was an idiot. Aren't porn stars always surrounded by sadness?

"Oh, Alice. I'm not talking about the old daddy-was-abusive sadness, but something relatively new is bothering her and it's bothering you, too."

Okay, I think. *Not bad, Faye. Not bad.*

"Sometimes it's hard for me to believe the choices she's made. It seems they'll haunt her for the rest of her life. I just wish I could help her as much as she's helped me."

Faye clapped her hands together and sighed. "Yes. I felt that. I could see you reaching out to her. I could feel you thinking that you failed in some way."

I told Faye how Ruth has a young son and how she doesn't want Connor or his friends to stumble on her movies when he gets older. I explained how Ruth has been trying to buy back every video and DVD she stars in, but how it's impossible because the porn man up the street keeps cranking out more.

"And what is this porn man's name," she asked. "Do I see a B and an S? B.S.?"

"Oh my God," I said excitedly, suddenly believing for the first time that Faye was psychic. "Yes! Bob! Bob Stone."

She nodded and smiled as if she'd had a vision.

"Tell me more. Tell me more. What do you see?" I practically was panting.

Faye chuckled. "I thought you didn't believe in such things."

"Well, maybe I do . . . So what do you see?"

"Nothing."

"Nothing?" I felt deflated. "Nothing? Why do you look like you have the answer?"

She smiled cryptically. "Maybe I do. Bob Stone comes here once a week."

"He does?"

"Yes. He only shoots his movies on the days I deem auspicious. He only hires actors that I approve. And he makes me do readings with everyone he works with." Her eyes bore into me. "He, unlike you, believes in my powers. So maybe I could help you, Ally."

I nodded my head, unsure of what she could possibly do.

I take the spoon from Trinity so Trinity can run some errands. Then I load the spoon up with mashed potatoes and try to feed Mom. I take a deep breath. Even in her Alzheimer's fog, Mom seems to sense my frustration. But she doesn't help me. She clamps her mouth shut. I struggle to pry it open the way Trinity has taught me, but it won't work. She wants to die. Who wants to live like this? But I can't accept it. I am selfishly angry with her for refusing to accommodate me, for wanting to leave. I grip the spoon so tight my hand cramps.

"Mom, come on, open up. Don't do this," I say, my voice quivering.

She violently shakes her head and moans like a sick animal. She's telling me to go away. It dawns on me that she's stopped speaking all together. When did that happen? Even the motherfuckers and cocksuckers have disappeared. I'm relieved about that. If she could speak, I feel she'd be calling me one or the other right now.

She narrows her eyes at me and growls. She's furious with me. "Leave me alone," she seems to be saying.

Trinity and I couldn't get anything into her tonight or this morning. Not even vanilla ice cream. She only drank a few sips of water and she spit most of it up. Maybe all of it. At this rate, she will die any day. I can't do this. I can't watch my mother die. Do I call an ambulance and rush her to the hospital? I'll tell them no feeding tube, but at least they can put an IV in her arm for a few days.

But she would hate being in a hospital. When Dad was sick, she turned to me and said, "Never let me die in a hospital." I laughed and shrugged it off. Mom would never leave me. She seemed so invincible then. She'd always be around to say, "There, there, angel, everything will be all right."

I throw the spoon on the table and sob. Every time I get a grip on my sorrow, another reason to cry emerges. I cry for my mother. I cry because I imagine she must be so scared. I cry because she will be gone soon. I cry for my motherless self. I cry because I married Alex and believed that he'd be here for me at times like this—my head on his shoulder, his hand on my back. I cry because I've never felt so alone in my life. I cry because I have no one to console me. Not my mother. Not my father. Not my husband. It's just me. Alone.

I rest my head on the table and collapse into these heavy, desperate sobs I didn't even know I was capable of. I haven't cried this hard in my life. I'm crying so hard because I can't believe how many reasons I have to be crying.

And then I feel it. A strong hand on my back. I don't open my eyes. Mom, I think. There is still part of her that understands.

"Shh," the voice says. "Shh."

I keep my eyes closed while the hand massages my back. I can feel my mother's love, just like when I was a little girl. She is soothing me, just like she always did. This is why it is so hard to let go, even now. I can't imagine life without my mother being there for me, to soothe me. I begin to cry all over again.

"Shh," the voice says again. "Shhh, Mommy."

Mommy?

I slowly open my eyes and look into Gabby's sweet face.

She speaks to me using the words I've used so often to console her; the words my mother once used to console me.

"There, there, my little angel, everything will be all right."

7

Moms' Night Out

The Giggling Gull is packed with what appears to be every mom in the Valley. They are an eclectic group: career women still in their work clothes; overexcited stay-at-home moms a little too dressed up for a dive bar; moms in sweats and ponytails who look like they bolted the minute they were sprung from kiddie jail. There are moms who look like they haven't left the house in years. Moms who look like they haven't talked to adults in decades. Moms who look desperate to make friends. Moms who look overwhelmed. And moms who look like they just got off a photo shoot, or a porn shoot, for that matter. There is plenty of silicon. Plenty of Restylane. Plenty of Botox. And plenty of booze.

Renee and Amy pass out appetizers of chicken sate, tomato, basil and mozzarella, and stuffed mushrooms. Renee whispers in my ear. "Amy's been complaining about another headache. I think she'll be splitting on us any minute."

Many of the women are eagerly awaiting Ruth's arrival. There's a long list of people who've signed up for consultations with her. We decided to bill her as a relationship expert. I realized that everyone in the world is having sex except me. But Ruth is nowhere to be found, which has me slightly worried. Ruth is always punctual.

Celia, my babysitter, is a bartender. She works alongside Nancy, who told me she has a knack for whipping up cocktails with flair. She looks happier than I've ever seen her.

"You should have seen the place the other night," Nancy says. "It was bursting with single guys trying to get a peak at Ceel in her spandex. I think she collected quite a lot of phone numbers. She's having a blast."

"Guess I lost a babysitter."

"Sorry about that," Nancy says as she hands me a frothy concoction. "Margarita."

I smile and take a sip. "Delicious." I survey the bar. "Look at this place. You're doing great."

"Thanks to you. This was a brilliant idea, Ally. And you promoted the hell out of it. We framed the blurb that ran in the *L.A. Times.*"

She points to the spot behind the bar by the cash register. I'd called up a contact at the Valley section of the *L.A. Times* and there it is:

MOMMY BEEREST: The Giggling Gull will host the first of what promises to be weekly moms only nights this evening, featuring food, drink, a manicurist, a psychic comic, and a screening of Four Weddings and a Funeral *in the back room.*

"You deserve a crowd. It's a great bar," I say.

It is. Nancy and her husband Mark grew up along the coast of Maine and moved here so Mark could pursue his acting career. When it didn't work out, they both took jobs for one company or another, but hated working for other people. They imagined one day moving back to Bar Harbor to open a rustic bar right near the beach. They'd call it The Giggling Gull. But they decided they couldn't leave their friends, change their kids' schools, and most importantly, cope with the harsh Maine winters. Instead, they brought the Maine coast to a San Fernando Valley strip mall. With its worn wooden tables, sawdusty floor, and lobster traps and buoys dangling from the ceiling, the bar resembles many of the places along the eastern coast. You can practically smell the salt water and hear the crashing waves.

Someone gently taps my shoulder. I turn around. It's Ruth. She looks like she's been crying.

"What's wrong? Are you okay?"

She wipes her eyes with the tip of her index finger, nods her head and smiles wide. "I'm better than okay. I'm wonderful. Thank you. Thank you. Thank you." She hugs me hard and twirls me around.

I giggle. "Ruth, what are you talking about? What's going on?"

"Well, I had a visitor today. Guess who it was?"

I shrug my shoulders. "I have no idea."

She looks like she's about to burst. "Bob Stone! And he brought me a present—all the master copies of my movies. Every single one of them. It's like he was a different person. He apologized for being such a prick. He actually said he'd help me any way he could to make sure my little boy never has to see any of my movies. He's having his staff call all their retailers and contacts to retrieve every DVD and video out there. He's taking my images off the Internet, too. He's a changed man. It's like he saw God or something."

She eyes me. "Somehow I feel you had something to do with it. You're like my angel."

I laugh. "Me? An angel?"

My eyes land on Faye, standing alone nursing a cranberry cocktail. She waves at me. I know she's little, but out of her element, she looks downright microscopic. She's dressed in white linen pants with flared legs and a long button-down white linen shirt, which I'm sure she must have purchased in the children's department some-where.

"Excuse me," I say to Ruth. I head to Faye.

"Okay. 'Fess up, Faye."

"What?" She widens her eyes and puts her hands on her chest. *Who me?*

"So, how did you do it?" It feels strange looking down into her eyes. I feel like she should tower over me.

She bites her cheeks. "Excuse me?"

"How did you get B.S. to return the movies?"

She arches her brows.

"What did you do, Faye?"

"Are you suggesting I discuss my clients with you, Alice? That would be highly unethical."

"Faye . . ."

She clears her throat. "Let's just say I predicted a bleak demise for him if he didn't return those master copies. I had a vision. It may have involved dismemberment."

I burst out laughing. "Faye, you devil."

"Maybe it wasn't too far of a stretch. You aren't someone I'd want to mess with, Alice."

I wrap my arms around her. "Oh, Faye. Thank you for whatever you did," I say. "You changed that woman's life. I've never seen her look so happy. She's beaming. I can't thank you enough. Thank you, thank you, thank you."

Faye squints her eyes and points a finger at my chest. "It's you, Alice. You are blessed. And I'm not talking as a psychic, but as an ob-server. I've been watching you tonight. A person who has so many people grateful to her is truly, truly blessed."

I give her a confused look.

She gives me a stern look. "Don't be so hard on yourself, Alice. Appreciate yourself more."

My eyes tear. "Thanks," I choke out.

"By the way, I don't think I'm going to perform tonight. I have a premonition that I'll bomb," Faye says.

"No you won't," I say.

She puts her hands on my shoulders. I instinctively look up. Then I shift my eyes downward.

"Alice, I have to go. I'm seeing too much for one psychic to handle. There's a lot of drama in the Valley. You have no idea. Your problems seem pretty mild compared to some of the visions I'm having right now."

I nod. We hug. Then she holds my shoulders and stares at me.

"Now, put all the past sadness behind you."

"I am," I say, smiling too widely.

She appears to be lost in thought for a few seconds. "Yes and no," she finally says. "You are still letting the stuff from the past control who you are. Are you really completely living in the present?" She puts her hand on my hand. "Call that photographer guy with the cute bottom."

"But . . ."

"But nothing. Tell him you want to see his latest photographs. Meet him for coffee and ask to look at his portfolio. Anything."

"Why? Do you see something I don't?"

She squints. I lean in. She shakes her head.

"What I see is someone who is not making any effort. And without an effort, there's no future to predict. You don't have to fall in love. Have a fling, a one-night stand, a quickie in the back of your car. And if he does turn out to be sleazy, well, the sleazy ones are usually great in the sack."

I laugh. "Faye!"

She smiles and then turns solemn. "Just make an effort. He already did. Maybe that's what he's waiting for."

"Maybe it isn't. Maybe I misunderstood. Maybe he's not interested in me at all."

"Why," Faye asks. "Look at you. You're beautiful, Ally. You have no idea how beautiful you are and that makes you even more beautiful. Now, move forward."

"Okay," I sigh out, just as a woman in her early twenties hesitantly approaches.

"Hi," she says. "My name's Deirdre Sarlow. I'm with the *L.A. Daily News*. We want to run a piece on this event."

"Great." We shake hands. "But you should really be talking to my friend, Nancy. She owns the bar."

Faye clears her throat. "You should talk to *both* of them. This was Ally's brainchild."

"Well." Deirdre fidgets with her pen as she speaks. "I pretty much have all the information on the event. It's really a great idea and I'm going to tell all the older ladies at work about it. They'd love it here."

"Okay," I say. *Older ladies, you little bitch!*

Deirdre looks down at her notebook as if she's trying to find a question there. "But, um, well, my editors just had a few questions they wanted me to ask you."

"Me?" I suddenly know where this is going. Faye is about to walk away, so I grab her by the arm.

"Um, they just wanted to know what it was, um, like, um, to have your husband leave you for Rose Maris."

I gulp hard and turn to Faye. "Move forward? Do you really think it's possible?"

8

Life Is Sweet

Mom hasn't eaten anything in at least a week. She's too weak to get out of bed, so she lays there, her body barely making a bump underneath the covers. Trinity and I have been holding vigil for days while Gabby is in school. We feed her ice chips, which she sucks on with a vengeance. When we bring her food, she clamps her lips.

"Maybe you should talk to him and tell him it is okay to go," Trinity says. "Tell him you are a big girl and you will miss him, but you will be okay without your mommy. He is holding on for you. You must let go and then your mommy can."

Why can't I do this? After all this time, all this preparation, why can't I let her go? Instead, I say, "Please, Mommy, just eat a little bit."

My mom tilts her head up at me, narrows her eyes, and growls.

Trinity laughs softly as she rubs Mom's face with a wet cloth. "It's okay, Mary. It's okay. That's just Alice, your daughter. He loves you very, very much."

Trinity turns to me sternly. "You go out for a while, missus. You've been here day and night. You need a break from your mommy."

"But . . ."

"And your mommy need a break from you."

"But . . ."

She puts her arms on my shoulders and turns me toward the door. "Go out for the afternoon. Please. You will be more useful when you come back."

I shower and dress. Then I get in my car and drive, but I don't know where to go. I run some errands. A few things from the grocery store. Shirts from the dry cleaners that have been there so long some of them are Alex's. Money from an ATM even though I never use cash. But what next?

I hear Faye's voice. It's been more than a week since moms' night out at The Giggling Gull. And despite the fact that the *Daily News* billed it as a "*Whatever happened to Alice Hirsh?*" event, the night had been a success. But I still hadn't heeded Faye's advice. If she asked me about it, I would say I've been busy with Mom and Gabby and life. I know how she would reply.

"How long does it take to have a cup of coffee, Ally? A half hour? Go. Have a little fun, please!"

I have Johnny's number in my wallet. He had taped a business card to the back of his photograph. I had pulled it off and carried it around, just in case I ever got the nerve.

It's not so much that I suddenly have the nerve. I haven't slept in days so I'm not thinking clearly. I just call him up. My palms sweat and my heart pounds. When his voice mail picks up, I sigh, relieved.

"Hi, it's Alice Hirsh," I say. "I have a lot of empty space in my house and I'm in the market for artwork. So, anyway, if you're around, I'd love to see more of your photographs. I'm actually heading to that coffee shop, so if you feel like stopping by with your portfolio, I'll be there in, oh, about an hour. Or, if you're busy, maybe some other time."

Why did I say an hour? The coffee shop is down the street, but now I can't go there for an hour. I think about other errands to run, but come up blank. So I go to the bookstore at the mall. I haven't bought a novel in a long time. I know there's a bunch of books I've wanted to read, but I can't remember the names of any of them. So I peruse the shelves, hoping something will sound interesting. After a few minutes of this aimlessness, I go to the magazine racks.

Alex stares at me from the *Star*.

RX: TROUBLE, the headline blares. I grab the tabloid and turn to the story. My heart goes nuts and I can't catch my breath. There's a two-page spread featuring photos of Xander and Rose. They don't look happy.

It's hard to believe that just a few months ago, Rose Maris and Xander Hirsh couldn't get enough of each other, but sources close to the couple say that it looks like there's trouble in paradise.

"This relationship is pretty much over," says a friend. "They realize that despite their intense physical attraction, they really don't have much in common."

According to friends, Maris has been seeking solace in her old boyfriend, Finn Mooney, frontman for Hardfax. They were recently spotted canoodling at Bar Marmont.

As a former publicist, I know *Star* isn't the paradigm of truth. Yet I believe the story wholeheartedly. I can't help but smile. Karma's a bitch, Alex.

I head to the coffee shop, convinced Johnny won't show up. Doesn't everyone have their cell phone with them all the time? So he probably got my message. If he was the slightest bit interested in me, he would have called back to say he was on his way. But he most likely heard my message and decided it was better to ignore it. I wish I'd bought a book to have something to read at the table. I scan the car for reading material. All I have is *Star* with Alex's photo on the cover. I leave that buried in the backseat.

But Johnny is there, sitting at a booth, sipping coffee. He grins wide at me. Then he stands and kisses me on the cheek.

"It took you this long to come up with the let-me-look-at-your-portfolio bit? Like I haven't heard that one a million times already."

"And here I thought I was being original."

He smiles at me and I see that his nose is slightly crocked. He must have broken it somehow. Maybe a car accident. Or a sports injury. Or a bar fight. Or maybe a celebrity punched him when he took nude photos of him or his wife or his child.

What was I thinking? It's not like me to be serendipitous. I know nothing about this man, except for what I Googled. And I hadn't liked what I Googled. He'd been arrested a bunch of times for trespassing on the lawns of one celebrity or another. He'd snuck into weddings and hospitals and funerals. He hid in parking lots at nursery and elementary schools. He took photos with a zoom lens of many naked celebrities and has been sued a gazillion times. His photos made him rich and lawsuits made him poor. Angelina Jolie, George Clooney, and Lindsay Lohan all have been quoted saying how much they hate him.

I know nothing else. I don't know if he's been married or has children or dogs, cats, or pot-bellied pigs. Is he a native Los Angelino or is he from somewhere else? Is he a vegan? Is he a ladies' man? Does he like jazz? Country music? Rock and roll? Heavy metal? Rap? If I ran into an ex, would she tell me to stay away, he's bad news? I know if I banged into Angelina Jolie, she'd tell me to run.

What does it matter? Can't I just relax and have fun? I don't need love or commitment or Angelina's seal of approval. I just need a diversion. A cup of coffee with another adult.

We order coffees. He asks how I am and I say fine. I decide not to mention that my mother is about to die.

"What is it?"

"Nothing," I say. "So, where's your portfolio?"

He chuckles. "Actually, I don't have it with me. I was already here setting up my new coffee shop exhibit when you called."

"And three of them have already sold," Debbie announces as she slams down the coffees.

"Yeah, to Deb," Johnny says. "She's my best customer."

I look at the walls. Hanging there are black-and-whites of abandoned farms and dilapidated country homes, and children running in fields, and cows, horses, and pigs.

"I took a trip through some back roads in Gold Country a few weeks ago to clear my head."

I stare at the photos for a while. "They're great," I say. I don't know what else to stay, so I just keep staring.

I feel him studying me. "So what are you looking for, Alice?"

I know from the smirk on his face that he's no longer talking about his photos. His eyes tug at my soul. I'm usually an expert at the witty retort. But I come up blank. Do I keep up the conversation about his portfolio or do I go deeper?

"I have no idea," I finally say.

Johnny's face doesn't change expression as he stares at me for what seems like minutes. "You know, I just turned forty," he says. "And I've never been married." He pauses.

"So?" I say.

"Well, lots of people think that's weird. Like, if you haven't been married by then, it's because you're too damaged or something."

I don't know what to say, so I shrug like it's no big deal to me; like I have no interest in his personal life.

"It's just that maybe after doing what I've done and seeing it all, I don't even believe in marriage. I made most of my money photographing the ugly side of it. The fights. The breakups. I've seen the horrible things people can do when love goes bad."

I flash on that day. There's Gabby in her filthy Cinderella gown and matted down hair, holding her magic wand as she sings while running across the lawn, away from me. I see the anonymous photographers greedily clicking away. Johnny is one of them—ravenous and detached—until Gabby bangs into him.

I bristle. "I can imagine," I say flatly.

"Yeah," he says, shaking his head. "I know what you're thinking."

Do you, I wonder.

"That time, well, it was the same old story on another day at another address. But there was something about you that was different. Maybe part of it was the love you had for your daughter. Maybe part of it was your deep, deep sadness. But I'd never been so ashamed of what I did before."

I shrug. *Yeah, you should be.*

"You're not the first person who's mouthed off at me. Over the years, I've developed quite a Teflon coating. But, I dunno, you made me want to be something more than I was. You made me feel, well, embarrassed of my life."

He rakes his fingers through his hair. I see it's slightly receding in front. "And then when you liked my photos, well . . ."

How did his photos end up here? Right next to my house, I wonder. He seems to guess what I'm thinking.

He tells me that when he left my house that day, he stopped here for a cup of coffee.

"I sat at this table, thinking about you and what I did for a living. And then I noticed the walls. They were bare. Walls should never be bare. So I got to talking to Deb. I showed her some of my photos and she liked them. So I told her she should put them on the walls here and try to sell them. She said okay. I thought that was as good as any first step."

He sips his coffee. "And you know what happened a few days after I hung 'em up?"

He waits for me, so I shake my head.

"You were here. With your friends. Sure, you ran out as soon as you saw me. But still, I took it as a sign. And then when I found out you asked about my favorite one, well, it was . . . Forget it."

"What?"

"Nothing. I've said too much as it is."

I wait for him to say more, but he doesn't. He clamps his mouth shut for emphasis. My mouth instinctively curls in a goofy grin. It's the kind of exercise my lips haven't known since I was, well, single and flirting.

After a few moments of silence, I say, "So, have you . . . changed, that is?"

He takes a long sip of his coffee. "Two days ago, I drove right by Kitson's just as Lindsay was coming out. And guess what?" He leans in towards me like he's about to divulge some great piece of gossip.

"What?"

"I didn't even stop. I kept on going. Okay. I did slow down a bit, but only for a second."

"Wow," I say sarcastically.

"I know. Although I did feel a little sick about it. It would have been an easy few grand."

I laugh.

"So anyway, we can be friends, if you'd like. No expectations. We can have this sort of hesitant friendship for two people who don't believe in love or romance anymore."

I wince a bit. Here the guy has spent the last half hour wooing me, for what? To be friends? How anticlimactic. Here I thought he'd already fallen madly in love with me and then he tells me he doesn't even believe in love?

But isn't that exactly what I want?

His eyes move over my face like he's reading me. Then he smiles. "And if somehow we end up screwing like rabbits on Viagra, so be it," he says. "So let's just have some coffee, and if there's no bad omens, we'll take it from there."

My phone rings as if on cue. I check the number. It's my house. Trinity.

I snatch it. "Trinity? Is everything okay?"

"Yes," Trinity says.

I sigh.

"It's just that your mother is going to die in about an hour."

"*What*?"

"You mommy is going to die very, very soon."

"Is the doctor there?"

"No."

"Well, how do you know then?"

"Missus, I know these things. I've been around death all my life. It is time. You should hurry home."

I stand. My hands shake. My head feels woozy. "I've got to go," I say. "My mother . . . is going to . . . die."

Johnny drives because my hands tremble so bad I can't get the key into the ignition. We pass Gabby's school, so I jump out and retrieve her. I know she'd want to say good-bye to Gaima.

She climbs into the car. I'm about to explain what's going on when she practically shouts, "It's the man who rescued us!"

Johnny grins while he squints at the road.

"He didn't rescue us," I say.

"He's the prince! He's the prince! Are you going to marry him, Mommy? Is this why you picked me up? Are we going to live happily ever after?"

Johnny stares hard at the road, pretending to be preoccupied with driving.

"Gabby, stop it," I say a little too sternly. "Grandma is really, really sick."

"I know, Mommy," Gabby says quietly. "She's been really, really sick for a long, long time. Almost as long as I've been alive."

How do I explain?

"Well, it looks like she's going to die very soon. Maybe today. Maybe in just a little while. I wanted you to be able to say good-bye."

"Okay," Gabby says, as if none of this is really a big deal, as if Grandma's going on a trip somewhere.

There are cars parked in front of the house. I don't recognize any of them. When I head inside, I get that Trinity has called her friends, all the caregivers she knows. There are about ten people huddled around Mom's bed.

"Who are they supposed to be," Gabby whispers in awe as she enters the guest house. They've lit candles and are praying around Mom. Their faces flicker with the candlelight. It is quiet and serene. The only sounds are the murmur of prayers, the soft smacking of lips.

"Gaima," Gabby whispers.

Mom's eyes blaze with an awareness that disappeared years and years ago. It makes me shudder. I can feel her presence in this room like I've never felt it here, in this house, before. Life is burning inside her.

Somehow, Mommy is back.

"She seems, well, so aware," I whisper to Trinity.

"Yes," Trinity whispers. "I've seen it many, many times before. It is all your mommy's energy pouring out of the body. The body is getting rid of everything it has."

For a moment I had almost wanted to believe in a miracle. But now I remember hearing about this before. The rush of life before death. A fierce, brilliant energy burns through Mom. It's just like a candle that flickers the brightest right before it expires. Or a light bulb that blazes before it burns out. Mom's face glows. Her eyes are clear and lucid.

Gabby and I move closer to Mom. The Filipinos look at us to see if they should leave the room, give us privacy. But I don't want them to go. They are comforting, like priests and saints and angels standing vigil. They are not afraid of Death who hovers around us.

"We love your mommy very much," one of them says to me, tears glistening in her eyes.

I believe her, even though I'm sure she's never met my mom before today.

Gabby and I each hold one of my mom's hands. Trinity puts an arm around Gabby. And while I watch Gabby as she strokes my mother's face, I suddenly think about Alex, how upset he'd be by this if he still lived here. He'd insist Mom die in a hospital so we wouldn't subject Gabby to this unpleasantness. But why? Why should she be shielded from this? It's part of life. It's a much better part of life than divorce is. Death is natural. Divorce isn't. Why should Gabby be denied her chance to say good-bye?

My mom squeezes Gabby's hand. She hasn't done this in a long, long time. She beams at Gabby. And it dawns on me than that Gabby is in dress-up clothes from school. She's a fairy with nylon wings and a halo of plastic flowers on her head. She looks just like an angel. I wonder if Mom imagines she's come to fly her away.

Then Mom's lips begin to tremble. She is struggling to say something to Gabby.

Please, Mom, please don't say cocksucker, I pray. *Please don't let that be your last word. Please, please, please.*

Mom closes her eyes in fierce concentration. Her face tightens and her lips quiver. She's using all her remaining energy to tell my daughter something.

The praying becomes louder. I look up at the faces around me.

The room is dark except for the candlelight, and the Filipino faces flicker with the flames. I see some people are crying. Tears stream down Trinity's face. But most of the people are smiling, despite their tears. These people are around death and dying so much that it is not something foreign or frightening or horrible to them. They see it like a friend who has come to visit yet again. They know what it looks like and sounds like and smells like. They nod to me and tilt their head towards my mother. They are silently telling me not to look away, to watch, to not be afraid, to savor every moment of her extinguishing flame.

Her lips continue to quiver. She squeezes her eyes and tenses her mouth. She wants to tell us all something.

The prayers stop as if someone has given a signal. We wait, expectantly. Gabby leans in closer. Mom's face relaxes. She smiles at Gabby as if she's never seen anything so beautiful before. As if she's a new mother looking at her baby for the first time. She opens her mouth and sucks in air. She lifts her hand and touches Gabby's cheek.

"Life is sweet," Mom whispers. "Life is sweet."

She tilts her head back onto the pillow as if to rest from this exertion. She looks like she's sleeping peacefully. But I know she is gone.

9

Life Is Sweat

The Laugher is laughing at all the wrong moments. The priest tells us that while death may be frightening, Jesus is always with us. "Jesus holds our hands throughout all our trials and tribulations."

The Laugher is hysterical. This is the funniest thing she's ever heard. Even better than Dr. Phil. People shush her. Father Gregory looks flummoxed.

My Aunt Maddy jerks her head around and gives The Laugher a dirty look. "*Shhhh.*"

"Aunt Maddy, she has Alzheimer's," I hiss.

The church isn't packed, but there are more people than I ever imagined. Trinity must have invited every Filipino in the San Fernando Valley. There are close to three dozen. I was shocked to see The Laugher and The Satellite. Surprisingly, Hilda's son, Hans, has brought them with him. Thankfully, I don't see Hilda. The Satellite makes everyone uneasy as she does laps around the casket.

I spot Johnny in the back row and smile. The day Mom died, he had stayed at the house, playing Barbie dolls with Gabby. Gabby told me later he talked dolls better than anyone she ever met.

"You could learn a lot from him," she had said.

"What?"

"You could learn a lot from him about talking dolls. He really knows what Barbie likes. And he can do a really good Barbie voice, too, much better than yours."

Ruth, Renee, Nancy, and Amy are here. Judy didn't show up, although she sent an enormous bouquet of flowers. Claire is here. Lauren flew in from Rochester and has been taking care of Gabby.

And then, just as the service began, I heard the church door creak open. For some reason, I shivered. Then Aunt Maddy made a loud tsking sound. A hush seemed to fall over the church. I turned just as Alex snuck into the same pew as Johnny.

This morning, as we prepared for the funeral, Gabby handed me a piece of paper. It was a painting of Mom right before she died. She lay in her bed, a stick figure with a smile on her face, surrounded by candles and angels. Above the picture was a title in Gabby's child-like handwriting: "LIFE IS SWEAT."

I chuckled. Gabby looked at me strangely. I didn't feel like explaining her faux pas, so I just hugged her tight.

"It's beautiful. We'll frame it and hang it on one of our walls. We have so many walls to fill with your beautiful pictures."

After the service, as Mom's body is loaded in the back of the hearse, Hans comes up to me. Despite his lineage, Hans is okay, and it was very nice of him to attend the service. I actually feel sorry for him, with his doughy countenance, nondescript features, and inability to look me in the eye. But he was gentle and patient with Mom.

"I'm sorry about your mother," he says, staring at his worn loafers. "She was a very nice person. I'm also sorry about what my mother did. It wasn't very nice of her. I want you to know, I tried to talk her out of it. But you know my mother. She doesn't listen to anybody."

Just as I'm about to reply, his whole body twitches and his face contorts. "Cocksucker. Motherfucker."

Everyone within earshot snaps their heads toward us in horror. "*Hans?*"

"Yes," he calmly says, looking at his shoes. He lifts his head up and sees all eyes are on him. Horrified.

"Oh," he says, as if he's realized something. His face turns purple. He quickly looks down again. He kicks at some pebbles. "Did I just, well, curse or something?"

I nod slowly. "Um, yeah."

He laughs nervously. "I have Tourette's Syndrome and it somehow comes out when I'm nervous. I'm so sorry, Mrs. Hirsh."

"You know, your mother kicked my mother out of her place because of her language. And all the time, she was imitating you."

Hans's gaze stays glued to his shoes. He nods his head.

"My mother knew it, too, but she wouldn't accept it. She's been in denial about it for a long time. Her son can't have a flaw. She thought I was doing it on purpose for some reason or another. But why would a forty-year-old man work for his mother, changing diapers and cleaning bedpans?" He forces out a laugh and then shuffles his feet along the gravel. "I just wanted to say I'm sorry for everything."

I give him a quick hug. "It's okay, Hans. Forget about it. It worked out for the best. I got to have my mom live—and die—in my house. So thank you for that."

Hans picks his head up and smiles, but he still won't look me in the eye. "Well, I'm glad," he says as other people begin to approach. They wait for Hans to step aside, but he remains there, pushing gravel with his feet and staring at his shoes.

"Well, it was nice seeing you again. Thanks for coming," I say as I look at the line of people collecting behind him.

"Well, sure. I'm glad to be here," he says, intent on kicking pebbles. He coughs into his hand. "I, um, was wondering if maybe you and I, well, could go out for drinks or coffee sometime. Maybe in a week or so?"

I am too stunned to say anything. The man who polluted my sweet mother's vocabulary is asking me out on a date! At my mother's funeral! Before I can respond, Johnny puts his arm on my shoulder.

"I'm sorry, but you'll have to fight me for her," he says, kissing my cheek and pulling me closer.

Hans mumbles something, says good-bye, and walks away.

Johnny kisses my forehead. "Don't read anything into what I just said. I could see you were struggling and I was just helping a friend."

I smile at him. "Thanks, buddy."

After Mom is buried, everyone comes to my house where Ruth, Lauren, Nancy, and Claire have set out platters of sandwiches, salads, and lasagna. Trinity and her friends have brought some traditional Filipino food, too. There are eggrolls, paella, and pancit, which is stir-fried noodles with chicken.

The smells hit my nose like a bomb. I am suddenly famished. I haven't eaten in days and days. I haven't even thought about food in weeks. Now I am ravenous. My stomach growls and my hands shake. It's like I've been marooned on some island and am smelling food for the first time in a very long time. Garlic, onion, tomato sauce, peppers, noodles, chicken, beef, all mix and mingle and waft through my house for the first time in a long time.

I grab a plate and heap mounds of food onto it. I eat it as quickly as I shovel it onto my plate. I stand in front of the platters and gobble it up there. Then I pile on more food. I don't remember the last time I really enjoyed food, but it could be that night, more than a year ago, at a sushi restaurant when I first met a certain celebrity who told me how lucky I was to have Alex.

I look around the room and I make a promise. No more bland smells. No more blank walls and empty spaces. No more abstinence from pleasure, from life. I exhale and smile.

"You look great," Nancy tells me. "How are you holding up?"

"I'm good. Really good," I say in between mouthfuls. "I just wanted to thank you for everything, but especially for helping me that day with my mom. I don't know if I could have ever gotten her here without you."

Nancy smiles and brushes her hand in the air. "That's what friends are for," she says. "Besides, you would have managed fine. I'll never forget that day when your mom danced around the room to disco. Remember? She seemed happy. There was so much love."

I take inventory of the room. More people than I imagined have shown up for Mom. I smile as I bite into an eggroll. When Mom died, I didn't feel sad in the way I thought I would. Instead, I strangely feel happier than I have in a long time. Maybe because in the end she seemed happy. Even though she couldn't taste mashed potatoes or speak or really move, there was still some joy because there was love. Maybe if you can be stripped of everything, you can still have something that can make you happy in the end—the love of a caregiver, a daughter, a granddaughter, even strangers. Maybe if you have that, death is not so bad. Mom still had something left. I saw it in the way she looked at Gabby. She still felt love. She still gave love.

Gabby squeezes my hand. I know she knows this, too, even if she doesn't understand yet. But she will remember all this one day and it will comfort her. For now she takes an eggroll and looks at me strangely. It's as if something's been lifted off of me and she's seeing me for the first time.

"You look really beautiful, Mommy," she says.

"Thank you, sweetie." I hug her.

"Daddy and I are going to play outside for a little while with Connor, okay?"

"Sure."

Alex is here? I hadn't expected him to come back to the house. But then again, where else is he going to go now that Rose has dumped him? I watch Gabby as she heads toward the sliding glass door to go outside. Alex is in the yard. He's taken his jacket off and is throwing a Nerf football to Connor.

Just when I feel like I'm getting it all together, Alex returns. Isn't this always how it works? He must sense my gaze because he turns, smiles, and waves at me. I give him a quick smile and turn my head.

"*No, Ally, you cannot go back to him,*" I hear my mother say.

"I can't believe he's got the nerve to be here," Lauren says, as if reading my mind.

"It's okay," I say.

"Remember, you're very vulnerable right now," Lauren says. "Don't let him convince you of anything."

I roll my eyes at her. Sherri, my neighbor, approaches. She's brought a tray of some kind of casserole. She hands it to me then gives me a hug.

"I'm so sorry, Alice," she says. "My mother died a little while ago. No matter how old you are, it still hurts."

"Thanks, Sherri."

"I'm also sorry about how crazy I got. Hopefully we can get past it and work toward a great, festive holiday this year."

"Absolutely," I say. "Now get yourself some food."

"Why hasn't he left yet," Lauren asks later as we carry plates into the kitchen. She's talking about Alex. It's been three hours since the guests arrived and most of them have left or are leaving, except for a few good friends—and Alex.

I'd been thinking the same thing, but I didn't feel like drawing attention to it. I shrug my shoulders. "I don't know. I guess he's having fun playing with Gabby."

"Oh, please. He never played with Gabby before."

"Maybe he's changed."

Lauren eyes me severely. "Don't you even say something like that."

"What do you mean, Laur?"

"It sounds like you're considering him and you can't ever. Not after the way he treated you."

I flinch. "I'm not considering anything. I'm the one who filed for divorce, remember?"

"I'm just warning you. I know he can be charming." She looks past me. "Oh, look," she says flatly. "Here he comes now."

I turn. Alex is heading right toward me. His clothes are rumpled and the knot in his tie is loose. He smiles at us uncomfortably.

"Lauren," he says, nodding.

"Hi Alex," she says, devoid of any expression.

"Um, Ally, can I talk to you privately for a moment?"

Lauren bugs her eyes out at me.

I give her a look that says, "Don't worry."

But I am a little bit worried.

10

The Cycle of Life

I don't know where to talk to him. Usually, we'd go into our bedroom when we needed to speak privately, but that seems strange and charged with hidden meaning. So instead we head into Gabby's room, surrounded by her princess motif. I sit at the edge of her pink canopied bed while Alex sits in her pink princess throne chair.

He clears his throat. "How are you holding up?"

"Fine," I say.

"Good, good," he says, picking at something underneath his nail. "You know, Ally, I really admire the way you took care of your mother. I know I had my doubts, but I think it was good for Gabby. I think she's learned that life isn't all about princesses and princes and magic spells and happily ever afters."

No, you already taught her that lesson.

Instead, I nod my head. Where is he going with this?

"Ally, I've made a terrible mistake. Can you ever forgive me? I love you. I always did. I must have been going through some weird midlife crises. Rose never meant anything to me. Please, take me

back. Please, forgive me. I promise I will make it up to you. I'll do whatever it takes to win you back."

I lean back on the bed a bit and smirk. I'm looking forward to hearing him grovel.

But what would I do? Would I even consider it? No, right? He dumped me. Actually, he didn't just dump me—he humiliated me. I could never ever consider it. Never.

But what am I doing right here?

"There was a guy at the church today. You seemed to know him. He's a photographer."

Johnny. He's jealous of Johnny!

I stare at him blankly, as if I have too many admirers to keep track of just one.

"Just watch out for him. He's a piece of shit scumbag."

He studies me, gauging my expression, to see if Johnny means anything to me. To see if his opinion of Johnny means anything to me. But I keep a poker face.

"Just watch out. He's after something."

He looks at me, expecting me to jump up, panicked and shriek, "What? What? What is he after?"

"Is that why you wanted to talk to me," I say, annoyed. "Because I can take care of myself."

Alex nervously shakes his head.

"What is it that you want then, Alex? Because I really should get back out there and—"

"Rose is pregnant."

He blurts it out so fast that I have to replay the words in my head to figure out what he said. Then I have to replay them again even to decipher their meaning. Rose is pregnant? How could that be? I thought it was over. A source said there was trouble in paradise. Besides, Alex was supposed to try to win me back.

Despite all I've been through with Alex, this is shocking. It's beyond shocking. It's like a sucker punch to the soul. I can't breathe. I
can't talk. I just stare at him, struggling to swallow.

Is it yours, I want to say. But I clamp my mouth shut just like Mom.

Alex nervously coughs. "We're getting married."

We stare at each other. I feel tears well in my eyes. I'm not sure
why. I've known for a long time that this was over. He cheated on
me. Hell, we're divorced. But now, despite how cruel he was, he still
gets the fairy tale.

And I still don't.

"Oh," I finally say.

Alex nods and takes a deep breath. He wants to escape, but he
doesn't quite know how to. I suddenly understand that this is the
last time we'll ever be alone again. I decide to make the most of it.

"What happened," I say. "To us. What was it?"

I figure he'll just give an annoyed shrug and say, "Let it go." But
instead, his eyes tear.

"I dunno. I'm really sorry, Al. I guess everything just seemed so
serious all the time. With your mom and Gabby and work, you
seemed stressed and unhappy. I probably did, too. But, I dunno, it
just seemed to take over everything. We used to have fun. We used
to laugh. Everything just felt so heavy. We never had fun anymore."
He runs his hand along the fluffy pink armrest of the throne. "I just
wanted to run away, I guess. I'm sorry."

I want to defend myself. I want to say I was not stressed and unhappy. But I was. I want to say, Alex, my mother was dying, of course
things felt heavy, but I don't. I want to say life *is* serious. Life can
make us unhappy. We grow up and become adults. We can't run away
from it, because you can't run away from yourself. Maybe Rose is in
that rarefied air where she never really has to be serious or sad or too
heavy, but still, that doesn't mean her mother won't get Alzheimer's or

her father won't die of cancer. After all, whether you're driving a Hyundai or a Rolls Royce, there are no free rides.

Instead, I say, "Well, that's great. Good luck."

He stands up and gives me an awkward hug that's over as soon as it begins.

"Thanks, Ally," he says. He turns toward the door. Then he stops and turns back. "Just watch out for that guy, okay?"

"He's actually not so bad," I say cheerfully. "Besides, he's no longer a paparazzo. He stopped months ago."

Alex shakes his head. "Ally, yesterday he took photos of Rose leaving her obstetrician. She just found out she was pregnant and now it's going to be all over the tabs, because of him."

Another shock. Another sucker punch to the soul. Another "But wait, there's more!"

I nod at Alex and smile, as if this news is quite pleasant.

"You okay," he asks.

I can't speak. I feel like I'm choking. I just nod my head again and smile even wider. *I'm terrif!* But tears are streaming down my face. I hate myself for crying in front of Alex.

"Well, 'bye, Ally," Alex says slowly.

Then he turns and is gone.

Part Three

Happily Ever After

I

Chasing Butterflies

T he poo-poo's coming! The poo-poo's coming!"

Gabby and I are sampling peaches from one of the ven-
dors at the Calabasas Farmer's Market when two girls about
twelve years old shout this and laugh hysterically. I glance over at
Gabby. Her face gets red and her eyes water. I put my hand on her
shoulder and am about to whisk her toward the flower stand, where
Gabby goes each week to collect the stray flowers that have fallen on
the ground.

Then one of the girls puts out her hand to high-five Gabby.

"You were totally awesome," she says.

"Yeah. I made my mom buy me a box of that cereal. Then every
time I finish, I say, 'The poo-poo's coming!' And I grab my butt. It
totally cracks her up," the other girl says.

"Really? It totally drives my mother nuts," the first girl adds.

Gabby's face lights up.

One of the girls hangs her head and asks sheepishly, "Can we get
your autograph?"

Is this for real, I wonder. I look at the girl, trying to decide if this is a gag. But she is completely sincere—and almost embarrassed. She hands Gabby a piece of paper.

"Sure," Gabby says, sucking in her cheeks.

She painstakingly prints out her name, leaning the paper on one of the girls' backs.

And, of course, this being Los Angeles, where residents are equipped with celebrity radar, soon Gabby is surrounded. It's not like they all recognize her, but they think they should, so they pretend they do. And even though she has one line in a TV commercial, she is a star—at least here in Calabasas, where Howie Mandel is as big as it gets.

"Say it. Say it. Please. Please," one of the girls begs.

The crowd begins to chant along.

Gabby looks at me, beaming. I smile at her and nod. "Go ahead, Gabs."

Part of me is completely bewildered by this attention, part of me is completely proud, and part of me is horrified that this will create a monster. After all, Gabby has high diva potential.

Gabby squeezes her eyes shut as if she's struggling to get into character. She takes a deep breath and then exhales slowly out her nose. I imagine this is something Rose taught her. Maybe not. She's been a drama queen for years without any coaching.

A few of the adults titter.

Then Gabby opens her eyes, widens them as if something's just dawned on her and scrunches her face in agony.

"The poo-poo's coming! The poo-poo's coming!"

The crowd bursts into applause and laughter.

Gabby takes a deep bow. Her hair brushes the pavement.

It turned out that despite what Alex had thought, the director had loved Gabby's ad-libbing. And so did the cereal's marketing department—so much so that they redefined the cereal. So now,

SUPERCrispyCrunch is a cereal that "keeps you regular—SUPERregular!"

"The poo-poo's coming! The poo-poo's coming." Kids and some adults imitate Gabby as they stroll through the farmer's market.

It dawns on me—Gabby has a catch phrase. Faye was right!

When I get in the car, I excitedly call Faye from my cell.

"You won't believe what happened," I tell her. Then I breathlessly explain.

But Faye is unmoved.

"I keep telling you, I'm good at what I do," she says. I can picture her shaking her head at me and frowning. "You're the one with all the doubts."

"But it was exactly what you predicted!"

"And?"

"Well . . ."

"It's like I'm psychic!" Faye laughs.

I don't want to bring her down with how wrong she was about Johnny. He called me the day after Mom's funeral to see how I was doing. I didn't call him back. He called me a few more times. Then he left me a message, saying that he wouldn't bug me anymore. And he hasn't.

"I'm a pebble star," Gabby announces from the backseat. "Can I call Daddy to tell him?"

"Sure," I say. I tell Faye I'd see her soon.

Then I hand the phone to Gabby.

Gabby is going to be a flower girl at the nuptials of Rose and Xander—"Rx." She says she's wearing a princess gown and a diamond tiara. They're getting married on New Year's Eve at a top secret location, she tells me. It's so secret that she doesn't even know where it will be. She tells me that the guests will meet at Van Nuys airport, where a private jet will whisk them away to some remote island somewhere. She said they hope it's so remote that no horrible pepperonis will be there to take photos of them.

"I don't understand why they hate getting their picture taken, because I love it," Gabby had said.

Rose's agent wants to cast Gabby in a movie. It's just a small part. A friend of the daughter of the lead. But she'll have to head to Salt Lake City for a week right before Christmas. My first instinct was to tell her no way, but I see how her face lights up when she sings and dances and, well, signs autographs.

Maybe I'll let her do it just this once. Then back to school. Back to a normal life.

I wonder if this is what every future stage mom has once uttered.

As we drive home, Gabby says, "Can we please not put those ugly things on the lawn again?"

"What ugly things?"

"Those blow-up snowmen. I had a nightmare about them last night. I got stuck in that snow globe with 'em and couldn't breathe. It was very scary."

"It was just a bad dream, honey."

"Can we do something beautiful this year?"

"Yes."

"I mean it, Mommy."

"I promise it will be better than last year. I also promise you'll get that puppy," I say. I turn in my seat and look into Gabby's eyes. "I know I've made a lot of promises and some of them haven't happened yet, but they will."

"A puppy! A puppy! Finally. Can it be a Chihuahua?"

I don't tell her that Chihuahuas should be considered rodents, not canines. Instead, I nod my head. "Yes, you can get a Chihuahua. We can even buy it a fancy outfit and everything."

"Yay! Yay!"

As we pull into the driveway, Gabby bangs on the window and shrieks. "Pepperoni! Pepperoni!"

My first thought is that a pizza delivery man has come to the wrong address. But it's Johnny. My heart pounds. My stomach tightens. Gabby runs out of the car and leaps into his arms.

He didn't expect this kind of greeting from Gabby and he stumbles backwards.

"Hello, Gabs," he says. "You seem extra happy today."

"I signed my first autograph and I'm finally getting the Chihuahua my mommy's been promising me for about one hundred and sixty thousand years."

He laughs and kisses her cheek. "Well, that's the most perfect day I've ever heard about." He looks over at me and smiles. "Can I take you ladies to the coffee shop for some ice cream to celebrate?"

Gabby squeezes him tighter. "*Yes!?*"

She looks over at me. Unconsciously, a scowl spreads across my face. I shake my head.

"Oh, Mom! Just when I thought you were starting to be fun for once in your life."

"Yeah, Mom," Johnny chimes in.

He must have caught a look on my face because his smile disappears. He sees Gabby's the only one happy to see him.

I don't know what I should say to him. So what if he took pictures of Rose? What does that have to do with me? It's not like Johnny and I are anything to each other, really. Nothing's happened beyond some flirtatious banter. As far as I'm concerned, now nothing will ever happen. Although it would have been nice. Why the hell did he have to ruin it by lying?

Gabby spots a butterfly flitting around the lavender in our front yard. She grabs her net and races to catch it.

"Are you having a tough time still with your mom and all?" I hear that slight Smoky Mountain twang. "You still need some space?"

"That's not it," I say, my eyes blazing into him.

He steps back and puts his hands on his chest. "Is it something I did? What could I have done? I thought we were becoming friends."

I don't want to get into this with him. What purpose would it serve? He's a liar.

"No. I've just been busy." I want to sound casual, but I can hear the snap in my voice.

"So cold. Okay, Alice, what did I do?"

"It's just . . . nothing."

He searches my face, confused. "What does that mean? Does that mean it's just nothing? Or does that mean it's just something you were going to tell me and then you thought better of it?"

I'm going to get into this. Why? What do I want from him? I can't like a liar. They're in the same category as a cheater. Actually, they're inextricable. If you lie, you will eventually cheat. And when you cheat, you will lie about it.

"It's just . . . well, it's really none of my business," I say. I can feel my voice quiver. I wish it didn't do that when I'm upset—it gives me away. "Well, I wish you hadn't told me you were done with all that paparazzi stuff when you weren't."

"What?"

"Alex told me you took photos of Rose at her doctor's office. I saw the pictures in the *Enquirer* myself."

The cover featured a photo of Rose leaving her gyno office with a big grin on her face. In one hand, she held a bag of baby books, in the other was an ultrasound photo that the *Enquirer* had enlarged.

He bites his lip and nods his head at me. "And why does that bother you? You still in love with Alex?"

I'm infuriated that he sees it this way. "This has nothing to do with Rose and Alex. It has to do with you."

"Me?"

"You lied to me. I trusted you and you lied."

He gulps hard and speaks softly. "Here I thought all this time you were avoiding me because you needed time alone and it's not that at all."

He sadly shakes his head. "Why didn't you just say something? You could have asked me about this. It's all so simple."

He pauses, waiting for me to say something. I feel my eyebrows furrow.

"I did a favor for a friend, okay? She's an editor at the *Enquirer* and she was very close to being fired. She had heard Rose was pregnant, but couldn't confirm it. Rose's publicist said it was a lie. I guess Rose was negotiating some big movie deal and she didn't want to lose the part because she was pregnant."

"Uh-huh."

"Anyway, I know a friend of a friend who works for this gyno to the stars. And, well, she gave me great access. So instead of being fired, my friend was promoted. But I didn't know it was Alex's. I thought that had been over for a long time. I thought she was back with that singer, Flipper."

"Finn," I say.

He smiles. "Of course, the money was great. I can't deny that. You know, it's not the easiest thing in the world to go from making tons and tons of money to begging art dealers to show my work. I'm slowly building a clientele. But it wasn't like I planned this at all. When I told you I was through, I thought I was. But I guess I wasn't. Sometimes things just come up."

"Oh" is all I can say.

"It's like me being a vegetarian."

"Huh?" I close my eyes and shake my head. *Ridiculous.*

"A few years ago, I swore off meat. I told people I was a vegetarian. I just ate beans and rice and tofu. And then, after about a year, I was at a barbecue and the smell of those grilled hamburgers got the best of me. So I became a carnivore again."

"Okay," I say, sighing. "I understand what you're saying, but the logic seems off a bit."

"It's just that sometimes the temptation is too great. But that doesn't make me a liar."

"Hmmm."

"You should have asked," Johnny says, a bit sadly. "And, I swear, if I had known it had anything to do with Alex, I would have told you. But I really thought they were over." He pauses for a moment, smiles at me and then shakes his head. "I guess we're off to a bad start." He turns and walks towards his black Subaru Outback.

" 'Bye," I say.

He turns and waves. "You know, you expect a lot from your friends."

I let out a sharp "HA!" before I ask, "Is that what you want, Johnny, to be friends?"

He looks annoyed with me. "Sure," he says. "No expectations, right?"

I walk towards him, my heart throbbing against my ribs. I can handle this two ways. I can agree with him and watch him drive away, and then wonder if I'll run into him again at the coffee shop. And maybe I will. Maybe we'll continue this game. Or maybe I'll see him with someone else who admires his photos and his piercing blue eyes.

Or I can make my own fairy tale.

So I march towards him. Then I wrap my hand around his neck and I kiss him. He doesn't move his lips and I think I've made a big mistake. Maybe all he wanted was a friend. So I stop, embarrassed. I begin to pull away. Then he grabs me tighter and kisses me back, hard, like he's been wanting this for a long, long time.

I don't know how long we kiss—a second, a minute, ten minutes.

He kisses so well that I'm at that place where time doesn't exist, where my body doesn't exist. I hear Gabby's tinny voice drifting into my consciousness from far away. And I am vacuumed back into my body.

"I caught one! I caught one and it's so beautiful," she shrieks. I wonder what she's talking about. Then I remember the butterflies. Johnny and I stop kissing. Our noses still touch.

Johnny looks into my eyes and whispers. "So did I, Gabby. So did I."

2

Freely and with Abandon

Gabby is in Salt Lake City with Alex for a little over a week. She's filming her part in a movie; its working title is *Forever Today*, whatever that means. It's one of those time warp movies that Hollywood likes to repackage every few years. Anyway, I'm alone. I can't remember the last time I've been by myself for more than a weekend. Even when I was single, I always had a roommate or two around. Maybe I've never been alone like this before in my whole life.

I don't like it one bit.

That's why I decide it's the perfect time to get that addition to the family: Gabby's Chihuahua.

Johnny is one of those people who has connections everywhere. So when I mentioned I was on a quest for a Chihuahua, he told me he knew a breeder in Santa Ynez, a town filled with vineyards and farms, just a little north of Santa Barbara.

"A few years ago, every celeb was accessorizing with Chihuahuas, so I spent a lot of time up there, taking photos of Paris and Britney cuddling 'em," he tells me.

It's been several weeks since our first kiss. And that's all there's

been, although I have signed J. D. Wolfe as a client at my fledgling
public relations company. But Johnny was away in San Francisco for
a few weeks, working on a gallery exhibit. When he returned, I was
busy preparing Gabby for her trip. When I did see him, Gabby was
around. So the relationship couldn't progress to anything but a few
stolen kisses, quick hugs, and some flirtatious banter.

And, in many, many ways, this is my idea of a perfect relationship. I feel I could continue like this forever. There is nothing scary
or unknown. We are like an old couple without the history.

Our relationship is safe.

Okay. Our relationship is boring.

But I'm not complaining. Boring is wonderful. Boring is all I am
capable of handling. I couldn't imagine having much more than a
few stolen kisses, quick hugs, some banter.

The truth is, I am horrified of sex for too many reasons to
count. First of all, I don't know what sex with Johnny would mean
exactly. When I was younger, sex was the next step in a serious relationship. At first, it was the step after "I love you." When I got a
little older, it was a few steps before "I love you," but I could see the
"I love you" hovering in the distance. I never had a one-night stand.
I never slept with someone I didn't think I loved. Maybe I didn't
love them, but at least when I screwed them, I thought I did.

But Johnny? Can't I put aside love and just have a meaningless
fling? Or is it already too late for that? Would it mean something to
me? To him? And what would it mean? And would we even agree
on its meaning?

The one thing I do know is Faye was right. I think too much. I
need to relax and enjoy life. Enjoy sex.

But even if I can get past our various interpretations of the act of
intercourse, I am terrified of the prospect of getting naked for Johnny.
I look great in clothes. All svelte and toned. My body is able to hide
its flaws well with the right material. But this might make things

worse. Because Johnny is in for a real shock. There's no way Johnny knows that I suck my stomach in all the time. He has no idea that I have cellulite and saggy breasts and a pouch of flesh dangling from my stomach. Or stretch marks across my hips and the tops of my legs. When I look at my body naked in the mirror I try to imagine what a man who has spent a lifetime photographing beautiful people would think of it.

I have to look away.

And Johnny's body looks impeccable. His arms are muscular and his stomach is flat. He still has the body of his former football player self.

Now Gabby is out of the picture for a week. She's no longer my scapegoat. I feel like I'm seventeen and my parents have gone away for a long weekend and my boyfriend is pressuring me to put out for him.

Although Johnny hasn't been pressuring me at all. He seems fine with our current status. I think.

"Thanks," I said to Johnny when he told me about the breeder over the phone one day. "So, if you could give me directions . . ."

Johnny laughed. "Well, I was proposing it as a kind of little excursion for the two of us. A trip out of the Valley to the country. Some touring. Some good eating. Some getting to know you time. And, of course, you could pick up that damn yappy vermin."

And then what, I wondered. The image of my naked body flashed before my eyes.

"Okay," I said, my heart throbbing, my stomach turning.

I pick Johnny up from his condo in Studio City. He looks handsome wearing a navy T-shirt and jeans, his hair wet and slicked back. We drive towards Santa Ynez, getting stuck in horrible traffic. But, of course, Johnny knows an alternate route. We breeze through winding country roads shaded by twisted eucalyptus trees, and their menthol fragrance fills the car. We pass fields dotted with grazing cows, horses, sheep, and pigs. Around lunchtime we stop at a rustic-looking country home, which turns out to be a winery and a restaurant.

And, of course, Johnny knows the owner. Some celebrity wedding was held there a few years ago. So we're given a secluded table in the corner near a small fireplace. The place smells slightly musty. It's the odor of antiques—everything in the place, from the dark wooden tables and benches to the vases and candle holders, seems to be meticulously collected from estate sales and antique shops. I gaze up to study the black-and-white on the wall. A series of dilapidated farmhouses, probably around here. I recognize the style and laugh.

"What?"

"Do you just take me places to show off?"

"Actually, I came here a few hours ago and begged them to put these up here. It's all part of my elaborate plan to get you in the sack."

He laughs. I smile, but I can feel my face turning deep purple.

"It's gonna take a lot more than a few photos," I finally blurt out. My heart thumps away. I know it's lame, but nothing else comes to mind.

"Don't I know it," he says, smiling slyly.

We stare at each other for a few moments.

"You know, I know absolutely nothing about you," I say.

"I'm pretty simple. What you see is what you get."

I feel my eyes narrow. "Somehow I don't believe it."

"It's true. What do you want to know? Ask me anything."

I think for a moment. There's so much I could ask. What was his childhood like? Where did he go to school? How did he become a photographer? But really, the truth is, there's one question that's been nagging at me.

"Okay, what's the real reason you never got married?"

Johnny smiles. "Never? You make it sound so hopeless. I'm not dead yet. It still could happen." He smiles at me. "You think it's weird, don't you? That I've never been married. You're wondering if something's wrong with me."

No, I know something's wrong with you.

"Of course not," I say.

"If it makes you feel any better, I was almost married once."

I can't help but lean closer. "Really? What happened?"

Johnny laughs. "If I told a guy this, he'd high-five me and then change the subject to sports or something. Why is it that chicks always want the sordid details?"

I shrug.

"If I tell you, you'll really lose respect for me."

Now I'm intrigued. Better to find this out sooner rather than later. "I promise I won't," I lie.

He leans in. "Well, I was with this woman for a few years."

"How many years?"

"Six."

"That's a long time."

Johnny shrugs. "I guess."

"What was her name?"

"What does it matter?"

I shrug. "I just want to know."

"Caroline."

I nod. "So . . . ?"

Johnny shakes his head and laughs. "Why am I telling you this? Okay, so we'd been together for a long time and figured it was time to get married, right?"

I nod.

"She's from San Francisco, so we figured we'd get married there. Her parents have a big house right in Nob Hill, so everyone flew or drove in for a long weekend. It was all going great. We had a really fun rehearsal dinner with drunken toasts and lots of singing. Then the next morning, I played golf with some buddies, even though I never golf. It was all going according to the plan."

"The plan?"

"The perfect wedding plan that all you girls have in your heads," Johnny says. He takes a deep breath and rubs his head. "Okay, so then I went back to the hotel to take a nap and get ready for the wedding. I had every intention of getting married that day. It never crossed my mind that I wouldn't."

My eyes widen. Johnny's enjoying my rapt attention. He pauses dramatically. Then takes a long sip of water.

"And then what?"

"You're not going to like this part," he says in a sing-songy voice. "I shouldn't continue."

"Continue."

He dramatically shudders. "Okay. You asked for it. So then, back at the room, I get a call from the bureau chief of the *Enquirer*. Turns out I wasn't the only one in San Fran getting married that weekend."

"Uh-huh."

"Courteney Cox and David Arquette were at the Grace Cathedral right in Nob Hill right at that moment!"

I sigh. "You didn't."

He nods his head slowly. "The editor just wanted a few pictures from me. And I had plenty of time to spare. I just wouldn't get to take my nap. So what? I figured no one would even notice I was gone."

He takes another long sip of water.

"But they did notice, right?"

He smirks. "I got carried away, as usual. It's like fishing. Or gambling. It's hard to stop. So I'm sneaking around. I get a few good photos of them from a tiny slit in a window at the church. They're up at the altar, exchanging vows. I could have left then and my boss would have been satisfied. But I figured I could get some better ones when they came out of the church. And I did. I got them kissing. But then I thought, why stop now? I could get some great candids of guests in front of the hotel where the reception is, right? So I go for it. I lose complete track of time. I'm actually at their wedding when I'm supposed to be at mine."

I let out a long breath. I don't know what to say. Johnny puts the water glass to his lips before realizing it's empty. He puts it back down on the table and runs his fingers around its rim. He looks at me. "Pretty awful, huh? I'm a real shithead."

"So what did Caroline do?"

"I showed up at her parents' house an hour late. She was gone. Her brothers beat me up. A year later, she married Tony, my best man. I just saw them when I was in San Francisco for my gallery exhibit."

I figured they'd bumped into each other somewhere. "Wow. That must have been awkward."

Johnny laughs. "No. I see them whenever I'm in San Francisco. I had dinner at their place. They've got three great kids. They named their son John after me."

I laugh.

"I'm not joking," Johnny says. "You know what their other kids' names are?"

"Courteney and David?" I'm being sarcastic.

"Very good!"

"You're kidding, right?"

"No. See, it all worked out in the end. Caroline and I weren't supposed to be married. We were both lying to each other. I was just looking for a way out. Courteney and David provided it."

"That's the weirdest breakup story I've ever heard," I finally say.

"Hey, it all worked out in the end. They got their happily ever after."

I raise my eyebrows. "Oh, yeah? And what did you get?"

He smiles and looks hard at me. It's like he's saying something without words. *If it wasn't for that, I wouldn't have met you.* Out loud, he says, "My freedom."

Garlic mingles with the musty antique smell. And soon plates of seafood pasta are brought to us by the Millie, the owner. She's a woman in her early sixties who was probably a hippie in the sixties. She has its residual effects—long frizzy gray hair, no makeup, a long, flowing brown gauzy skirt and shirt, dangling earrings, and clanging bracelets.

"I see my cows are all gone," Johnny says to her. "Did some big art connoisseur buy the whole series?"

Millie looks like she's stifling a laugh. "Something like that."

"Tell us more," Johnny says. He winks at me.

She lets out a sigh. "A couple. The wife's pregnant. She's due any day. She thought the cows would go nicely in the nursery. She's got a farm motif going. Pigs. Horses. Sheep. Cows. Said your stuff would work well with the wallpaper."

"Egads, Millie, can't you see I'm trying to impress someone? I might have ruined my chances already with the Courteney Cox story."

"Johnny, why the hell did you go and do that?"

"I dunno. She looked like she'd get it."

Millie checks me out slowly. "She has smart eyes. Maybe too smart for you, John."

She leaves us alone with our food, but I'm not hungry at all. I move the pasta around on the plate and force a few strands into my mouth. My stomach is in turmoil. I can't remember the last time I felt this way. Probably about when I was seventeen and dating the football star who wanted me to put out. How can I lust after a sleazy paparazzo who ditched his fiancé at the altar? I'll just tell Johnny that I'm not ready for any of this yet—all this honesty, all this hope, all this pre-foreplay foreplay. It's too soon. I'm too damaged. Plus, my body needs a year of intense boot camp along with a boob job and some lipo and God knows what else.

"You, too?"

I had been so busy trying to cover up my lack of an appetite that I didn't notice Johnny wasn't eating either. I didn't know this happened to guys. I thought guys could eat no matter what. A week-old corpse could be rotting next to them and they'd still tear through a steak. But not Johnny. The mound of pasta remains in front of him, untouched. We smile. Then we go back to struggling with our food.

Millie returns a little while later. She looks at our plates. I'm afraid we've offended her. I scan my brain for a good excuse. Millie flashes a knowing grin.

"Touch of the flu, John?"

"Something like that."

"Don't worry," she says as she collects the plates. "I'll give it to the dogs. They love my cooking." She pauses and a mischievous look spreads across her face. "Plus, they're too stupid to get nervous jitters over sex. They just hump each other freely and without reservation. You two should try it sometime."

She guffaws as she turns and heads into the kitchen, leaving Johnny and me facing each other. There's an uncomfortable moment of silence. What is this about? I'm an adult. I've had sex before. We stare at each other for a few moments.

Johnny clears his throat.

"Speaking of dogs, let's go get that Chihuahua," he finally says.

Johnny drives home while the Chihuahua sits on my lap. It's so small, skinny and skittish, way too fragile for Gabby and me. How will it ever handle Gabby's temper tantrums? The screams? The slamming doors? The I-hate-yous? Just this car ride home seems too stressful for it. Why couldn't Gabby have wanted a black Lab or something more suitable for us? Like maybe a pitbull? But a Chihuahua? They're not pets. As Johnny said, they're accessories for the red carpet.

"Do you ever listen to anything else," Johnny asks.

"What do you mean?"

"Some of the tunes are pretty catchy. Who can resist Angela Lansbury singing 'Beauty and the Beast'? But this princess music has been on the entire trip. I was going to say something earlier, but you looked kinda cute, singing along to it."

"What? I have?"

"Yeah, you seemed really into it, so I decided not to say anything."

Gabby's princess music CD has been on the whole time and I didn't even know it. This happens to me often lately. I'll be so preoccupied that I don't notice I'm listening and singing along to Gabby's music even when she's not in the car. Sometimes I'll catch myself, shut it off, and scan the radio for something more, well, age appropriate, as they say. I used to be very current, when it came to music. And I had eclectic tastes—I listened to rap, country, pop, anything really. Now I can't name any top ten hit, but I recite every song ever recorded by The Wiggles or Hannah Montana. Truth be told, lately I like Gabby's princess CD more than most top ten songs.

I move to eject the CD but Johnny puts his hand out to block me.

"Wait a second, they're playing our song."

"Huh?"

He turns up the volume. It's "Once Upon A Dream," the song Sleeping Beauty sings to Prince Phillip. Johnny starts belting out the lyrics.

" 'I know you, I walked with you, once upon a dream . . . ' "

I laugh, thinking he's just mocking the music. But then it hits me with a wallop. This is what Gabby sang that day when the paparazzi were staked outside my house. This was the song Gabby trilled out while I chased her around the lawn until she banged into

Johnny. And when she finally stopped, I reamed out Johnny, telling him how utterly loathsome he was.

It was one of the worst days of my life. Maybe the worst ever. And now I am remembering it and laughing at the same time. I never would have imagined this moment in a million years. It doesn't make sense. So I blot out all thoughts by mangling the lyrics along with Johnny. He sings in a crazy falsetto and we burst into laughter. Then we resume singing at the top of our lungs. Johnny opens the windows. Then he squeezes my hand.

It all feels great. The wind whipping my hair. Johnny holding my hand. Screaming the lyrics.

" 'Ohhh, I know you, I know what you do, you love me at once, the way you did once upon a dream!' "

Strangely, our singing lulls the Chihuahua to sleep.

All the nervousness I experienced at lunch has evaporated. I wish we'd taken a doggie bag with us because I am suddenly starving. I feel light and free and famished. Johnny must feel the same way because he gets off the 101 before our exit and drives along Ventura until he spots a French bistro.

"What about her?" I say, pointing to the Chihuahua on my lap.

"Let's take her with us. She's so small, no one will even notice."

We are scanning the menu when I see Amy. She's sitting at a dark corner table, looking deeply into someone's eyes. I stand to say hello to her when I see that the man across from her isn't her husband. It's a personal trainer I've seen a few times at the gym. His name's Merritt and all the women talk about him in hushed tones as if he's God, or at least Brad Pitt. His exercise regimen—a fusion of pilates, kickboxing, and Tai Chi—is a religion to them.

Amy and Merritt are holding hands and grinning crazily at each other. I had been right all along. Amy doesn't have migraines. She has a lover. A lover who is maybe twenty-five, at the most.

I quickly sit back down and cover my face with the menu. She doesn't see me. I don't want her to. She's doing what she's doing and I don't want to be part of her drama. If she sees me here, she'll call me tomorrow, ask to meet with me, cry, beg me not to tell anyone, then tell me all her problems, confide in me when they finally break up. She's such a cliché, I think. But then again, who am I to talk? A divorced woman whose husband had an affair. Is there anyone who is not a cliché? We think we're so different. We struggle so hard to differentiate ourselves from everyone else on this spinning orb. But even being that person striving to be unique is just being another version of a cliché.

"Let's get out of here," I whisper to Johnny.

"Sounds good to me. I'm not big on Frog food anyway."

We order take out from In-N-Out Burger. Double double cheeseburgers. Chocolate milkshakes. Fries. Johnny drives to a side street off Ventura and we chow down right in the car. I slip my legs on top of Johnny's as if I've done it a million times before. Then I take big delicious bite of my burger. But after just a few bites, I look over at Johnny and I'm not hungry anymore at all. I'm just horny. He's staring hard at me. He leans in and we kiss.

We make out in the car like teenagers. He kisses my neck, my face, my lips. His hands get underneath my shirt.

I am a middle-aged mom of a six-year-old and I'm being felt up in my Volkswagen Passat. This is pure bliss.

The Chihuahua begins to yip from the backseat.

Back at my house, we practically fall on top of each other the minute I open the door. I pull off his shirt and kiss his chest. My hand massages his stomach. I'm surprised that he's got a bit of a gut. I had expected a six-pack. But instead of being a turnoff, this arouses me even more. I like that he's not a gym freak.

I unbuckle his belt.

Johnny moans. "You're more aggressive than I expected."

"Beware. It's been a long, long time," I say, panting. "I might be a little rusty."

"Oh yeah, that's just what I was thinking. Poor Rusty Alice," Johnny says breathlessly. "I hope I won't need a tetanus shot."

As soon as he pulls off my black lace underpants, the Chihuahua yips and yips and yips as if on cue. This was just the distraction I had prayed for at lunchtime, but it's the last thing I want now. I want to ignore the little varmint and forge ahead. But she has other ideas. She keeps yipping and yipping. Then she makes a sound like she's gurgling mouthwash.

"Shit," Johnny says. He sighs.

"Flush her down the toilet and continue what we're doing. Gabby will never know."

Johnny—wearing Fruit of the Loom briefs—gets up and heads toward the sofa where we've left the dog. He squats next to her and begins petting the dog and speaking gently to it. I wonder if I should get dressed and get up to help. The moment seems lost.

As if reading my thoughts, Johnny says, "Don't even think of moving. Stay exactly where you are. We've had our share of false starts."

Is he talking to me or the dog?

He whispers something soothing to the dog and then pets her gently. I look at his hands. They're big and strong with long, graceful fingers—another turn-on. I hate stumpy, dwarf-like digits on men. It's almost too much for me to watch these strong hands petting this dog. It feels like I'm watching porno without the porno. I feel like I might explode.

"Does she have a name yet?" He speaks in a whisper.

"I guess I'll leave that up to Gabby. I'm sure it will be something like Ariel or Cinderella. I just hope Gabby and I don't scare it away."

"Why?"

"Well, it can get pretty loud here. You've probably seen it. Gabby has quite a temper."

He turns from the sofa and looks at me strangely. "Gabby? I don't picture that at all. You guys are so calm."

I wonder if he's being sarcastic, but then I understand he's right. Gabby hasn't had a temper tantrum in . . . well, I can't even remember the last time. It *has* been calm here. There's been no screaming. No slamming doors. No I-hate-yous. No drama in quite a long time. Maybe a Chihuahua would fit our temperament perfectly. Maybe this will all be easier than I thought.

I smile so hard the muscles in my face ache.

"What is it," he asks.

How do I answer this? "It's complicated."

"Try me."

"Well, I'm just really happy right now. But don't be scared, I don't mean because of you or anything."

"Gee, thanks."

"I just mean that you're not the sole reason for my happiness. I'm happy for so many reasons. Of course, you're one of them. I'm happy that you're here. But it's more than that. I'm happy because I can be happy. Does that even make sense? For a while being happy seemed impossible."

The Chihuahua's asleep again. Johnny had mentioned when we left Santa Ynez that he had special powers that could put a dog to sleep in minutes. He said this came in handy when he needed to get past guard dogs and trespass onto celebrity estates. I thought he was kidding around, but it seems his technique has worked with this as-yet-unnamed pooch.

I am sitting up with Johnny's T-shirt wrapped around me as I wait for him to take that long walk from the couch back to me. He comes toward me and pulls the shirt off. Then he takes in my body, pushes me down and kisses all of it, including my breasts, my stomach, my stretch-mark-riddled hips. My first impulse it to apologize for it. I want to say, "Sorry. I know my breasts are saggy, but I breastfed Gabby for six months and they've never been the same. But they were really perfect and perky a few years back. And my stomach? Well, it used to be flat and hard, but ever since I was pregnant, well, I haven't been able to get rid of it, despite all the crunches at the gym. Ditto those stretch marks. They say shea butter prevents them. But that's a downright lie, because I rubbed it on my belly and hips for nine months, and guess what? Didn't work. But my skin used to be blemish free."

Shut up, Alice, I tell myself. *Listen to Millie.*

Enjoy.

Hump freely and without reservation.

Which is exactly what I do.

3

Who Are You Supposed To Be?

I have on a frilly, puffy, sparkly gown. I wear an enormous crown that looks like a silver chandelier perched atop my head. I carry a magic wand that lights up like a firework when I wave it. I look pretty ridiculous. It's a costume I've cobbled together from some vintage stores on Sherman Way in Canoga Park. Each item seemed perfect on its own. Together, I'm not quite sure I know who I'm supposed to be. But I do look festive. I do look as though I'm in the spirit of things. And isn't that all that really matters?

Fake snow—resembling soap bubbles instead of flakes—swirls around me. I'm surrounded by mechanical princesses and fairies.

It's Christmas Eve in the Valley.

We are putting the finishing touches on my front lawn. It looks incredible. Multicolored lights drape the house and the trees. A mechanical Cinderella lifts up her leg while an attendant prepares to slide a glass slipper on her foot. Snow White lays motionless as her prince leans in, frozen, his lips puckered. Sleeping Beauty prepares to dance with her prince. Fairies wait expectantly on the roof for the electricity to be switched on so they can pirouette and spin.

Irving Berlin's "White Christmas" blasts through a speaker. I recently read that Berlin's infant son, Irving Berlin, Jr., died on Christmas Day. So when I hear this song I think about the bad connotations it must have had for the Berlin family. Christmastime was probably never happy or merry or—since they lived in Los Angeles—white, for that matter. But soon "Deck the Halls" begins and I put these thoughts out of my head. We all sing or hum along.

Johnny has a friend who is a set designer. He loaned us the princesses, the fairies, the snow machine. Everything.

Gabby will be returning from Salt Lake City any minute and I want this perfect. The lights. The princesses. The fairies. The snow. The carols. It doesn't look like my house anymore, but a fairy tale trapped in a snowstorm. A perfect fairy tale for a six-year-old. It's exactly what Gabby had envisioned for the house last year when I opted for inflatable abominable snowmen instead.

But alas, yesterday I was reminded of how fleeting a child's wishes can be.

Gabby called to tell me that she hopes Santa doesn't bring her princess clothes this year.

"Why?" I asked.

"Well, princesses are for babies. I'm a big girl now," she said.

"*What*?"

"It's true, Mommy. I'm almost seven. I wanna get a Hannah Montana poster for my bedroom."

Another little death. Another phase outgrown.

Ruth puts a big red bow on the as-yet-unnamed dog's head. At least Gabby didn't say she no longer wanted a Chihuahua. Nancy and her kids are struggling to upright Ariel, but her fin makes it impossible. Renee passes out egg nog. Trinity visits with a plate of freshly baked chocolate chip cookies. She's leaving in the morning for Manila, for the holidays and her daughter's wedding. She hasn't seen her daughter in ten years, she tells me.

"The last time I see Melissa, he was Gabby's age. Now he getting married. My family has grown up without me," she tells me. "Soon I will be a grandmother."

I cringe. Trinity is only a few years older than I am.

Johnny is on the roof, plugging in the last string of lights. He looks so handsome in his leather jacket and Santa Claus hat. Yesterday, he spent the entire day and night. We never left the house—no details necessary. But halfway through the day, we flopped on the couch, exhausted, and watched *It's a Wonderful Life.* No matter what, that movie always gets me. When Harry says that George is the richest man in town, I lose it. Never fails. There George stands in the midst of this eclectic group of friends and family and he realizes he has everything in the world to live for. I've watched this movie every year for as long as I can remember, except for last year. It came on, and for a while I struggled through it, but halfway in I knew the magic had been lost for me. Nothing about my life had seemed wonderful. I couldn't quite understand why George just didn't off himself. But next year I want Gabby to watch it with me. "See, you don't need a handsome prince. You can be rescued by your friends. By their love," I'll tell her.

Two days ago, I went to see Faye to say good-bye. Just when I started believing she was psychic, she decides to move to Sonoma.

"I don't want to be a psychic in L.A. anymore," she offered by way of explanation. "Everyone here wants me to tell them they'll sell the screenplay or the TV pilot or get the role in the movie. When I don't, they get angry at me. People in other parts of the country just want the truth."

She studied me. "You look radiant, Alice. What's going on?"

I told her how I just converted Mom's guest house into an office. My public relations company is taking off, partly because I'm damned good at what I do and partly because every mom in the Valley is looking for press for their start-up businesses. I've been so busy, I've hired

Claire part-time (she had a baby and wanted to scale back anyway). She takes over when Gabby returns from school. That's part of my deal with Gabby.

"What will I do without you, Faye?" I asked. "Everything you predicted is coming true and now that I believe in you, you're leaving. It's not fair."

Faye laughed. "Do you want to know my secret?"

"Sure," I said.

"The truth about psychics is that we're all psychics. You. Me. Ruth. The Winnie the Pooh mom. Gabby. Everyone. Why do you think your friend Johnny took photos of someone else's wedding on his wedding day? Because he knew his marriage would be doomed. But very few people appreciate their psychic ability. Psychics are the only ones who truly understand this and tap into it."

I nodded.

"Think about it." She laughed. "Maybe it's a government conspiracy. Maybe if people understood that they could predict the future, they wouldn't be so afraid of everything. And then they wouldn't need the government to give them a false feeling of security."

I looked at Faye like she was nuts.

"Alice, did you ever notice the noise? You can't think with all the noise out there. It's in your car. In the mall. In the stores. In the restaurants. On the street. Just as you're humming one song, you enter a new place to be bombarded with another song. And these teenagers today don't have a chance. They have on their iPods while they text message their friends who are standing right next to them. Or they're on MySpace or Facebook. Soon there'll be no such thing as psychic ability."

"That's why I need you here. If I could predict the future, none of this would have happened."

Faye hugs me tight. "Best of luck, Alice," she says cryptically.

"What does that mean?"

She laughed. "You know. You've always known."

My heart thumped wildly. I wanted to ask her about Johnny, but I was terrified.

"What is it, Alice?"

I opened my mouth, but the words felt stuck in my throat.

"Alice?"

"Well, Johnny," I blurted.

She downright guffawed.

"What?"

She touched my cheek. "Look at yourself, Alice. You can't help but smile when you say his name. You figure it out."

If Faye is right and I am psychic, then I feel very good about the future with Johnny. He's a former sleazy photographer who left his bride at the altar. He stalked me on the worst day of my life. He harassed lots of people. He's loathed by celebrities. There are no pretenses with Johnny. Maybe that counts for something. He told me exactly who he is, and I believe him. Plus, he talked Barbies with Gabby for hours—that's more than I could ever do.

An enormous white star on the house above us lights up. The people who have moved into the porn house have created a nativity scene with a crèche and real lambs whose bleating can be heard throughout our impressionist neighborhood. I guess Bob Stone was so disturbed by whatever Faye told him that he moved somewhere else. Anyway, the young couple who live there have no idea about their house's past. The wife is pregnant and due in a few weeks. They're born-again Christians, the wife told me when I rang her doorbell with a casserole last week. She explained to me that when her husband Ronnie walked into the house, he knew it was perfect for them.

"He had total déjà vu," she said. "He felt like he'd been in the bedroom and living room before. Even the hot tub seemed familiar to him."

I sucked in my cheeks and squelched a laugh. So Ronnie the born-again watched porn! I'm sure one day Gabby will tell their child that she once thought she had rescued a princess there.

Rose and Xander are getting married on New Year's Eve on some Caribbean island. I hope it works out—not because I'm suddenly altruistic, because I'm not at all. But I do want Gabby to be happy. And for her to be truly happy, she needs her daddy to be happy.

Gabby. I don't have to be psychic to know that your love for your child is a heartbreaking kind. I love her so much but I also know one day she will leave me and be out on her own. One day she'll say good-bye to princesses, then Barbies, then Bratz, then *High School Musical*, then Hannah Montana. And then, one day, me. As much as I love her, she is not mine forever.

You hold her hand. She holds yours. One day she holds it only when she's sure no one's looking. But she eventually lets go and doesn't hold it for years and years and years. Then one day she holds it again. But this time it's because you need her to. She helps you cross the street.

And one day, if your life is as perfect as it can be, she buries you and continues on without you. She'll long for your hand in hers. She'll imagine it in her dreams. And the best you can hope for is that you've taught her well. You hope she doesn't make mistakes, but of course she will. And hopefully, she'll feel your phantom hand holding onto her and comforting her through it all.

I see the white lights of a stretch limo.

"It's Gabby." I give one of those yells that I try to disguise as a whisper. I wipe tears from my eyes. "Gabby's here, Gabby's here!"

There's a flurry of activity. Johnny flicks the Christmas lights on. Someone turns on the snow machine. The fairies pirouette on the roof. Cinderella's shoe fits. Ariel's fin wiggles. Snow White and the prince kiss. Sleeping Beauty waltzes around with her prince. It's more awesome than I imagined and it takes my breath away.

I want Gabby to have a fairy tale because life is sweet, but there are no happily ever afters. Let my daughter believe in them for as long as she can, because the truth is, Cinderella and her prince get old. Maybe he leaves her. Maybe she suffers from senile dementia, a Waxie hanging out of her ball gown. Maybe he has a heart attack on the toilet. Snow White. Sleeping Beauty. Ruth. Renee. Faye. Nancy. Amy. Alex. Johnny. We can all have our happily ever afters for a few brief moments, which is the best we can do. And it's still pretty good.

Gabby races out of the limo. Her eyes are wide. She gasps. The Chihuahua nips at her feet as she runs through the snow, squealing. She sticks her tongue out, trying to lick the flakes. She twirls round and round. Then she bends down and pets the panting dog.

For a few moments, she is lost in this winter wonderland. I bask in her excitement. Then she stops, searching the lawn for something. I feel my stomach drop. I wonder what she thinks is missing. I thought we'd covered it all, but there's such a look of longing on Gabby's face that I feel I've somehow screwed up. What could it be?

Finally, her eyes settle on me and she brightens. She was searching for me! She races toward me and wraps her arms around me. I pick her up and our noses touch.

"I love it, I love it, I love it."

She unclasps her hands and studies me in my mishmash of a costume. She giggles. "Oh, Mommy, who are you supposed to be?"

I think about this for a moment. I honestly don't know. I had originally planned to be a princess, but then I added the magic wand, which would be more fairyish. And the crown on my head looks regal, like something a queen would wear. And my red sparkly shoes must belong to Dorothy from *The Wizard of Oz*.

Who am I supposed to be? Who am I supposed to be? Who am I supposed to be?

I run through the answers. A fairy? A princess? A queen? A combination of all three? None of the above? Something I've invented?

Gabby will question all of it. And she will never be satisfied with my answer.

So I say, "I'm just a mommy who will do anything for her little girl."

Gabby smiles and squeezes me tighter.

We're silent as we breathe in the moment, both knowing we'll remember this forever. Our little piece of happily ever after.